PRAISE FOR CALIA WILDE

Wilde splices the action with heated scenes that breathe intimacy and urgency

— BOOKLIFE

The way in which Wilde displayed sexual passion upon the page was a fair mix of realism and metaphor, which is what I like…I think *the payoff* can be more explosive or have a greater impact if much of what happens on the page can be experienced through the reader's imagination. Wilde hit the nail on the head.

— LIVE FREE LIVE RICH

DEVLIN'S LUCK

A SINISTER LEGACY DUET

CALIA WILDE

Copyright ©2026 by A.R. Case writing as Calia Wilde

All rights reserved. No part of this publication may be reproduced, distributed, or transmitted in any form or by any means, including photocopying, recording, or other electronic or mechanical methods, without the prior written permission of the publisher, except in the case of brief quotations embodied in critical reviews and certain other noncommercial uses permitted by copyright law. For permission requests, write to the author, addressed "Attention: Permissions" at theAuthor@CaliaWilde.com.

Misfit Ink

5257 Buckeystown Pike, #215

Frederick, MD 21704

MisfitInkBooks.com

Ordering Information:

For details, contact theAuthor@CaliaWilde.com.

Disclaimer:

This book is a work of fiction. Any references to historical events, real people, or real locales are used fictitiously. Other names, characters, places, and incidents are the product of the author's imagination, and any resemblance to actual events or locales or persons, living or dead, is entirely coincidental.

Language, translation, and use: Not all phrases are translated. As the lead characters use/learn the varying languages, some notation of translation will occur (as the character understands it) is made. Whenever same-language speakers are the only characters on page, language use is inferred and not italicized. Translations may not be accurate for regional dialects due to author error. Certain phrases are taken from colloquial sayings and do not translate one-to-one to English - which this book is primarily written in.

The following is an indication and acknowledgement of potential content that may be upsetting or triggering, but is clearly not exhaustive:

Vulgar language, excessive or gratuitous violence, kidnapping (forceful deprivation of/disregard for personal autonomy), death or dying, and blood.

Devlin's Luck is a work of fiction that may contain emotionally disturbing content. Please be aware of your own tolerance for the triggering content mentioned as well as use your best judgement about reading when your own emotional reserves are low. Sometimes it is the little things that can tip the balance into dark spaces.

Cover design, interior artwork, and layout: created by Misfit Ink Books (MisfitInkBooks.com)

Front cover photography and interior art: Photography, background, interior art, and font treatments used under license through Adobe Stock. Any other fonts purchased under license or are supplied under open license for publishing use.

AI Disclaimer and Restriction: The author expressly prohibits any entity from using this publication for purposes of training artificial intelligence (AI) technologies to generate text, including without limitation technologies that are capable of generating works in the same style or genre as this publication. The author reserves all rights to license uses of this work for generative AI training and development of machine learning language models.

Generative AI was not used in the creation of this written work or the published content. Non-generative AI may be indicated as AI use in the metadata due to software-induced processing or false positives in detection software. Misfit Ink Books and the author believe in the power of human imagination and creativity, and supports creators who pursue their unique vision through dedication to craft and hard work.

INTRODUCTION

Notes on languages and translations, and deviations from the Chicago Manual of Style:

1. Google translate is *not* perfect. While the author did use it as a resource to double-check the meaning of certain words; phrasing and dialects required more in-depth research to represent a more accurate snapshot of how the exchanges would be spoken. Mistakes are my own.

2. Chicago Manual of Style: "generally advises italics for foreign words not in standard English dictionaries to signal them to the reader, but for fiction, especially by multilingual authors, it allows flexibility, suggesting regular text for words part of a character's natural speech to build authenticity (like Spanish in a Latinx character's dialogue), using italics primarily to distinguish truly unfamiliar terms or to avoid misreading as typos, and noting that frequently used words might only need italics on the first mention." That is an advisement. This author opted for regular text for all

instances, except when emphasis is implied as part of speech.

If you're curious why the "rule" was broken, read my bio, or watch this: https://youtu.be/24gCI3Ur7FM?si=fvzeLFaWa2Tj2kR_

Italic use on English words in conversation are spoken in Italian or the Galluric dialect and other Sardo dialects common to Sardinia (known as a "Romanza Insulare" - a Latin branch of its own separate from Italian) indicate what the character (commonly Mario across the two books) understands and is represented using grammatically-correct English phrasing, not the literal phrasing that was common during the Modernist literary movement. Some author liberty is taken with this as well.

3. If you're curious where some of the reference material is for Sardo (the language) is feel free to wade through the references listed here:

CaliaWilde.com/language

and

CaliaWilde.com/language-part-deux

THE HUNTERS' CODE

The Thumb: Life
    (The Grip and Foundation)
    Live by the code.
    Live with purpose.
    Live with clarity.
    Life is the reward.

The Index Finger: Honor
    (The Direction and Guide)
    Honor the code.
    Honor every marker.
    Honor the family.
    Honor rewards itself

The Middle Finger: Discipline
    (The Spine and Trade)
    Finish the job.

Eliminate complications.
　　　Deceive wisely.
　　　Guard your secrets.

The Ring Finger: Respect
　　(The Vow to Elements)
　　　Respect the sea.
　　　Respect your elders.
　　　Respect your home.
　　　Cherish innocence.

The Pinky: Death
　　(The End/Finality)
　　　Die by the code.
　　　Die with dignity.
　　　Die without regret.
　　　Death is your gift.

TRAVELS

9.
5.
    13.
6.
    10.   14.
    DISCIPLINE   RESPECT
    HONOR
7.   11.   15.   17.
            18.
        12.   16.   19. DEATH
1.   20.
LIFE
2.
        THE HUNTER
        THE ASSASSIN
3.   THE SHADOWS
        THE LEFT HAND
    4.
                        SWORD COMPASS

To my father and uncle.

Identical twins, rascals, and great men.

Your tall tales and pranks taught me how to laugh, and how differently two people could retell the same story when the other was obviously omitting pertinent details like who was chasing who that day Dad chipped his front teeth. Or, exactly who was at fault for the infamous root beer stand incident.

It also was so much fun watching you play 'steal the grandbaby' if the other showed up late for family reunions. That was a hoot.

DEVLIN'S LUCK

1

ELLIE

Nailing the little gilt shamrocks between the trim strips and the door frame seemed like a good idea at the time. But the sixth one down was crooked, canting at an eight-degree angle—not a perfect fifteen, which made it stand out. Everyone touched it on the way in. Their dirty fingertips turned the gold leaf black.

Lucky, they called it.

A visual pox, it was, even though that's likely a bit overdramatic. Then again, no one ever accused me of subtlety.

I set my carry-on down to unlock the front door of the tavern I owned.

The building was still standing. That was because I hired only the best help, and with the exception of Casey Kelly, each one of them could run the bar with their eyes shut.

Sgt. Casey, on the other hand, had run the bar into the ground with both eyes open almost ruining a neighborhood institution. But everyone loved him anyway. That's why he still had a key and was listed as co-owner despite not having a say in the business anymore.

Didn't stop him, though.

With a little jiggle and a hard shove to combat the stickiness of the swollen wood, I pried the door open. Dragging my bag behind me so no neighborhood kid would snatch it as a prank, I tapped my code into the alarm and blinked off jet lag for a minute, maybe longer.

Then I shivered because the damp March chill had seeped into my bones and was currently wreaking havoc on the pristinely refinished hardwood I'd paid for.

I shoved the door shut and examined the frame for issues. It had been a reclaim from a salvage done on a bar in Milwaukee. I went up with Kat, my bestie, to check out fixtures and came home with a hundred and some year-old slab of oak that didn't fit inside the tiny U-Haul we'd rented. But I knew it was perfect for the place.

The Blarney Zone melded old with new. State of the art big screens, five cable sports subscriptions, one fully-balanced surround sound system, and old-world Irish Pub aesthetics, sandwiched together with a touch of class, a little brass, and a lot of sass. It was home.

More of one than my condo, which was seven blocks south and a world away. I'd hit O'Hare at an ungodly early hour, still lit up from an international flight I didn't sleep on and heartbreak. I sent my luggage with the driver who had strict instructions to, and I quote, "Just dump the bags inside the main door. If you can't do that, leave 'em in a fucking snowbank. I could give a shit."

Yes, world traveling was not my forte. Neither was censoring my mouth.

But running a bar filled with a mix of the eclectic neighborhood misfits, more than one gangster, and a trauma-whipped, retired police sergeant? Hell, yeah. That was my jam.

And I'd made it home from Europe with just over a week to spare before the momentous St. Patrick's Day weekend. That was barely enough time to prepare.

One thing that made the Blarney Zone a gem was the annual Chicago St. Patrick's Day celebrations. While the dyed-green river pulls a guaranteed fifty thousand visitors braving the precarious lure of spring haunted by the very real winter zephyrs that tore down the concrete canyons of downtown, the neighborhood parades attracted a lot more. Having a reputation to uphold kept this neighborhood intact.

We could boast two hundred K on a sunny day.

And the Blarney Zone was the smack dab center of the parade route.

Mental note: I needed to buy more sawdust for the vomit-fest. Somewhere I heard peanut shells helped oil the wood floor below. But for the life of me, I couldn't figure out where to find over a bucketful of those, let alone the cubic yards I'd need to cover three thousand square feet of oak.

That's if I didn't open the basement bar. Which I'd have to do. But that would be "locals only." There was a back-alley entrance everyone knew about, but only used for Sunday pot lucks and the occasional Christmas party.

However, this year it would be the perfect spot for my regulars to hide from the crowds.

The door squeaked against the jam as Kat shoved it open.

"Oh, you're home?" she asked.

If I'd had more coffee, I'd come up with something better than… "No, I'm a fucking ghost. Boo."

"You're white enough," she fired back.

Only Kat could get away with that. At just under six-foot, with lower west side Chicago street smarts, Rhianna-esque sleepy eyeliner, Beyonce snap, and a ton of pre-PhD cred in Business Management, she was formidable. And the very best of best friends I could ever hope for.

"Did you know Italy shuts down their beaches in winter?"

"You're the one who wanted to get married in February." She clasped her hands together and switched on her falsetto. "It will be *so* romantic!" Her face skewered into a grimace. "How's Pornstach anyways?"

The question hit my gut like a punch. Not only had my bestie picked up my twin sister's nickname for Johnny, but she nailed a sore spot… one of many.

I held up my hand—my ringless hand. "You tell me."

Kat's mouth fell open. "No… oh sweetie."

And that was why I came here instead of crash-landing at my house. Her hug felt like the best cozy blanket, the ultimate in posh luxury spa wraps, and had just enough Katali Musk 12 notes to transport me back into a million awesome memories.

She squeezed twice, giving me the option to let go. For once, I didn't. I kept hanging on.

"You want to talk about it?" she asked.

"No."

She waited a beat. Knowing I needed to spill.

"He was fucking around on me."

"I *knew* it. No one with that thick of a caterpillar on their upper lip and peach fuzz on their jaw is worth more than a trash panda's puked up pizza."

My shoulders shook. Only Kat could make me laugh when I wanted to cry. "That wasn't the worst of it."

She pushed me out to arm's length. "You're messing with me, right?"

I shook my head.

It was so hard to admit, but if anyone would understand, it would be Kat. I sucked in a bracing breath. "Did you watch the live stream?"

Kat nodded. "The mask was a nice touch. Was he wearing lifts?"

"No, that was… oh geesh—" I tried not to laugh, but it would not be contained. "—It's-a-me-Mar-ee-oh."

"Who?" She was understandably confused.

"Allie's husband."

She searched the empty room for her sanity. "Whoa, wait a minute. Your sister isn't married. She ain' even dating. Not since that disaster with the epi-pen dude."

"I know, it's a shocker, but get this… my stick up her butt twin bumped into a guy who stole her rideshare, they ended up at the chapel together and, boom. Married. I think she's pregnant already."

Kat blinked and held her breath. Her thoughts were *loud*.

"I *know*."

"His name is Mario?"

I cackled. Sue me. Making fun of my "big" sis was ingrained into my DNA. I mocked his name for a second time just for a laugh.

"Gurrlll…" Kat wiped fake moisture from her eyes.

I dug in my pockets for my phone. "To be fair, you might want to walk that back." It took me a minute to find the photo I'd snapped of Allie and her hubs before I left. It was a great picture. They were doing their usual disgustingly sweet snuggling right at sunset with the brilliantly blue Mediterranean peeking out around the edges of their love fest. If I were in a better headspace, I'd have it framed for her.

But it brought tears to my eyes. I turned the phone away mostly to escape the memories, but Kat grabbed onto it like a starved tiger. "Who in the *365 Days* is that?" Her fingers glommed tighter.

"Mario."

"It's-a—uh-unh. He's too gorgeous to make fun of. For real? Allie?"

I nodded. "Bagged and tagged with a whole family heirloom signet ring and everything." Omitted was the whole capital F, "Family" detail, because while it was outrageous enough that my straighter than an orthodontist's-child's-teeth sister did something spontaneous, Kat would *never* believe she married a mobster. Worse… an assassin-mobster.

Which pinched. Because that would be something I'd do. I mean... *Johnny Porciello?*

Kat was speechless. "Whoa," she finally breathed.

I nodded.

"Deets. Now."

No. There were too many land mines in that story. "We have a bar to open."

"Fuck the bar. This calls for... I don't know what, but *damn*, Allie?"

Then she folded in on herself. "And you. You didn't get the fantasy. I'm so sorry."

I let out a defeated breath. She was partially right. I didn't "get" the fantasy. I dropped it like a volcanic internal temperature, 7-11-nuked, apple pie. Which was a great descriptor for my personal "he who shall not be named" dilemma. Johnny was barely a blip compared to—

Mental nope. Blocked, deleted, wiped out of the database.

"Fill me in on the prep for the big holiday," I begged.

She stared at me for a moment, and then at the bag sitting near the security panel. "When did you get off the plane?"

"Two coffees ago."

Her face fell. "Oh honey, you need rest."

"Can't sleep, the clowns'll eat me."

Kat scanned me from head to toe. "Are those Allie's jeggings?"

"That's just *one* of the issues. I lost my luggage."

She knew that was a lie.

"Allie has my underwear bag."

The snort that came out of her was unflattering. "Your

four thousand dollar 'it must be skimpy' shopping spree landed with Allie? *Shee-it*. No wonder she's married."

That deserved another evil laugh. "I'm definitely going to be an aunt soon."

"Gimme that phone again."

"Why?" I handed it to her despite my fake protest.

She studied the photo. "Shoot. Those are going to be some pretty babies. 'Just saying."

"Plural?" I was still wrapping my head around one.

Kat laughed. "She isn't going to stop at one. You know your sister. She'll get all wrapped up in baby fever and soon there will be three or four little *It's-a-me's* out there."

Now, *that* cheered me up. Kat giggled right along with me as I laid out the scene.

"He's from a *huge* family in Sardinia. His grandfather has to be a hundred years old, and his father's a big politician or something in finance. Nicely padded portfolio if you get my drift?"

"She deserves a little something after all the scrimping. Is she staying there?"

Probably. Although she did ask me to check on her house once I got settled. It was about a half mile northwest of the bar and tucked into a quiet little suburban pocket that clung to the 1970s something fierce. Postage-stamp lawn, three cramped bedrooms, detached one-car garage with a wonky door, and …paneling. It made me want to puke every time I visited.

With grandfather's inheritance she could have remodeled it ten times over. Or bought something much newer. But she clung to it like a safety blanket because she'd worked for the money that bought it.

"They're jet-setting."

"Ugh."

Kat's single-syllable benign envy echoed mine. The silence weighed on the tattered threads of my heart.

"I met someone."

Her head tilted at my one-eighty. "And?"

I shrugged. "It was a rebound thing, you know? But at least he can grow a beard if he wanted."

"Any photos?"

None I wanted to look at. *Ever.* I shook my head.

Never leave incriminating evidence behind.

2

RINGO

In my career, I've met hundreds of unlucky guys. But none quite as fucked as Signore Gesualdo Conti. "Don" Conti if you gave two fucks about hierarchy.

His office looked a hell of a lot different than the last time I was here. A freshly gouged chunk of wood was torn out of the heavy door. The hospital bed was new, too.

The carpet was gone, exposing wooden planks that were definitely not new. At least the blood stains were scrubbed away.

A heart monitor, oxygen monitor, and a bazillion other devices kept him alive. I almost felt sorry for the guy. Paralyzed from the shoulders down, he probably thought this was Hell. My only consolation was that he'd see the real place soon enough.

Underneath the changes was an ever-present taint of excrement. Weirder? Sulfur.

Like someone had lit a fresh match. But that wouldn't

happen. The big warning label on the oxygen tank made even me think twice about that foolishness.

I sat where directed by the secretary and stared at the man propped up in his death bed. His nurse was a suited, looming, meathead with hands like hams. I doubted his role entailed bedpans.

"They took all my weapons at the gate," I complained.

Don Conti wheezed a laugh. "Next time you visit, don't walk in the front door."

"Will there be a next time?" I asked. It was on everyone's mind. From the Italian officials who'd locked up his daughter on attempted murder, to my adopted family, the Mancas…or as they liked to call themselves, "The Left Hand." And no, that wasn't a play on words. They took that shit seriously. Apparently, it was a thing that went back at least eight thousand years. From cradle to early grave, they mastered the art of death, and sundry other more lucrative professions from kidnapping to piracy, but their main calling was assassination. As one of theirs, and the Devil's own, I was the rare outsider who'd taken up the blade.

Don Conti pondered my question. "I think my solicitor will kill me first."

I glanced at the lawyer in the corner. The stacks of paperwork in his purview were on the verge of toppling over. The Conti family was in arrears due to bank fines. Their assets were being liquidated, and only the American holdings were left out of the vulture pit because they'd been signed over to Adelmo Conti's trust as son and heir to the Conti name. Unluckily, he'd died just a short time ago, without a will. Therefore, the entire block of assets were in limbo as they reverted to Don Conti.

And once he died, the next closest heir was in jail, waiting for her attempted murder charges to be upgraded to murder. Because she fired the magical bullet that lodged in her father's spine which was slowly killing him.

Having a lawyer present was highly unusual. This reeked of a setup. I faked a relaxed air. "Why did you need me then?" Dianora would suffer more alive. But if Don Conti was exacting revenge for a certain duplicity I'd committed, then a lawyer would be the perfect assassin for the assassin.

Don Conti nodded toward the solicitor. That triggered a rush to uncover a binder, and an even more concerning rush toward me.

If I had a dagger, he'd be dead.

Instead, I took the hefty package he offered. I flipped it open, knowing no one was going to voice a hit contract out loud in front of witnesses, but having it documented was a step outside my comfort zone.

The first page didn't look like any workup I'd ever seen. The second didn't either. I flipped through the detailed summary of assets, double-checked addresses mentioned, and got highly confused.

To be thorough, I fanned through the stack to the final pages. Just spreadsheets and ledgers, no details about a mark, no special requests to bring back proof. It was as if I stepped through the twilight zone door into a world run by…businessmen.

I set the binder down. "Mario or his father would be

better suited for this." As I prepared to stand, Don Conti grew agitated. He flapped his shoulder to attract the lawyer's attention. Once he had it, he ordered, "Leave us for a moment all of you."

The solicitor followed orders, as did everyone else.

A month ago, that guard tried to kill me.

Of course, I was actively trying to kill him at the time, so I guess the animosity was warranted.

Once they were gone, I spoke freely. "What the fuck?"

Don Conti grimaced. "I have secrets."

That wasn't a surprise. "Don't we all?"

He changed tactics. "Have you ever wondered who your father is?"

A cold thread slithered up and around my neck. The whole reason I'd ended up with the Left Hand was because my mother didn't bother keeping track of who she partied with, or fell into bed with. And when I came along, she lied her ass off about my parentage. No one believed her. But naming me after an aging, and married, rock musician got attention—and settlements. With enough money, she dumped me at a boarding school in the Alps and never looked back.

Had I wondered who my father was? Sure. Until I got that fantasy beaten out of me by punk-ass kids.

Then Mario stepped in. My life changed.

I had a home. A family. A profession I was well-suited for. I didn't need a father or a mother when I had uncles, grandfathers, brothers, cousins, and the hoards of women they attached to, or attracted, who fluctuated between the ones wanting to feed me and the ones who wanted to fuck me. I steered clear of both unless I was hungry.

So, did I wonder? "Frankly? No."

Don Conti frowned. "Go to the table, there is a yellow folder." His voice was weak. If he died while I was in here, I'd be locked up, assuming his guards didn't try to kill me first.

I glanced at the door, hoping it didn't come down to that.

The yellow folder was really thin. One photo was in it.

This asshole and his photos. I hadn't even looked at the image before shutting the folder.

"That's your mother when she was twenty-four."

As if it explained things?

Warily, I reopened the folder to take a good look at the scene. Sure as shit, there was Mom in all her half-dressed glory, sandwiched between two equally disheveled men. One of them was famous. Not name-sake famous, but richer than God famous. He was on the left.

Don Conti leaned in on her right.

I tossed the folder onto the bed, disgusted. "Fuck."

Don Conti started to speak, and I warned him, "Don't. Don't say it."

He laughed, then coughed. When he caught his breath, he spoke quickly.

"When the solicitor comes back in, sign the papers for the Chicago holdings. They go to my son. Don Manca will be pleased with you, bringing that fatted cow home.

"But before you open that door, I ask one thing."

Here it went. "I'm not calling you, Dad."

"Kill the man in Chicago. The one who murdered Adelmo. I want *you* to do it. I *know* you can."

Hell, I was slated to kill Johnny Porciello, anyway. Don Manca, his grandson Mario, and I discussed it at length. Mario wanted to wait for the dust to settle first. His grandfather wanted it done yesterday so his new granddaughter, Mario's wife, would sleep easier, and me?

I wanted that son of a bitch dead. It didn't matter when or where, but it was going to be me. Gesualdo wasn't asking for much at all.

"Are you sure?" Rumor had it that Dianora Conti might be pregnant. And that child was likely a little Porciello.

"More certain of that than I am of your parentage."

"There were two of you that night, huh?"

"At least one of us had a broken condom."

Damn. I called that one.

"Although, when I'm angry, I used to clench my fist. Just like you are. I can't do that anymore."

His gaze was on my left hand. The one I'd clamped down hard. "I'm not Italian, I'm Irish."

"You tell yourself that, but have you ever wondered why Don Manca agreed to take you in? Perhaps he recognized the snake he fostered."

The evil chuckle turned into another coughing fit.

I opened the door so everyone could see he was still alive.

When the ruckus calmed down, the solicitor led me to the door with the binder of American holdings, that fucking yellow folder, and a copy of the transfer with my signature on it. He retained the originals of the latter two items when he bid me a good afternoon.

There was nothing good about it. At least for me.

Eight hours later, I was in the heart of Sardinia getting patted down, again.

"Don Manca is waiting." Loppa, one of the uncles, opened the door for me. Unlike Don Conti's domain, Don Manca sat in his kitchen surrounded by comfortable things that reminded me of life, not death.

A casserole pan sat on some hot mats. The zuppa gallurese had been decimated by whoever beat me to it. Rough brown bowls sat in a short stack next to the pan. I helped myself. I skipped the leafy greens and added the fried zucchini and leeks to my plate.

Mario's grandfather sipped on an after-dinner drink. Probably mirto.

I dove into the layers of cheese and bread. Imagine the best stack of toasted cheese sandwiches soaked in rich beef stew broth and then oven-baked like a savory lasagna. It was the very first thing I ever fell in love with.

I was eight. I've never gotten over that crush. The first bite I met with a groan of pleasure. The second and third went down so fast I barely breathed let alone vocalized.

"Long trip?"

At least he waited until I set my fork down. I shoved the binder at him. "The Conti's Chicago holdings and the totality of the late Adelmo Conti's trust. Mario will want to look at that. Check out the top page."

He flipped the binder open.

"This is your signature."

I lifted my fork and gave him a quick nod to acknowledge that yes, I'd signed my name to something other than someone's dying breath.

Don Conti stared at the top page for a long time, waiting for me to elaborate. Unlike most, he didn't bluster or threaten. If he was angry with you, you died. Plain as that.

I swallowed a sip of beer. "Did you know that Don Conti might be my biological father?"

The gaze he had on the page snapped to read my face.

I relaxed. He didn't know. The relief was almost instant. I'd been stuffing my face like a dying man. I could finally breathe. I wasn't going to lose my family.

"He showed me a photo of my mom. You can guess the scenario, right?"

Don Conti frowned, but didn't shove his disgust at me.

"Yeah, well, with Adelmo dead and Dianora locked up, I guess he needed a new heir."

That goaded the family patriarch to review the documents under my signed albatross.

"There was a solicitor there, it's legit."

He closed the binder. "This is his way of apologizing to the family, yes?"

Perhaps. "He also wants me to kill Johnny Pornstach."

"We have men for that."

"You know I want to."

He grunted in that way he did when he didn't precisely

agree but was being diplomatic enough not to outright say so.

He finally spoke. "Mario thinks it is prudent to wait."

"Mario doesn't run the family." Yet. Hopefully, that would be at least a dozen years, or maybe even a few decades before he was tapped. Because I hated to lose my best friend to more paperwork and headaches.

"Neither do you."

Aw, fuck. "Touché."

Don Manca chuckled. "You are emotionally close to this one."

Bullshit.

His finger rose into the air, shaking as if I'd said the word out loud. "Don't lie to me."

"Even emotionally compromised, I'm still the best you got. And this was a…" dying wish? A vow to a parent I never knew?

Don Manca leaned in and spoke softly. "A set-up. Wrapped in a very expensive package."

I hadn't thought of it that way. As Adelmo's replacement, I'd be the first person on the short list of suspects if his killer turned up dead.

"What do we do?"

He smiled. It wasn't the one he saved for grandchildren or the nieces who brought him sweets. No, it was the one he got when he was especially pleased with a diabolical plot. "You need to go to Chicago and watch over Mario's lovely bride's twin sister. Perhaps begin the transition of the Conti assets to ours, and should ends fall loose, tie them up. Very discreetly, of course."

He set his thumb on his middle finger between the first and second joint.

Eliminate complications.

I was better at making them, yet I was looking forward to eliminating at least one.

3

ELLIE

Casey Kelly fit the physical description for an ex-cop, a limp, a barrel chest, a grayed crew cut that showed slightly more sunburnt skin each season, and a penchant for creative cussing.

He also hated anything regimented, buttoned down, or serene. That's why the straight from work crowd loved him. Once I shoved my way through the sticky main door, the wall of music, laughter, TVs, and heavily-slurred drunken blather slammed into me.

I took a moment to soak it in.

This familiar ground was *why* I came home. Not to sit in my too-small condo ruminating on how long it had been since I'd been kissed senseless. Two weeks wasn't that long. Yet, it felt like an eternity.

"El!" A regular dubbed "Tall Bob" spotted me and waved me to the empty stool next to him. Casey looked up and grinned.

"Kat said you'd made it back. How was the honeymoon?"

Crap. All the goodness I'd soaked in slid away leaving me like an empty bucket with too many holes. I plastered on a grin I didn't feel and lied my ass off. "It took me at least a day to remember how to walk again." Utter and complete fabrication woven, I graced the roar of laughter with a queenly smile and a wave. Then plunked my ass next to Tall Bob and ordered a cherry bomb.

Casey's laughter skipped a beat. He didn't have to glance at the clock. He knew what time it was because he'd practically lived at a bar for the last twenty years.

I was beginning to see the appeal.

He set the tumbler down and dropped the shot glass inside. "Careful now," he warned.

I ignored his words and slammed the fruity combo of energy drink and cherry vodka.

He set a glass of seltzer down next to the empty glasses almost before I'd finished. His eyes lingered on my left hand.

Tall Bob, not big on details, peppered me with questions about Italy. *Did you get to the Trevi Fountain? Did you see the Vatican? Where is the best pizza?*

I could barely answer before he had four more questions lined up. Because of my sister's little side trip, which included getting married, all the plans she'd helped me arrange were blown out of the water.

"I got to see Carnival in Venice." Where I "dropped" my phone in the water. It truly had been knocked out of my hand when… damn that bastard… elbowed me to show me a landmark or some shit. It had been so smooth I'd thought it was an accident. But around he-who-must-not-be-named, nothing was an accident.

I'd never felt safer in my life.

A shiver worked up my spine and stabbed me between the shoulder blades. I shook it off, attributing it to the chilly March wind I fought all seven blocks of my sloppy trudge to get a drink. Or five drinks, if you didn't count the seltzers Casey pushed at me between shots.

Everyone wanted a chance to welcome me home with a hug and a shot. I was swaying by eight o'clock.

"That's all for her tonight." Casey handed off the bar to Rosco, who unfortunately took one look at me and agreed with his old boss. When I bought the place, I took everyone with me. The first year sucked because I discovered not everyone enjoyed working here as much as I did. Rosco, Casey, and Kat stuck. And for that, they all were given raises and responsibilities. Then I found new employees who were young enough to deal with the bullshit, work hard, and build the dream.

"Walk with me, El." Casey pulled me to the back booth, and I sobered, knowing he was going to ask the hard questions.

I poured myself into the wooden bench opposite him. "What's up?"

He opened his mouth and tasted his words before speaking. "You ain't wearing your ring."

"Long-ass story." My chest heaved, barely carrying the weight that dragged it right back down again.

"Yeah? I heard a rumor from an old friend."

I braced myself for something awful. Casey's *old* friends

were *all* cops. If they weren't, they were still friends. "What's the scuttle?"

His eyebrow barely twitched. "Heard the FBI is sniffing around again."

No. There wasn't enough alcohol in the world to deal with *that* again. "We own the bar fair and square. You're good."

"I ain't talking about the bar. I'm talking about you."

Movement out of the corner of my eye had me checking the source. A man snagged my attention. I must be hallucinating because he moved just like… damn it. Whoever he was, he disappeared into the back hall where the bathrooms were. It couldn't be that asshole. I left him in Sardinia.

The jukebox shifted to a sad song.

Since Casey only allowed Irish music on his nights, it had fife and pipes. The haunting whistles and screeches felt like heartbreak in a cold rain. My soul sang along as I tried to keep the warm wash of sorrow-soaked booze from taking over.

"I'm good, Casey. I haven't done anything wrong, illegal, or immoral since…yesterday." I laughed at my joke.

He didn't. He shifted in his seat. "Apparently, you picked the wrong man."

No shit.

"I pick a lot of wrong men. It's a gift."

His gaze didn't leave my ring finger. "Is that why you're here alone?"

"Casey. Don't."

He sighed and scratched at his scrub brush straight scalp. "I worry about you."

"When haven't you?" I'd known him forever. All the neighborhood kids did.

He sipped his coffee, waiting me out. My sarcasm wasn't going to win points tonight. "Are you sure he's in your past?"

Most definitely. "It was a temporary blip. I'm good now."

His eyes lifted. "Yet you're drunk."

"It's still technically my vacation."

He leaned back to scan the bar. A habit that carried over from his days on the force. "Have someone follow you home, or take a rideshare tonight. Do not walk there alone. Understand?"

"Yes, Dad."

"I mean it. There are people asking questions. And you coming in here and lying about your honeymoon and marital status isn't going to fly. Those folks scrutinize any inconsistency."

I knew that. But the file the FBI had on me must mention at least twice that I was a pathological liar who couldn't provide a straight story if you held me at knife point.

A memory flashed through my mind. One of many I'd like to forget. Maybe it was mentioning Carnival earlier, or the way my rabid brain couldn't let go of one douchebag assassin, but that moment was frozen at the forefront of my thoughts.

I caught myself gazing into space. Something Casey Kelly

did often. It was called "a thousand-yard stare." What it really was could be summed up as PTSD trauma processing. Sergeant Kelly earned his during a shootout gone horribly wrong. It stripped him of his rigid moral code and replaced it with blood, dishonor, and nightmares best solved through liquid therapy.

Mine was more insidious. I'd lived with little cuts to my psyche ever since my Grandfather was dubbed, "The Outfit's Accountant." His life work reduced to headlines and sensationalized stories.

While he embraced the Family—capital F—he kept his *family* out of it. But the FBI decided that his weak spot was an avenue to harass, exploit, and torture. They were given legal means to terrorize a simple suburban family for over fourteen years.

Then Jaja died.

And the trouble got worse because all the money he'd scraped together to provide for us when he was gone was tainted with sin.

The nightmares never stopped. They just got worse. I should have at least tried to fight them off. Instead, I embraced them…made fun of them… crafted an entire persona that couldn't be wounded.

I was too sober for this shit. "I need another drink."

"Like hell ya do." Casey motioned to Molly so he could order a second coffee, plain, and one for me.

"I'm going to be up all night." The caffeine wouldn't be fully to blame, but it certainly wouldn't help.

"Better than a having a hangover. Are you taking my opener tomorrow?"

I nodded. I'd be here whether I was working or not. Might as well give everyone a break and do something.

Molly set my mug down, doctored exactly as I liked it, except for the Baileys. I knew it was missing as soon as I raised it to sniff.

"Then, cheers." He lifted his cup to match mine.

No sooner than I finished sipping, a shadow moved from the hallway back toward the bar.

And my heart stuttered before picking up the pace to flight *and* fight levels.

Ringo-fucking-Devlin was in my bar. I tracked him the entire distance from the back hallway to his seat in the prime spot where the curve of the bar hit the north wall. There were two stools tucked into the corner where the bar flap interrupted the short leg of the "J." I liked to sit there because you could watch everything that happened in the main bar as well as check out anyone taking the stairs to the overflow lounge in the basement.

That bar was only a third the size of the main floor's. Most nights the door to it was locked. That didn't stop curious folks from tugging the brass handle. And, if I wanted to escape there tonight to ignore Casey's no-drinking decree, I'd have to walk right past my nemesis to get there.

I'd rather gnaw my arm off.

Casey finished saying something I'd completely missed. He stared at me, waiting for a quip or a snarky reply.

He got silence instead.

"You're off your game."

"You drop a bombshell like gooberment hounds sniffing around my booty hole, and I'm supposed to just ignore it?"

He frowned. Apparently, the conversation had moved past that point, and I'd handed him proof of my distraction.

His gaze followed the trail I'd inadvertently exposed. "Who is he?"

Oh, sweet Jesus. Once a cop, always a… "No one."

Casey laughed once. "You don't fool me. I know what that is. It's kryptonite. At least for you."

"I ain't Superman. I have no weaknesses."

He laughed long and hard at that one. Once he got it out of his system, he cleared his throat. "You know, I hated Johnny Pornstach."

If everyone could stop reminding me of my faults, it would be really nice of them. "What was it, the caterpillar on his upper lip or the weasel-like set of his shoulders?"

"He was all wrong for you."

I groaned. "And who's right for me?"

Casey's grin fell. "Not him." He glanced to the front of the room. "And probably not the guy who caught your eye. That's trouble."

"How can you tell?" This was insightful. Because when I first met "He-who-shall-not-be-named" I had picked up on the swagger, the careless hair, the grin that hid secrets, but Ringo had done nothing more than any other normal man would have done when bumping into a pretty woman.

"He's a wolf." Casey leaned in and lowered his volume. "Without looking, he sees everything. You don't do that unless someone somewhere has taught you how."

I kept my eyes on Casey.

"Are you saying the newcomer is dangerous?"

His icy blue eyes met mine. He gave me a little shake of the head. "Dangerous doesn't describe it. I know that thrills little girls like you, but steer clear of that one."

I feigned offense. "Little girls like me? Come on! I've got at least two handfuls right here." I grabbed my breasts and lifted them with a squish.

His face wrinkled into a sardonic grin. "He's the kind you think can protect you, but they only draw you into the darkness."

If he only knew how true his words were.

I leaned in with a flirty pout on my lips. "Sounds like you. Why do you think I love you?"

He laughed. "If only I were thirty years younger."

"Spank me and call me baby-girl."

Luckily, the song had switched to something raucous and mindless. Because I was in a mood. Casey picked up my lies, and we joked until he deemed his bedtime nigh.

As he took his leave, he tapped the table to get my attention. "Hey. Watch your back."

It wasn't delivered with his usual cadence. This warning held weight. Behind the words was insistence and sincerity.

I nodded, finally sobering past the false clarity booze goggles provided. "I will."

His words haunted me an hour later as I scanned the streets while the rideshare driver chatted.

Ringo had disappeared, and I suspected I was being followed.

Maybe the wolf was hunting?

But I wasn't a helpless little girl. I had teeth, too.

4

RINGO

You'd think I'd be used to being ignored by now. I cultivated the art of not being spotted, yet Ellie and the older bartender were hyper-aware. I'd managed to slip past their radar the entire night until I made the mistake of eavesdropping on their conversation once it moved from the bar to the back.

The booth was built for secrets. High walls, shadowy lighting, the cover of a speaker mounted just off center from the high half wall and the bathroom hall. I couldn't design a better blind.

And no sooner than I walked away, I felt her eyes on me.

Knowing I'd been made, I took the chair guaranteed to attract attention. Regular patrons avoided it, as if it had "reserved" on it. Only one of the stools there didn't wobble. Which meant it was a solo seat.

Rosco kept me entertained between spurts of activity. I asked the usual questions. Where's a good spot to eat? How does he think the local team is going to do? That sort of thing.

He pegged me as new to the neighborhood, but native to the land. Anything more foreign would raise suspicions.

And when Ellie finally emerged for the rideshare she'd called, I was waiting in my car parked across the street and slightly back so she wouldn't spot me.

What I didn't expect was the car two spots ahead to pull out in front of me.

I waited, giving another car space to fill the gap between me and whoever followed Ellie.

She hadn't had more than thirty hours to relax at home before she picked up a tail. Don Manca would need to know.

The rideshare turned left into her condo's parking lot. The black sedan hunting her braked but pulled past. He'd circle the block and return.

I flipped on my blinker and waited for traffic to clear before pulling into her lot. I took a spot near the dumpsters and got out.

Ellie was inside, no doubt thinking she was safe. But she absolutely wasn't. I entered the lobby of the units across from hers so I could mark her position as she flipped on the lights in her home.

The living room light came on. Seconds later, the kitchen lit up. I relaxed into the wait. There were two entrances into her unit. The lobby door, which often didn't lock behind her like it should. This side's lock had a misaligned bolt that made it impossible for the door to secure unless you lifted the door as it shut. A familiar issue, sagging from wear, construction mistakes, or deliberate sabotage. Like one heavy object dropped onto the handle which threw the whole mechanism out of alignment.

Then there was the slider she walked past. Her living room had a little balcony slab that was fenced off with a short, spiked fence. As if that was a deterrent?

One jump, a heavy screwdriver wedged into the frame corner, and with a twist-lift you were in. Unless you dropped the security bar into the track.

The curtains rustled, and Ellie bent over to lock it in place.

"Good girl."

She stared out at the lot silhouetted by the lights inside. Her gaze slipped past me in the shadows. But she was searching for something.

A car parked near the entrance. The lights illuminated the side of her building.

Ellie slipped behind the curtains and flicked off all her lights.

If it were me, I wouldn't have turned on the lights at all. But she was new to this.

Only the faint shift of the curtain gave her away this time as she watched the lot's entrance. But nothing came from that direction.

As one who always looks for weak points, I monitored the shadows by the dumpsters. An alley led to the two bins hidden behind a wooden fence.

There was a gate there for tenants to drag their bags through. The path had been shoveled clean, and the melted snow puddles plaguing their trek had dried up today.

Ellie's high bedroom window faced that breach.

I should have remained in my car. I'd be able to watch it better from there.

"Fuck." Did something move behind the fence? I couldn't tell. And I couldn't just stroll over there without Ellie noticing. What I really needed was to be in her home, guarding her personally.

Don Manca was right. I was too emotionally close to this. Because my first thoughts after forming the desire to be inside with Ellie were not about protection at all.

Which meant I should leave. I should call for reinforcements to put on Ellie and focus on the business that brought me here.

But honestly? Business wasn't why I came. Damn Conti, his dying wish or his stupid photo—not even all the money in the world was enough to drag me here.

Killing Ellie's ex? Well… I should be doing that, not watching her like some pervert. My justification was simple. She'd draw him out. Sooner or later, Johnny Pornstach would want closure. Any man who fell in love with Ellie Jacobs would. It was inevitable, like the ocean tides, or death.

I smiled. He'd die all right. As I waited for the right diversion to slip out of the hiding spot I'd chosen, I plotted at least a hundred ways to murder the man who'd broken promises to my Ellie.

My heart sped up. *My* Ellie?

When had I claimed her? She wasn't mine. In fact, she flew seventy-three thousand kilometers to get away from me. She cut her vacation short by three days to not see my face.

Yet, from the moment I first saw her, drunk, jilted, and belligerent, I claimed her.

There was something that sparked deep inside my chest that pushed aside every other thought and took notice. I'd been working a complicated mission. Save Mario, my best friend, from dying. That was easiest if I were the man charged with killing him. I could eliminate all the competition if I was racing for the payout. The target wouldn't be on me. Yet being close enough to stab him was the perfect spot to trap others attempting to make the same mistake.

And then Ellie happened. She wore that damn glittery wedding gown. Its design was guaranteed to catch the eye and tantalize the senses with little glimpses of flesh. Its purpose was to scintillate a man into madness with the way it pushed her creamy breasts up to form two perfect spheres of temptation.

I blew out a breath. The nose of the black car was still in place. Whoever it was must be freezing their nuts off. March in Chicago was like a roulette wheel of weather choices. One moment sunny and mild, the next it would be icy rain driven by bitter winds. Even the nights were capricious.

The sedan's lights came on and it pulled away.

I slipped out of the blind and circled the block to check the alley. The plows had piled up a stubborn bank of snow that had deflated into a mass of gray and black ice clinging to the wooden privacy fence. There were footprints grooved deep from tenants climbing it to reach the far corners of the bins. I ignored those. The fresher ones weren't deep because they hadn't had time to melt. Two stood out because they pointed the wrong way. I couldn't gauge the size because the snow melted into ice pellets— only the shallow shape of a work shoe was visible.

The shoe-wearer's attention wasn't focused on the dumpsters, but instead pointed toward Ellie's bedroom window.

My imagination placed Johnny into those indents. His beguiling baby face peeking above the slats. His spindly arms clinging to the fence in a vain attempt to pull his body over.

What the hell did she see in him?

My hand closed, imagining the knife I'd cut his throat with. Generally, I didn't hate my targets. They were a job, nothing more. The means to a very final end.

I followed the twisted trail of marks to the pavement. One drying footprint pointed out of the alley to the street.

He'd circled the block the same way I'd come, peeked into Ellie's bedroom window, then got in his car and left.

I stood on the mark, and angled my body to see the world from his view. Something was off. A man obsessed wouldn't exit cleanly. Especially not one twisted enough to peek over a fence into a bedroom window. I took a second and third look at the evidence and came up with more questions than answers.

Even the answers I could form pointed toward the conclusion that this man wasn't stalking Ellie for the obvious emotional reasons. It was too…

Professional.

Damn it.

Now I really needed to plant myself at her side. I hadn't gotten a good look at the driver. And the car was deliberately common. Nice enough to be out of the price range of street criminals, but not ostentatious, which would attract attention. That attention to detail was something Mario would appreciate.

Johnny didn't possess that subtlety.

I crept away and made a choice. I was damned, so I might as well enjoy the trip to Hell.

Fifteen minutes later, a car pulled into the lot. I got a message on my phone informing me of the delivery. I met the driver at the door to Ellie's building and tipped him in cash.

Yes, that would stand out. But I wasn't hiding anymore. I couldn't.

I tapped in the code for Ellie's unit and waited.

"Hello?"

"You didn't eat supper."

"What the—? Ringo, you fucking asshole. I'm sick and tired of—"

I cut her off. "You didn't eat. I got food. Let me in."

"Are you insane?"

"Obviously, let me in. It's cold out here."

"Freeze."

The intercom shut off abruptly. I dialed her number, hoping she hadn't blocked me yet.

"Who the, goddammit Ringo. Go to hell."

"Mexican. Street tacos, enchiladas, and chips. It's getting cold. Open the fucking door."

"Or what?"

Well, that was an easy reply. "I'll show you exactly how secure your so-called security is. Easy way or hard way, El, which is it?"

Her sigh was audible. "What kind of street tacos?"

"Barbacoa. I'm not a heathen."

The door buzzed, letting me know she'd unlocked it. I slipped in, and she opened her door. Light streamed from her apartment illuminating the hallway around her figure.

I had to ignore the urge to drop the food and bum rush her into her living room. She was way too trusting, and shouldn't have opened the door before confirming it was me, not some random asswipe.

"Put the food on my table, then leave."

"I'm not going anywhere."

Her eyes spit fire. Instead of arguing with me, she lifted her phone. Her fingers scrolled on the screen.

"Are you calling the cops?"

"No. Don Manca."

Shit. I grabbed the phone. "Don't do that." He didn't like business calls in the early mornings.

"Give me my phone."

Absolutely not. I did a quick calculation of time zone difference. He'd be awake, probably feeding goats or eating breakfast, but still. "Are you trying to kill me?"

Her eyebrow quirked up as if what I suggested was a novel idea. One worth exploring…immediately.

It was time to come clean. "You were followed."

She scanned me from head to toe and back. "I see that."

"Not by me. I followed the guy who followed you."

Her nostrils flared. "You're not scoring any points, dumbass."

Yeah… I could see that. Time to regroup. "Okay, your sister worries about you," I started.

"And she let me go home all by myself with Firenze as a guard right up to the ferry where she knew I'd be just fine without Don Manca's dogs on my ass. And, speaking of dogs…what are you doing here?"

My brain scrambled for something other than the truth that crawled up my throat and begged to leak out. "I'm here on business." *Whew.*

"Business."

"Yes."

Her eyes rolled upward, and she groaned before snatching the food from my grip. "If I'm going to go to prison for aiding and abetting, I'm eating first. Damn you."

"Aiding and abetting what?"

Her glare said something, but I couldn't figure out what. "You know what. Who's the target this time, me?"

I got a little hung up on the way her yoga pants clung to her ass so my reply didn't come out quickly enough to erase suspicion. "It's real work. There's a company here that—"

Her hand shot into the air. "Shut up. Don't talk, I don't want to know. I'm tired, still half drunk, and really don't want to hear your voice."

We should really talk about her anger. It was unjustified. *Maybe?*

"Listen, I know we didn't exactly part on the best terms, but you gotta—"

Ellie set down the bags and dug in a drawer while I was

talking. I stopped when she pulled out a wicked-looking taser and then a fresh cartridge.

"Sweetheart. Put that down."

She loaded it instead.

"Baby, those things hurt an awful lot."

"Good." She depressed the button and nothing happened.

"They also need to be charged once in a while." Thank God.

She threw the whole thing at my head. I caught it, barely. "Let's talk."

Ellie went to the kitchen window and picked up a potted plant. The novelty pot was a heavy, white, ceramic piece cast in the shape of an octopus pointing middle fingers up from each tentacle. It would hurt like heck if it broke on my face.

"Okay, no talking. Let's eat instead, please? Your poor plant doesn't deserve to die because you're mad at me." Although, it did appear to be dying from embarrassment.

She stared at the vessel in her hands. It took her a long time to weigh the choice, but eventually she set it down, and I breathed a little easier.

I opened my mouth to ask about plates, but caught her glare before I could squeak out anything more than a "Wh—" Instead, I mimed the circular platter with my hands and pointed at her cabinets.

"I hate you."

The h-word. *Yikes*. But I wasn't being forcefully removed yet. Her hands were empty. And her phone was abandoned on the table.

I edged around her carefully, holding my hands high to

show I wasn't a threat to her. After opening a few cabinets, I found plates. Utensils were easier to locate. There were only three drawers in her tiny-ass kitchen. One was situated between the dishwasher and the sink, so I opened that first and hit the jackpot. I placed two settings on her tiny table as she unpacked the food.

There was a lot. I hadn't really factored in much more than purchasing a variety so she could pick her favorites. I'd eat whatever was left. It didn't matter much to me. Food was a means to an end.

Staying right at her side was the most important thing.

5

ELLIE

As scared as I was, Ringo did one thing well. Piss me off until I wasn't shaking anymore. And even if I was still shaking, I could blame it on being angry.

Yet, he brought tacos.

Was that enough to forgive him for following me? And I didn't buy his whole schtick about following someone who was following me for one damn minute. He had to be following me first in order to spot whoever it was. If it was anyone at all.

I replayed the last half hour in my head. While I hadn't figured for certain if someone actually followed me on my ride home, obviously someone, specifically *him*, evaded detection. How could I concentrate? He'd showed up at my bar, sat in my favorite chair, and let's not forget something *really important*, the FBI were targeting me…again.

How would I avoid their notice with an assassin dumping takeout on my table at two A.M.?

My nerves were shot. During my usual sweep of the house to check windows and confirm the bar was in place to lock the sliding door to the patio, I thought I saw something in the parking lot. But aside from one or two new cars in the lot, nothing seemed out of place. Until I swore I heard someone by the dumpsters.

That was my one complaint about this place. I'd bought it before realizing that my unit's bedroom was right next to where the garbage trucks backed into the short alley at seven A.M., *every* Tuesday.

I owned a bar that shut its doors at two and had a nightly cleaning routine. Do the math.

And right after that noise, there was *nothing*. Which was more than odd, it was terrifying. Because if there had been the expected noise of a garbage bag landing inside with its clanging echo, or the crunch of footsteps walking away, or even the rusty creak of someone pushing the wooden gate closed, then I would have relaxed.

But there was no sound.

Not out there. It was all in my head. My imagination supplied a horror-soundtrack complete with heavy breathing and an ominous music bed perfectly designed to scare the shit out of me.

I'd finally written it off and was getting ready for bed when Ringo buzzed the intercom.

No one friendly used my intercom. They called. Even the food delivery people called or texted. Duh.

Then I heard his voice and lost my damn mind.

Why did I let him in?

Savory slow-cooked beef was not a valid excuse.

Bone chilling terror? Plausible, but wimpy as heck. *EVS?*

Quite possibly. But an empty vagina was easily solved.

I had the mortifying suspicion that the real reason I opened that damn door was because my dumb broken heart had poisoned my entire body and was slowly taking over my brain.

A flesh-eating zombie virus would be more welcome.

Ringo handed me two extra-spicy sauce packets as I unwrapped my second taco.

I didn't move. He set them down next to the crumpled wrapper and continued eating as if he hadn't just shoved the foundations of my soul ten feet sideways.

There were three varieties of sauces to choose from, and he picked the right kind. Proving he was not only observant, but damn him, watching out for my needs.

Or maybe he was just manipulating me?

Whatever. Eat first, question the dubious morals of an international hitman later.

He's the kind you think can protect you, but they only draw you into the darkness. Casey's words rang through my brain.

"Do I have sauce on my chin or something?" Ringo asked.

Busted. But two could play at that. I picked up a napkin, spit on the corner and wiped his face.

He froze.

Even that wasn't normal. I mean, most guys would freeze in terror because they'd basically just been spit on, or they'd recoil in disgust.

With Ringo, it was the stillness of a predator who'd just spotted his next meal.

I was sick of being a target. "I told you not to talk."

He tossed his food to the plate. A whole minute went by as he debated breaking my rules and pissing me off more, or whether he really wanted to escalate the war to DEFCON four.

"You're a piece of work."

Straight to nukes.

"Says the guy who stalked me from a tiny ass villa in the hills of Barbagia all the way to suburban Chicago."

"I'm not stalking you."

"You are a liar."

"Like that's a crime?"

I growled. He was infuriating. "Since you brought it up, let's talk about crime for a minute."

His face blanked. "Let's not and say we did." He glanced at the windows next to us.

From age nine I'd known exactly why he said that and looked where he did. And I also knew a million and one ways to say something completely harmless just in case you were being eavesdropped on but really needed to say something un-harmless.

"Did you know that Chicago averages over 600 homicides in a year?"

His eyes went cold.

"And that the local FBI building houses over 600 employees. They can do 700 if they experience a high volume in case load."

"Did you know your hands are shaking?"

I set my taco down and tucked my fingers between my knees where he couldn't see them. "Did you know you that an erect blue whale's penis is over twelve inches in diameter and that still isn't the biggest dick on the planet?"

Ringo snorted. "No, I didn't know that. But I suppose the biggest dick is exactly one hundred and eighty-one centimeters tall, weighs 81 kilograms, and knows exactly what your face looks like when you orgasm."

My breath stalled in my throat. With it, my eyes got that funnily warm tingle of excess moisture pooling at the edges, and my hearing got fuzzy in the corners.

I tried to form words and failed.

"Breathe, Ellie."

As if I needed his permission? "You're a bastard."

"Everyone knows that." He tried to laugh at his own joke and failed. Oddly, he broke eye contact with me, and I could suck in air without the weight of his scrutiny clamping my throat shut.

"I found out who he is…was." He stared at the plate in front of him.

"Wh-who?"

He sighed. "Someone awful. They… uh… were in hospice care for complications from a gunshot wound, and last night their breathing stopped. Attempts at revival were unsuccessful."

"Did you know he was in a bad way?"

Ringo snorted bitterly. His gaze drifted to the window. "Let's say it's one of those occupational hazards of mine."

My eyes bugged out. It was on the tip of my tongue to blurt out, "Did you do it?"

And he must have read it on my face. "I'd just landed at O'Hare this morning when Mario called me to let me know. He thought I would need that information." Ringo licked his lips and resumed his vacant perusal of the food we'd both abandoned.

My brain worked overtime to process everything. It almost sounded like I should know who his father was, but the only person I knew who'd been shot was—

Holy shit.

I must have muttered the words out loud because his eyes snapped up to trap mine.

"Yeah. I'm here on real business. Call it a hostile takeover, or something." He frowned and picked up his food.

"Does his daughter...?"

God, my mind went blank. Dianora was in jail awaiting trial for shooting her father. Now it would be upgraded to murder. And since there was still the unsolved murder of her brother which she helped organize with the help of my ex—

"That's why." It wasn't just a lightbulb but one of those super-strong searchlight-type do-hickeys shooting off.

"Why what?" Ringo asked.

I wiggled my empty ring finger where he could see it.

His eyes went to it. An eyebrow went up. "Yeah. Eat... if you can."

Food and gory memories didn't mix. My head still felt fuzzy, and my body processed all these shocks after shocks with very little *comfort* between.

No sooner than I thought the word, I remembered how

nice it felt to have Ringo's arms around me. And it wasn't just one memory, but multiple. From the cute hug he gave me in the airport in Venice, to the way he picked me up in the piazza, one very long night of touches, and a heartfelt hug in the Galleria of Vittorio Emanuele II right after I finished my third twirl on top of the mosaic bull. Lastly, waking up in his arms as he ran out of a Tuscan fortress with guns blazing and…

His father. *Damn.*

"You really shouldn't be here." Once word got out that Don Conti was his father, the sharks would circle. Not just law enforcement, but other factions. Don Conti's family would also be gunning for him since he was an outsider. Worse? He was sitting right here at my little two-person cafe-style dining table, eating tacos with his half-brother's killer's ex.

It was a complete cluster fuck.

"Aiaiu wants me here. Right here." His finger pressed on the table, pinning him in place.

How does it feel to be one of those paper shooting targets? The words remained behind the secrecy of my thoughts. "Aiaiu" meant grandfather. A term of affection in Sardinia, but also the title of the patriarch of the familial organization Ringo was adopted into. No one called Don Manca that unless they were family. Shit. Family, capital F. My sister taught me that. She was allowed to call him that, and I wasn't.

But Ringo was, and worse? He uttered it in front of me, who wasn't Family.

My foolish heart whispered vain hopes. I stabbed that bitch with a flaming chopstick…mentally.

"I guess you'll have to let him know I don't want you here."

Ringo laughed silently. His shoulders shook even after his mouth closed and his face twisted into a mix of amusement and pain. "Nice try. I'm going to sleep on your couch tonight."

"No, you're not." I knew him better. He'd pretend to sleep, and instead stare through the plate glass watching the shadows until the sun rose. Even then, he wouldn't sleep.

"Your bed then. With you."

"Hell no."

"You say that now."

"I'll keep saying it."

This time his face didn't fall before the laughter died. But in the slow creep into seriousness, something shifted.

Longing.

Maybe I was misreading the emotion. Maybe I was simply pushing my own mixed signals there. Or maybe it was just…

Pain.

I tucked my hands between my knees again, shivering from a draft that had snuck up on me.

"I'm here."

I shook my head, trying to deny him. But it was weak. Fragile.

The brutal truth was, I still mourned his loss even though I was the one who'd pushed him away. I simply couldn't live my life with a killer. It would place me into a cage that I thought I'd escaped before.

The truth was, I hadn't escaped. I'd only dug back

under the fence and planted my stupid butt inside the zoo I knew.

Johnny Porciello was a killer. A guy who wanted to be "mobbed-up" so badly, he cheated on me with a twisted woman made even more evil by the patriarchal organization who'd never let her manage her own destiny. Her failure, as evilly executed as it was, meant yet another generation of women who would live their lives at best as commodities, and in the worst ways, as victims. I couldn't possibly want that, could I?

With every fiber of my being, my heart cried. It begged for Ringo's touch. His gentle care. His lies. I could easily settle into the false ignorance my sister embraced. Living with Ringo would be one long nightmare.

And probably the one great love of my lifetime.

I was smarter than that. I had to be.

With new determination, I cleaned up the mess on the table and forced myself to accept what I couldn't change tonight. He'd invoked Don Manca's name. Even I wasn't strong enough, or stupid enough to try to argue with the leader of a group of assassins.

Once the main kitchen-dining area was sorted, I moved to the bedroom to get Ringo a blanket for his cold camp on my couch. At least I wouldn't have to worry about getting murdered in my sleep. I had an assassin guard dog.

"Embrace the good." It was my new mantra. Or maybe an old one I'd resurrected.

"Wait." Ringo shoved past me and did a quick sweep of my bedroom, even going as far as rising on tiptoe to peer out my window at the dumpster fence.

"I heard a noise there earlier. Was that you?"

He glared at me. "No."

Crap.

I tugged the comforter I'd meant to retrieve off the shelf I'd crammed it into. "Grab a pillow, but not any of the feather ones. Those are mine."

He picked up one of the plush throw pillows I kept on my bed and stared at the fuzzy raised lettering crocheted into the cover. "Fuck off?"

"Turn it over."

He laughed as he read. "…You."

He missed a word.

"You're sleeping on the couch," I said as I flounced out.

6

RINGO

Ellie played a good game, but she was hiding in more ways than one.

She retreated to her room after dumping me on the couch with not only her foul-mouthed pillow, but a printed blanket that tossed me right back to my childhood. Except that dang cartoon handed out its advice peppered with profanity now. She had stuff like that all over her little two-bedroom condo. During my security search, I discovered tiny mustache stickers on her outlet covers, a rooster clock that really needed to be shot, and a bathroom word sign that read, "If you let them SHENAN once, they're just going to SHENANIGAN."

Cute, or a cry for help?

I played with the overlarge planchette on her coffee table as I pondered that question. Then noticed, even it had picked up her personality.

Maybe I would summon her last fuck like the plastic pointer directed.

The instant I thought the word I remembered the hot as hell night we spent outside Genoa at the sprawling mansion Mario and I bought. It was one of those places designed to impress. When I picked it out, I had the stupid idea I'd bring Mom there one day and rub her face in my success.

Ellie and I had been in Milan that morning. We spent the day looking for her sister. She was looking. I was distracting her. We did two of the touristy things she had detailed in her trip package. First, we went to the Duomo to get a good view of the penthouse Mario's father lived at. But with all the tourists milling around, I couldn't exactly pull out the rifle scope I'd carried with me. Frustrated and cold, I let Ellie drag me to the Galleria.

The stores were overpriced, and the crowds huge. It would be a great spot to shiv someone and disappear into the throng. Not even the twenty-seven cameras I'd spotted would be able to track me.

Ellie spun on her heel and laughed until she was dizzy. I caught her on the third turn, and she looked up at me, flushed and happy.

I had to have her that way.

So, I took her on a long trip home to my bed. The place I felt safe because I'd made it that way.

What a mistake. Yet I didn't regret a damn minute of that night. Only the next day when I led her up the coast to the villa Don Manca held. This time, I brought the whole rifle with me. Ellie didn't notice the bag I carried, being content to dance ahead, stop and smell early flowers, point at olive trees, and glow.

Just… glow. Like an ethereal angel filled with joy.

Then I spotted the sniper. I sent her ahead, pointing out the house where her sister and Mario were having breakfast on the fucking terrace. Right out in the goddamn open.

The hitman lined up his shot, and I scrambled to assemble the rifle and take aim. Ellie had her phone to her ear because she wanted to warn Allie we were on our way up.

I ignored her and focused on making the craziest shot of my life. There was a light crosswind, sun slightly behind the target, and an uphill angle, making the calculations shift by the millisecond.

Right as I squeezed the trigger, she asked, "What are you doing?"

Then all hell broke loose. She freaked out, following the line of my aim and seeing the sniper fall out of his perch, roll down the terrace, and disappear into the brush.

Worse? She was on the phone with her sister, and by proxy, Mario. I'd outed myself in the worst way possible.

At first, she screamed at me. I was compared to her no-good ex who'd killed Adelmo Conti.

Then she just froze me out.

It was for the best.

I was the rebound fuck. The guy to screw the bad taste out of her memories. I'd done my job, protected my best friend. Led him to the real killer. Got him out alive so he could live happily ever after with Ellie's twin.

And I'd lost the girl.

The bedroom door rubbed against the carpet as Ellie cracked it open. I'd turned off the lights so I could see out of the sliding glass door better. Her bedroom light was on. It reflected the outline of her head in the glass of the slider better than a mirror.

"Ringo?"

It took me a minute to push the anger out of my voice. "Yeah, babe?"

The swath of light grew larger as she slipped out and approached.

She had both hands in front of her.

Was she carrying a weapon? I tried to make out the details and fell short. But I wouldn't turn around. If she was going to stab me in the back, the hole would match the one I'd done to myself that horrible day.

"May I show you something and get your opinion?"

She'd stopped just behind the couch. I turned my head to get a look at her.

Her pajamas weren't from the trip.

She'd packed a whole bag of sexy lingerie that ended up with her sister. I heard the complaints for three days. She'd worn my T-shirts two of those days, and one very intimate night, not a damn thing.

But the fuzzy black and white…*thing* she wore looked like a child's costume. Except it was overlarge and swamped her perfect figure under about an inch-thick fake fur.

"What the hell is that?"

She looked down at her outfit. "It's a honey badger. As in—"

I stopped her before she got both of us sidetracked. "What do you have to show me?"

She handed over a piece of paper and slouched over the side of the couch. "It was tucked in my suitcase."

"From Italy?"

"It wasn't there in Italy. When I came home, I had the driver dump the bags in the lobby. But he couldn't get in, so he tucked them behind the fence."

This woman was too stupid to live. I unfolded the paper.

I breathed out a stream of air and tried to remind myself why the hell I was here.

She stared at me with her chin propped on her fists. "Well?"

I turned the paper in my hands. Johnny had signed his name to the death threat. "Is this his handwriting?"

Ellie's hopeful face fell. "Yeah."

I re-read the misspelled and grammar-less scribbles.

Pay me the 50k u owe me for the pre-nup, or your ded.

"Fifty grand?"

Ellie disappeared behind the arm of the couch. Only the little round ears of her hood peeked out. "I sent him a pre-nup contract the day of the wedding. In it, if we stayed married a year, he'd get fifty thousand. But that's it."

"Then you don't owe. You didn't marry his dumb ass."

"Tell him that."

I leaned a little to get a glimpse of her, but all I could see was the stupid cartoon face sewn onto the hood. "Get off the floor."

"But I like it down here."

"No, you don't."

Her head cleared the lip of the sofa arm. Her blond hair stuck out of the hood in disarray because she'd shoved it on too quickly to straighten the mess. "Don't tell me what I like."

Was that a dare? "Chiacchiere served with chocolate lattes—light on the chocolate, lemon creme tarts, strawberry vodka, and—"

"Shut up."

"—bad boys who can't spell for shit."

Her eyes narrowed.

"Tell me I'm wrong."

"Can you spell?"

"In four languages, sweetheart." Although my German was questionable.

"Don't call me that."

"What? Sweetheart?"

"Or babe, sweetie, darling, none of it." Her face turned pink.

"What should I call you?"

"Ellie. Just Ellie."

I shook my head. "No can do. You're a hell of a lot more to me than just Ellie."

Her mouth fell open. Slowly, she sank behind the arm of the couch.

I stood up and picked her up off the floor and sat down on the couch with her ugly sack of a costume and everything.

"You're going to be too hot to sleep in this." Already, I could feel her warmth through the fur.

The silence that stretched thin was uncomfortable.

"Ellie?"

"I get cold."

Right. Venice. The first night.

I tugged the blanket free and tried to get it to cover us both.

"I'm not sleeping out here."

"Shh." I was tired of arguing with her.

"I mean it, Ringo, I only came out to ask your opinion of that…"

"Threat?"

She squirmed until she could face me. "Will he do it?"

Since he'd already killed once, I doubted she was safe. But if I said that, she'd freak out. "I think he's an idiot."

"Is that your *professional* opinion?"

"Sweetheart, you don't want my professional opinion."

She blinked at me. "Yes, I think I do."

I swallowed. This close, I could smell her shampoo. And her warm skin. "I think Don Manca's right."

Her eyes went a little wider. I nodded because we both couldn't say a whole hell of a lot if she was being followed like she thought she was.

"Scooch."

"What?" I asked.

"Give me some room." She wiggled free and then unzipped her costume. Underneath she had a lightweight cotton shirt that drooped off her shoulder, and thin pajama bottoms that were soft as hell. I knew that because she slid over me and stretched out on the couch, giving me the outside and stealing the inside. "Now cover me up."

Her ass wiggled against my leg. I rolled until I was

stretched out against her. She was small enough to fit against me, but her couch wasn't long or wide enough to fit both of us. "This isn't going to work."

I stood up and collected her, blanket and all, and carried her into her bedroom. She'd turned down her covers, so I laid her down and flipped the rest of them back so I could crawl in beside her. "No funny business. This is… me being a professional only, okay?"

"I don't—"

"Ellie, don't argue with me. You'll lose. At least on this. Got it?"

She rolled over to face me. "Why are you such a *good* bad guy?"

"Excuse me?"

Her face scrunched. "You. All sexy and fun, and…" her fingers traced my chest, "…built. And you brought food. But you probably know at least a hundred ways to do—"

The quick glance she sent me was part fear.

"My job?"

Her hand flicked away. "Yeah, that."

"Try about five hundred ways. Or maybe just six."

"Only six?" She asked.

"That covers the main categories." I began to count them off as I whispered in her ear. "Firearms, bladed objects, strangulation, blunt force trauma, drowning…" I trailed off, distracted by the soft fuzz on her cheek.

"That's five."

I smiled. "Flame thrower."

"You're making that one up."

I was, but she didn't need to know that.

Our eyes met across her pillow.

"You think I'm sexy?"

She rolled her eyes. "*Four* languages?" she asked through narrowed eyes.

I nodded. "I went to boarding school in Switzerland. They had French, Italian, and German as required courses."

"That's three."

"What language are we talking in now?"

She shook her head. "Doesn't count."

"Oh, I think it does. Ol' Johnny Pornstach can't even spell his native words correctly."

"He knows Italian."

"It's not that hard to learn."

She pushed at me. "I've been trying to learn for six months."

Ah, that was her problem. "You don't try. You do."

"Okay, Yoda."

"Sei incantevole, I tuoi occhi sono come due stelle. Ti adoro. Per te farei di tutto." My words trailed off because they were too honest, too close to the edge of insanity for me to trap them if more spilled free.

"How does that sound in German?"

I snorted. "Like two hammers trying to fuck."

Her laughter died quickly. The light in her eyes, however, didn't. After two unsuccessful attempts to speak, she whispered, "Per te farei di tutto."

"I won't hold you to that."

"What's it mean?"

"Tutto, *everything*. Per te, *for you*." I translated only part of it.

She filled in the rest with a small nod. Her hand came to rest on my chest. "I don't want you here."

"I know. I'm just another bad boy. You don't want that in your life." She'd made that point perfectly clear.

Her fingers tightened, pulling my shirt away from my skin. "You're here because you're protecting me. You've been ordered to. I get that. What I mean is…"

There were tears clinging to her eyelashes. She swallowed.

"…I don't want you here like that."

You and me both, babe.

7

ELLIE

Warmth. I loved mornings when I didn't wake up shivering. I inhaled my little pocket of comfort and caught notes of cedar, warm skin, and the oddly sweet spicy fragrance that lingered on Ringo's skin.

Mmm… I ran my nose against his chest, reveling in the sensation of his hard muscles, wiry chest hair, and that aroma I couldn't quite pin down.

Wait. Ringo? What the fuck?

I tensed for a moment, then remembered last night, the food, that awful note, me trying to be as unsexy as possible before approaching him.

Oh my God, he'd seen the honey badger.

It had been a gag gift from Kat in retribution for gifting her with a whole series of books about honey badger shifters. Once I found out where she'd gotten it, I bought one for her and we named them. Mine was Stevie, hers was Max, and we reserved the final sister's name for when and if Allie would ever join the fandom. So far, she'd resisted.

Despite the ugly pajama incident, he was in my bed, shirtless and sexy as sin. Maybe I could?

Bam! Bam! Bam!

Ringo jolted awake. Within seconds he had a gun in his hand and a knife in the other.

I don't even think his eyes were open.

"Where the fuck did you have those?"

Another rapid set of pounding rattled my front door.

"What the fuck? Who is pounding on my door?" I blearily swung my feet out from under the covers and got them to the floor. Ringo, in contrast, had hidden the gun, but still had the knife in hand.

I walked past him to open the door.

"Ellie don't—"

Belatedly, I realized that opening doors without asking was pretty stupid, but also not as much of a crime as he seemed to think it was. I mean, they were in the building, so it had to be a neighbor, or someone I knew.

"Casey. Why didn't you call first?"

He was already dressed, spit-polished, and looked like he ran 4k before breakfast.

"I tried. You didn't answer."

My brain was not firing on all cylinders yet, because that didn't make sense.

I retreated to the bedroom to find my phone and check for messages or that sort of thing. That's when Casey spotted Ringo, and my carefully divided world collapsed in on itself.

"Who the hell are you?" Casey grumbled. He knew damn well who he was having pointed him out last night. I don't think that was the point of his questioning, however.

I hoped Ringo hid the knife. I cringed and waited for the telltale sound of a body hitting the floor or maybe even a scuffle. Casey might have a fighting chance, but he was about ten years past his prime and Ringo? He ate bodyguards for breakfast, figuratively, and could drop an assassin at over two hundred yards with a single bullet. I'd seen both firsthand.

"Ringo Devlin."

I ran out of my bedroom just in time to catch their brutal handshake.

No love lost there.

"Good, you've met." I looked at my phone and realized this was the one I'd bought in Milan when my other phone forgot its home like Dory, and never returned. "I forgot to switch this one to my old number. Sorry."

Casey let go of Ringo's hand. There were red marks where they'd tried to strangle each other palms-first. "Is that a new phone?"

I sighed.

"She lost hers."

"You knocked it out of my hand, jerk." So much for sexy-smelling chests. I opted for coffee instead. "What are you doing here, Casey?"

"Dropping off the bar keys."

As much as that made sense, it didn't. "Why? I have a set."

"You do, but Niall doesn't, and he's closing tonight."

Oh right. I was supposed to take care of that, but forgot. We had a brand-new bartender starting just in time for the holiday rush, and bonus, he was Irish. Or at the very least, Irish-American with a cool-sounding Gaelic name. The tourists would eat him up. Hopefully, he'd survive the weekend and become a regular part of our rotation.

Casey eyed Ringo. "You two know each other?"

"No."

"Yes."

Damn Ringo for outing my lie.

Casey should be used to me by now.

However, both men stared at me.

"What?" I asked because my addled brain was missing their subtext.

"How long?" Casey growled.

Ringo crossed his arms and took a step back, all while watching me for the implosion sure to begin any second now.

Where had he put that knife?

In my back, obviously. "About a month," I said.

"A month? As in *before* the wedding?" Casey was in full cop mode. I hated that setting.

"Reminder, there was *no* wedding."

His gaze swung from me to Ringo. "I'll bet."

Ringo held up a hand. "Hey, that's not fair."

"You wanna clarify that, buddy?"

Oh God… Buddy. Cop-speak for perpetrator, without technically being incorrect.

Ringo smiled. "We met in the airport on Valentine's Day."

That was a good day. It started awful, and turned into one of the most romantic, unromantic overseas flights I could have ever imagined. Ringo needed a last-minute ticket to Italy, and I was trying to cash one in. Fate. Dumb luck?

Or maybe forced opportunity. In hindsight, I'm certain Ringo could have arranged his own flight just fine, but used my predicament to weasel his way into my good graces.

And yet, spending seventeen hours on flights and in airports with a man pretending to be a perfect gentleman wasn't all bad.

"You bought me chocolates in Denver."

And coffee in Venice.

"Sounds cliche." Trust Casey to ruin my little fantasy. "And then you show up at the bar last night."

"She mentioned where she worked, so I thought I'd check it out while I was in town."

"And now you're here." Casey stared at his shirtless abs. There was a scar running up one side. I knew the lie about that one. Supposedly, Ringo got it while helping Mario's uncle on the farm.

But goats don't carry knives that can cut a man's side open like that.

A familiar little tingle pricked at my cheeks and my thighs trembled from locking my knees in place. I didn't even have to see the blood to know that line of scarring almost killed him. And that thought had me searching for a chair, because any second now, I was going down.

"Well?"

Ringo was staring at me, not answering Casey. "Are you okay?"

"Head rush from getting up too early."

His scrutiny was a little too suspicious. But he let it go. Casey, however, didn't. "What's wrong?"

"Nothing," I protested.

"She was going to faint."

"I was not."

Casey interrupted our argument. "You *know* about her fainting spells? When did she see blood?"

Christ on a cracker. Casey was too overprotective.

"Venice. A carnival play. She thought it was real."

It wasn't a play. It was the real damn thing. Someone chased me into an alley and had me at knifepoint. They were trying to get me to join them in some van somewhere for candy and possibly a cocktail. And when I woke, I'd be in Budapest or Dubai, or perhaps even Manilla without the promised books. Then Ringo swept in, took their knife right out of their kung-fu grip and sliced their throat open.

I fainted before I kissed the ground.

Luckily, I woke up in a five-diamond suite, with my nose against a really nice chest that smelled kind of sweet and kind of spicy. Just like this morning. Unlike today, we weren't interrupted.

"Ellie?"

Was Casey asking me to corroborate Ringo's lie? "Huh?"

"Are you okay?"

"I'm fine. No coffee yet. Maybe hungover." Funny, I didn't feel hungover. I was mostly mortified. These two weren't supposed to meet. Ever.

"How long 'you in town for?" Casey made small talk

while Ringo made coffee. He had already been through my cabinets once, so he found everything right away. That had to be making Casey super suspicious.

Ringo answered him. "At least two weeks. The company I work for sent me to check out an acquisition."

"That sounds fancy. Which company do you work for?"

"Casey, give it a rest."

He whipped his gaze to me. "You and I need to talk."

"No, we don't. I'm a big girl now, Dad," I fired back.

He leaned back in his chair and grimaced.

Ringo glanced over his shoulder and raised an eyebrow at me. He knew all about my mom and dad and their alpaca farm in northern Arizona. A shiver swept over me courtesy of the draft at my back.

The adult onesie was on the floor by the couch. I tossed off all shame and pulled it on.

Ringo set two cups on the table. Mine already had cream in it with a little sugar, just like I liked it. Casey's was black, but Ringo put my cream pitcher on the table. It was a black and white cow I'd picked up at a flea market. It color-matched the black and white sugar bowl labeled "cocaine" that sat proudly in the center of the table next to my Bert and Ernie salt and pepper shakers. Ringo took his mug, my favorite plain mug that was labeled "Tears of my enemies" on each side. He sipped first.

Assured it wasn't poisoned, Casey picked his cup up along with the conversation.

"Less than a month," he muttered into his mug.

"Well, if it weren't for the sniper incident and maybe the

major battle royal in Tuscany, we'd be married now," I snarked back.

Ringo's eyes went wide.

Casey laughed. "I have no clue where you come up with your ideas, Ellie." He leaned a little to include Ringo. "Has she blindsided you with anything so insane that you question your ears?"

His eyes dipped down my body. "No, but I've questioned my eyes at least twice."

That earned a table slap from Casey. "She's a pistol. Her and Kat both."

Speaking of…where did Ringo hide that gun? Maybe I'd shoot my male guests with it?

"Best damn women I've ever met, her and Kat. I was barely making rent. Those two took over and I can retire for real this time."

"You're not retiring." A pang of fear shot through my heart. What would I do without Casey? He was my rock. The boss-dad I never knew I needed.

"That's because you won't let me."

"Someone's got to take the Sunday mass crowd. Those folks are downright scary."

"Speaking of Sunday… Kat says we're opening the basement for the parade overflow?"

"That's right." I explained my idea of locals only to Casey. He and Molly would handle the patrons downstairs, while our main force took on the tourists. I'd doubled the shift coverage in hopes for a sunny day and a good crowd.

"And what are you doing on the Sunday before St. Patrick's Day, Ringo?" Casey had shifted to good cop, but he was still interrogating him in a very casual but friendly way.

"I'll probably be drinking with the tourists." He studied me as he spoke.

"You'll still be in town?" Casey asked.

Ringo shrugged. "It's open-ended. If the acquisition goes through, I'll have to stay for maybe a year or more. Then again, it might fall apart tomorrow. The owner died. Now it's being decided by committee, and lawyers."

Casey grunted in commiseration. He hated lawyers. Not only the ones that had cheated him out of good collars back in the day, but when he was fighting for his pension, those particular assholes screwed him over. The shitstorm was his partner's fault, but internal affairs thought Casey should have noticed and said something. Therefore, they fought to strip him of his life's work and all the compensation due it. Luckily, he'd had the family bar to fall back on. Otherwise, he would have been left with nothing.

Good ex-cop he was, Casey lobbed another noose. "Which business if I may ask?"

Ringo smiled. "Commerciare di Conti."

I froze. He'd added all the right-sounding accents in the words and everything.

"Conti Commercial Incorporated?" Casey's face fell. His eyes shifted to mine. There were all sorts of silent warning bells and lights and whistles going off in his. "Are you sure your company wants to buy that mess? I heard the owner was murdered."

"Yes. That's what our company heard as well."

Casey shifted to study Ringo. He wore his hastily-donned and wrinkled dress pants, but his bare feet and chest spoke volumes. His rumpled hair wasn't that way on purpose. There were slight circles under his eyes.

But I'm sure Casey was looking at his hands and arms. Tiny scars from fights told a grisly story of Ringo's true business. That eight-inch stripe on his flank told another.

"Which company is that?"

Ringo rattled his words off with a smile that even I could tell was faked. "Intesa sa Filonzana di Finanziario e Commerciale."

Casey's fingers twitched. He probably wanted to reach for the little notebook he used to carry everywhere. Once I bought the bar, he stopped carrying it in his breast pocket.

"You're Italian."

Ringo laughed at Casey, a real one this time. "Does Devlin sound Italian to you?"

With wary eyes, Casey admitted, "No, it sounds Irish."

That earned a nod. "My mother, not a saint, that's for sure, was from Dunmurry. Slipped off to London at age fifteen. Hopped to America and landed a rich music producer husband by age thirty. Somewhere in there before the rich guy, and after more than a lifetime of parties, I was born. The second she got money, she shipped me off to a boarding school where I met a bunch of Italian prep boys who needed a little street sense. Luckily, I found one who didn't. He became my best friend, and now I work with him."

"Dunmurry, huh?" Casey asked. As if, in that info dump, it was the most important thing.

"Yep."

Casey shifted in his seat. "My great-grandparents are from Banbridge, just a ways south of there."

Ringo changed stance. "Have you been there?"

My ex-boss smiled, and it lit him up from inside. "Twice since I left the force. Traveled all over the island the first time. But the second, I concentrated on finding kin in the northern half. Not difficult with the surname Kelly. You toss a stick and you hit one."

Ringo's smile fell. "I've never been closer than Edinburgh." His brow creased.

He'd spoken of his mother once. It wasn't flattering to put it kindly. I wondered if there was family who'd embrace him, or like most things in his life, he'd be shunned.

8

RINGO

After dropping Ellie off at the bar, I drove downtown. The Conti business, running under the simplified initials of CCI, occupied the fifteenth floor of an office building near the river. It had eight conference rooms, two co-working open spaces divided by a common area that was more lounge than office, and a reception atrium that resembled a spa, not a business.

Those couches looked comfortable.

It was a front, plain and simple.

I needed to talk to Mario about this. He'd been here a month ago and probably figured out exactly how to fix the structure and money flow before he even met with Adelmo.

Heck, he should be here. Not me. This wasn't my forte. I'd been groomed for messier battlefields than boardrooms. I requested a conference space for the call, and was led to a private room.

"Mario, how's the honeymoon?"

"Too short. I'm in Milan."

He sounded stressed. "The penthouse?" His father's place was conveniently situated near all the movers and shakers of the region, which suited his role as Italy's trade minister just fine. But it held bad memories for both Allie and Mario.

"Much to my bride's dismay."

He almost died there the last time they visited. "Is Loppa with you?"

"Firenze. No one is trying to kill me today. You're in Chicago."

Ha ha. He was never going to let me live that down. "I'm at CCI."

"I know."

Wait, I hadn't given him any information about my plans. Don Manca trusted me to work it on my time table, and Ellie was at the bar. Unless she talked to her sister, no one knew. "Did Ellie call her sister?"

"No, a gentleman named Alfonzo Messina-Conti reached out to my father when you checked in."

"They *do* know I'm here." Fuckers. I'd been led around by a junior VP, from marketing no less, just to add insult to the diversion.

"Are you endearing yourself to the natives?"

That was one way to put it. "I haven't killed anyone yet, if that's what you're asking. I just might, though. These dilettantes wouldn't understand a threat if I gift-wrapped it. Adelmo's operation is a front for laundering. It's only saving grace is that it's got a nice view of the river." No wonder he was losing money.

"What about the shipyards?"

"Rail yards. Most of the product comes through by train or trucks, not boats. The Great Lakes cargo ships are only ten percent of the business."

"Any routes that reach international ports?"

"Plenty. There are locks and canals that offer a water route to the Gulf via the Mississippi River. Land routes to Canada or Mexico, the trains, and air freight."

And that gave Mario all the information he needed to pressure the players who controlled points north, south, east, and west. Plus, line up a real meeting for me. It took him an hour.

It was held at an empty restaurant just west of Halsted.

Four members of the Conti organization's faction met me there. None of them were closer than fourth, maybe fifth cousin to me. The question was, had they gotten the memo about their newest family member?

"Mr. Devlin. It isn't often we have a member of the Left Hand in Chicago, yet this is now two months in a row. Is there a problem?" Their leader's tone insinuated the problem was solely *ours*, not his.

I'd done my homework. Every man present hid behind legitimate businesses. Two of the men were so clean, I doubted they even knew what their leader meant about the Left Hand. It was a polite term for assassins. Don Manca's specialty even though the family controlled almost all of Sardinia's smuggling, kidnapping, finance, and extortion interests. The real claim to fame for the family was its ability to send a person anywhere in the world to eliminate problems.

These boys would be shaking in their boots if they weren't so clueless.

"You should have received word that Don Conti passed, but if you haven't, I can offer you my condolences in person. Had any of you met him?" I tossed the question out casually, as if seeking commiseration.

Only their leader nodded.

"But you all knew his late son, Adelmo." They had to. He would have needed each of them to coordinate the consortium in order to send their tributes back to Don Conti.

Nods passed through like a ripple.

Their mouthpiece, Alfonzo—the Conti-Messina man, spoke. "Did you know Adelmo, perhaps… *meet* him before he died?"

That was a loaded question. One I respected their mouthpiece for asking. "My brother did."

A man in the back cleared his throat. "Excuse me, when you say, brother—" He was probably wondering if there was yet another heir in line for the minor fortune in the trust.

"My adopted brother, Mario Valentini. *Apologies*. I never got a chance to meet my late *half*-brother."

There. If they hadn't gotten the memo, it was just served with all the grace of a bomb detonating. Which was how it was received. The farthest two looked highly uncomfortable. The nearest two schooled their expressions, but were fighting their instincts to wage war.

"Listen, I'm new to my role in the Conti Family. And because of that, I'm not going to use it as an anvil over your heads. What I really want to know is how do you think you're going to stay in business losing a minimum of 400k a year?"

"Profits have been down since the pandemic," Alfonzo argued.

"The tariffs have been eating into our margins," another added.

A number of excuses were tossed out. But none were the ones I wanted to hear. I stared at Alfonzo. "You're related to both the Conti family, and two other rather *large* families here, correct?"

He nodded.

"And you're in a unique position, as I am, to hear the rumors of the family's demise, no?"

If the temperature of the room was cold before, it was downright icy now. If I wasn't as accomplished of an assassin, and wasn't at the peak of my skills, I'd be nervous. But I knew I could take these four, both waiters, the five busboys, and the restaurant manager out before breaking a sweat.

Okay, I might sweat. But it would be a small thing.

"Rumors are rumors for a reason."

Ah. Not a denial, and definitely not an endorsement.

"I'll bite. I heard another rumor. That the daughter was here last month, and she arranged for her brother's death." I paused and snapped my fingers as if in afterthought. "Wait, that wasn't a rumor, I was with Don Conti when he found this out. What I want to know from your mouths, is *one* thing. Did my half-sister speak with any of you?"

There was a threat under my tone. One that came

naturally. Until about a week or more ago, I never knew that it sounded just like my biological father's voice. Now that I did, a part of me rallied against it. That emotion wasn't welcome here. I needed to channel Don Conti as quickly and as ruthlessly as possible to avoid losing control. One wrong move and I'd be a target. If I wasn't one already.

"She avoided most of us."

Most. Not all. Alfonzo's shadow spilled secrets too easily.

I let him continue selling his companions' souls to the Devil.

He indicated the mouthpiece. "Of course, Alfonzo here was not included. If word got out to the other families that Dianora wasn't loyal, they'd send in their vultures to pick the bones. She talked to me, but as the eldest of the family, not as someone disloyal."

He looked at the others before continuing. "Listen, I'm progressive, right? But if Don Conti wanted his daughter running the show, he'd've made that happen, tradition or not. He knew she was a loose cannon. She couldn't be trusted."

The rest nodded.

I picked out the most hesitant one in the back. "You, what did she say to you?"

"She had problems with how Adelmo coddled his employees."

So did I, but I wouldn't use the word, coddle. I'd use the word waste.

"And you?" I asked the other. His name was Vincent Grasso, or Vincenzo as Don Manca referred to him. He wasn't a Conti by name, but he was the next closest relation here. He was also connected to the D'Antonio faction through his sister's marriage. The leader of that group clawed his way to the top of the game just a few years back. The Left Hand had vested interest in their business, which meant I'd need to watch this one carefully.

He shifted in place. "She didn't talk to me directly. I've got crews, you know?"

No, I didn't. But knowing that he did raised my estimation of his business acumen.

"And one of them raised a flag to me."

I glanced at the others to see if that was news to them. It likely wasn't by their stoic expressions.

"Dianora was planning the hit." But not going through proper channels.

Everyone knew this, after the fact. But Vincent dug his grave by admitting it out loud.

If this were any other family, this man would be dead already. All of these men would be dead for the simple fact that they didn't escalate their insights to the top. You don't keep secrets like that from family.

I chose my words carefully and drenched them in retrained violence. "Why wasn't someone from my adopted family's faction contacted? Mario was here. Convenient. Yet you let Don Conti think it was him."

Their faces paled.

"It was supposed to be internal. A… misunderstanding. One using a disposable resource," Vincent said.

That's one way to describe Johnny Porciello. Not a word I'd ever use for Mario.

These men were fools. No wonder the Conti family was in decline. "How many of your men were involved?"

That's where he clammed up. Which was even more stupid. Protecting them would get him killed. "I want to *talk* to them."

"Talk? Are you sure that translated correctly?"

I glared at him. "Invite yourself to that meeting if you want to know exactly how it translates."

The leader motioned for the waitstaff to begin service, which effectively pushed the pause button on our conversation. These four were in tune with each other. They did business outside of normal protocols that were observed in most of the older families. I could chalk that up to being insulated here in Chicago.

But what they didn't realize was twofold. Foremost, you can't be passive and maintain control. There were international groups making inroads everywhere. Deep money, deep connections. Oil money from East Asia, mineral monopolies from two continents. Corruption grew from roots almost as old as the Sardinian heritage I followed. New faces with crypto and technical expertise. Political factions that favored money over country ideology. If anything worthy of protecting was to survive, you needed to have both hands in the ocean to fish out the wealth and eliminate the rot. That's why there was a Left Hand. To bring balance when the scales went out of alignment.

And I was more than happy to be that person. It fit me better than being some sacrificial lamb for Don Conti to exploit from beyond the grave.

After the lackluster lunch, I settled into the problem that

was Johnny Porciello, going as far as describing him by name.

"This disposable asset, Johnny Porciello, has he been found?"

There were glances around the table.

"We're working on it." Vincent said.

I pushed aside the mislabeled cheesecake they'd placed in front of me with fanfare and pride. One bite told me everything I needed to know about their tastes. "Stop."

The uneasy shifts in posture spoke their complaints without words.

"This is coming from the Left Hand. Any word of him on the streets, comes to *me*. Understand?"

"We can handle this." Vincent assured me.

I shook my head. "No, you can't. You weren't asked. I was. Personally."

Vincent laughed. "The bastard son of Don Conti doing this *job*. Convenient, no?"

"That's my problem, not yours."

He leaned back, anything but appeased. "Fine. Just make sure it doesn't… bring pressure on us." His smile was wicked. The veneer of his spit and polish, and the aw shucks, I'm just a businessman facade dropped, and I knew why he'd been included in this meeting. His youth made him weak. But give him one or two more decades, and the family would have a strong person in place to run the businesses here the right way.

Funny, I wasn't thinking about the Conti family. I was gauging how Don Manca would react.

The rest of these men were scared. Their livelihoods

were unbalanced with the regime change. They didn't have the fire in them to fight back. But this one did. I'd have to watch my back around him. The knife would come out soon.

I'd just finished updating Don Manca on the events when I got a call. The one I expected.

"I've arranged your meeting. We're square." Vincent rattled off a location north of the rail yards. It was a no-man's land of shipping containers, empty rail cars, and ubiquitous white storage sheds that ranged in size from garden tool sized to massive block-long monsters with overhead cranes rivaling most ports. The unit he specified was barely two thousand square feet. An aluminum-sided dumping ground for dusty boxes and two container offices. Outside, the snow had melted in the lot leaving plenty of dry patches, but also deceptively slick drifts that melted into icy black puddles of treachery.

I checked the lay of my weapons as I locked the car to begin the lonely walk from where they signaled I should pull into the building to their little cluster of three men. A fourth lurked in the rafters. He gave himself away by a tiny displacement of dust and mouse turds that trickled through the air like fairy dust.

If this ambush was planned by my team, I'd have a guy on the roof of the second trailer. Perhaps a floating guard behind that pile of boxes.

Were they outnumbered, or just stupid?

"Gentlemen."

"You don't look Italian."

What a thing to lead with. I smiled without showing

teeth. "My Irish half overpowered it." And my Sardinian half told me to stop right where I had room to maneuver but was close enough to grab a meat shield. "Where's Johnny Porciello?"

"He's not one of us."

The rest nodded along.

Liars.

"You're not one of us."

Not only liars, dumbasses. "What's your last name?"

"None of your business." The speaker was one hundred and eighty-seven centimeters of dead man.

I tested the rest. "Is that true?"

"Yeah hotshot, we're not scared of you." The shadows above the second trailer moved.

"You don't need to be scared of death. It comes for us all." Owning when it did was a blessing. I checked my watch for the time. The man in front reached for his gun.

Exactly two minutes and thirty-eight seconds later, there were only bodies. I pulled out my phone and dialed from memory. "Hi Charley, I'd like to make dinner reservation for five." I rattled off the address and waited for the cleaning crew.

9

ELLIE

For a Wednesday, the bar was crowded. Weekend regulars crowded the stools and filled the tables. Excitement was high, and the blarney was flying. I was in my element, tossing little verbal bombs into dying conversations and moving on to spike the next explosion of laughter.

Although not everyone was a local.

A woman sat at one of the tables. Slightly unusual. Singles usually gravitated toward the bar so they wouldn't be trapped. That spoke of confidence. Worse? She'd nursed a light beer most of the night. I stopped by the table while picking up messes and asked if she needed anything.

Instead of answering me, she asked, "I heard you got married." Her eyes dipped to my empty ring finger.

By now, most of my inner circle knew the wedding was a bust, but it still was a topic of conversation at the pub. Since I hadn't bothered coming clean, I lied.

"That's right."

"Where's your husband?"

While her tone was kind enough, there was some thread of pressure underneath the words that goaded me into action.

"He's fucking some chick. It's an open marriage. I'd be upset if it weren't for the sleep I'm finally getting."

Her face barely twitched.

And that's where the spiders working their way up my nerves started weaving overtime. I scanned her from sensible shoes to business-casual blazer. "Wanna threesome?"

Her eyes dipped to my ring finger again. "Why aren't you wearing your ring?"

"It's a bar. Do you honestly think I'm going to be dunking twenty-five carats in dirty dishwater all night?"

Here's where she pretended to accept my smokescreen.

I cleaned the table next to hers, then leaned over before I left. "If you want to interrogate someone, do it elsewhere, *agent*. I've been followed by the FBI my entire life. And *that* is not a lie."

"Ellie Jacobs-Porciello? That's a mouthful."

I cringed inside. She was calling me out. If I lied to her this time, I could get in big trouble.

"Just Jacobs, agent."

"So, tell me, is the rumor of him being hospitalized in Las Vegas on February thirteenth true?"

"Hospital?" While I knew exactly why he was admitted, I was supposed to be clueless about that part.

"And the one about you marrying someone else? What about that one?"

I turned and locked eyes with her. "What's your name?"

"Bridget, Bridget Perkins."

"Well, Agent Perkins, here's how it went down. I found out Johnny was cheating on me. I sent my sister to cancel the wedding, but she somehow found the love of her life and decided, 'what the hell,' and got married so Mom and Dad, and everyone tuned into the live stream got a show. They were going to get an annulment, but instead, decided to see how it all works. That's the whole story. Now, if you excuse me, I've got a bar to run."

"He checked out of the hospital, against orders, on February fourteenth. No one has heard from him since."

Maybe if I hadn't had the wild two weeks I'd had, or maybe if Ringo hadn't charmed his way into my house last night, I might have had some emotion about that. But all I could think was, "Good riddance."

"If he turns up dead, you're the first suspect."

How convenient. I glanced at the bar. Molly was doing an admirable job closing out orders but it wasn't her job, yet. "Suspect? A guy who was supposed to stay in the hospital dying? That would hardly be considered murder, if you ask me. Talk to Casey—he knows the law. And so do I. Unless you got a warrant for my arrest, I'm done talking to you, Agent Perkins. You can leave now."

But she didn't. I knew she wouldn't.

A few minutes before last call, Ringo sauntered in and took the stool on the end. My stool.

I finished filling Tall Bob's beer and rushed to intercept him before he did something to connect himself to Agent Perkin's web.

"I'm going to be another hour. Wait in the car or at my house."

"No." He was unusually abrupt tonight.

"Ringo, please? It's not cool for you to be here."

He glanced around and dismissed the thinning crowd. Unfortunately, he'd mistaken Agent Perkins as harmless. She was anything but. "I'll stay."

I quickly shifted subject. "What are you drinking?"

"Whiskey, top shelf, neat."

Figured. I pulled down our best Jameson triple. I dropped a small rocks glass in front of him and splashed two ounces in the bottom.

He picked it up and examined the glass. "It's dirty."

I didn't have enough fucks in my brain basket to be patient with him. "Exactly. Like a certain someone I know. You really need to wait in your car."

"You like me dirty."

My cheeks heated as I retreated to close out tabs and announce the final call.

"Ellie? When did you have your bridal shower?" Molly asked.

"I didn't have one." There wasn't time. Johnny pressured me to elope to Vegas, and I had to scramble to get the arrangements together. I barely had time to talk my sister into being my maid of honor.

"We can't have that." She turned to Tall Bob. "What do you think, Saturday, downstairs?"

Like a match to gunpowder, the word spread. These assholes did anything for an excuse to open the basement and embarrass me. "No…" I tried to protest, but the plans formed faster than my lies.

Agent Perkins approached the bar to cash out her tab and listened to the arrangements grow. She smiled wickedly at me and made a suggestion for the decorations.

I tried twice to quell the rabble.

Ringo shook his head and lifted his glass. "To the beautiful bride!"

Traitor.

I kicked a spare case of beer loose from its storage under the bar and stood on it to make my voice carry farther.

"I didn't get married!"

The chatter stopped. As one, the bar set their attention on me.

"I didn't get married."

"We saw you… on the live stream," Molly pointed out.

"That was my sister. You know… Allie?"

A whisper in the back was quickly shushed.

"I'm… sorry. No party."

"Bullshit!" Tall Bob called out. "We can still party. We *should* party. Ellie's back on the market!"

The roar that erupted was flattering, but also embarrassing. For some stupid reason, I glanced at the end stool. But Ringo wasn't there. A fifty-dollar bill was tucked under his empty glass. It echoed the hollow part of my heart.

"I got it, it will be an *un*-wedding party," Molly suggested.

A patron agreed and added to the concept. "We should

dress in black, like a funeral. Except this will be a hell of a lot more fun."

"Anything with a black label will be on special," Tall Bob suggested.

That would cut into profits. I narrowed my eyes at him. "I'll be sure to get you something special." There was an Icelandic schnapps certain to make even the worst alcoholic turn down a free drink. My evil laugh wiped the smile from his face.

Molly theatrically dropped to her knees. "Come on, Ellie. We're going to cheer you up. Say yes, *please*."

I stared at all the familiar faces. "Fine. We need to dust the cobwebs out of the space before next Saturday anyway." The more I thought about it, I grew to like the idea. I could gauge the extra inventory needed, and word would get around about the changes I made, further enticing the neighborhood to brave the crowds after the parade.

The bar finally cleared out. Agent Perkins stood at the bar flap, next to the empty chair Ringo had abandoned. "How'd you know?"

I'd had at least a hundred distractions between our conversations, so I was at a loss. "Know what?"

"That I'm an agent."

That.

"Like I said, I've been followed by agents my entire life. My grandfather was Alfred Pulaski, do you know about his file?" I watched her eyes carefully.

"Yes."

"So, that's how. Talk to my lawyer. He's listed in mine." I tried to walk away.

"Ellie?"

"What?"

"I'm sorry you got cheated on."

There went my opinion that FBI agents weren't human. "What would you know about being cheated on?"

She made a face. "First husband, second husband, six boyfriends, and I think my cat left me for a better house."

I could feel that. But she was still a Fed. "That sucks. Talk to Casey. He'll tell you that you are barking up the wrong tree."

"The owner?"

"Former owner. Two years ago, my best friend, Kat, and I bought the place."

"But you kept *him* on?"

While Casey didn't have anything that hadn't already been dug through at least a hundred times, I got defensive. "Why wouldn't we?"

"He's a cop."

"Was." I leaned in and stared Agent Perkins in the eye and spackled down a thick layer of truth. "You know that there is a saying 'honor among thieves?' But if you ask around, there isn't one like that for the police. Sure, they talk a big game about having each other's backs and holding that thin little line, but when your partner is a lying scumbag who cheated on his wife with a drug dealer's second mistress while running more meth through the south side than any real dealer, well… they get a hard-on about bad apples, even if they're innocent. Casey learned just how supportive his brotherhood truly was. I'm very glad he joined the other side and I will *die* on that hill, feel me?"

Something worked across her face before she masked it. "I get it. You were a spoiled kid who never learned there are folks putting their lives on the line to keep you safe."

"I was safe before all that. What I wasn't after, was a kid. I couldn't be because my childhood was one big game of hide and seek with your so-called protectors who liked staring through my window at night. I was eight!"

I hadn't meant to yell. And I really hadn't wanted to lose my cool around the nosy agent in sensible shoes.

Tall Bob loomed behind Agent Perkins. "Last call was ten minutes ago. Leave." He leaned a little, using every inch of his six feet four frame to intimidate. While I knew he was a pacifist, I couldn't confirm that a two-A.M.-drunken Tall Bob with a half a crush on me wouldn't toss a field agent from the FBI right out on her ass if she resisted.

Little Molly hustled up to join him.

And she *would* toss Bridget Perkins on her ass. That's why I hired her.

"Get your ass out. I'm not telling you twice," Molly warned.

The agent stepped away, hands held high. "Apologies. Have a good night."

It took much longer to get Bob out because he had this mistaken idea Molly and I needed a man around. I'd walked him out, pointed him in the direction of his apartment building, and was trying to talk him down for the fifth time when Ringo rolled down his car window.

"Yo, Bob. I got this. Go home."

Bob swayed a little and stared at Ringo leaning to the

passenger side so he could see his face more clearly. "I know you. You sat in Ellie's seat."

"Yeah, he did, Bob. He's my bodyguard for tonight. You can go home now."

Bob didn't listen to me. "Are you trying to date our Ellie? She's free, you know?"

"Bob, go home."

My words were drowned out by Ringo introducing himself to Bob. "I'll see you at the party, Saturday."

"Hell yeah. Wear black." And with that, he waved at me, Molly standing in the door, and shook Ringo's hand a second time. "Take care of our Ellie. But I get dibs on Molly, understand?'

"Loud and clear, Bob. Molly's yours."

I checked with Molly, who'd turned pink. She shook her head to deny Bob's words and then retreated into the bar to finish cleaning.

I leaned into the car. "I'll be an hour at least. I've got to close out the tills and wipe down the place. Are you going to wait?"

"Yes."

Okay… I didn't know how to feel about that. Two nights in a row he'd pushed his way into my routine. I should be angry, but I wasn't. Instead, I was happy he hadn't abandoned me.

"If the cops come by, drop the name, Rufus. He's our regular weekend bouncer. They know him pretty well. Say that he asked you to sit here, okay?"

His eyes searched mine. "You're asking me to lie?"

Yes. *Duh.* "No, I'm telling you that the cops get really

nosy around here. They'll pull up and have you frisked and cuffed if you don't know whose name to drop, got it?" I knew these streets.

That earned a smile. "Understood."

"Good. I'll make you Chicago street savvy yet."

I didn't want to leave, but closing wouldn't wait. The longer I lingered here, the later it would be until I tugged the sticky door shut and locked the last deadbolt. But Ringo licked his lips. And that motion beckoned me closer. I put my hands on his window frame and crouched a little.

"Ringo?"

"Yes." He shifted closer, not saying yes in response to his name, but yes to stealing a kiss.

His eyes locked on mine. But he stopped just outside of range. "You gotta breach the distance. I'm not doing all the work."

I shoved him away and fled inside the bar.

Now I *was* mad at him.

10

RINGO

Never underestimate women. This was impressed upon me from a very early age. Un-sainted mother aside, Don Manca raised me on tales of Sardinian pirate queens, spooky crones who dressed in black and took their euthanasia gig from door to door, and one really scary goddess who not only wove the thread of your life, she cut it, too. Add to the mix all the aunties, grandmotherly types, and everyday women who loved those crazy outlaws, and I should have picked her out right away.

A Fed.

Sure, Ellie didn't come right out and say it. That made things a little difficult to understand, but she knew enough to warn me from the middle-aged woman with pampered feet. One of Mario's cousins owned the same pair of heavy-duty, all-purpose walking shoes. They didn't slip, they didn't creak, and they made it easy to run, climb, kick, and be a general nuisance. She was also cleared to do jobs on her own.

Which meant, dangerous.

And as soon as I saw those shoes, I knew my problems in Chicago had just multiplied. The agent knew where Ellie lived. I knew that because she got into the car I followed last night. She took her time before driving off. I stared at her empty space, wondering what her angle was.

"Hey stranger, you looking for a good time?"

Ellie leaned against the car on the driver's side, breaking my concentration.

"Get out of the street." I shifted to exit the car and get her back on the sidewalk where she'd be safe... er.

"Give me the keys."

"You're not driving my car."

"You had alcohol tonight, buddy. I'm driving."

"It was an hour ago." I opened the passenger door for her.

Ellie scanned me up and down and relented. "I'm getting in under protest. If you wreck with me in the car I'm haunting you."

"It takes a lot more than two ounces of premium whiskey to get me drunk. That's one thing I inherited from the lush." I helped her get her seatbelt free so she could buckle it.

She caught my hand. "Is your mother really that bad?"

Now wasn't the time for analysis. I gave her as brief of an answer as I could without opening myself up to a longer discussion. "She dumped me at boarding school so her husband wouldn't find out about me."

Ellie's face fell.

I circled the car to sit in the driver's seat. As I did, I scanned for dark sedans and anything out of place. Nothing seemed wrong. The streets were almost dead. But as in any big city, there was traffic, albeit sparse, and some action near the intersection where a late bus picked up passengers. Normality. Or as normal as life could be for me.

I started the car. I hit the seat warmers so Ellie would be more comfortable, then started south.

My rental would be safer than her condo. But it was also almost a half hour away, even with the non-existent traffic. I pulled into the lane and circled her block before pulling in the parking lot.

"I'd thought you'd missed the place at first."

"I'm being careful."

She turned to face me. "Orders?"

I nodded. It was time to remind myself that I was here on business, not pleasure. Ellie would be safer if I wasn't visible in her life. What kind of insanity had gripped me when I promised to be at that party on Saturday?

"Well. Thanks for the ride."

Her hand hit the handle, and I barked out, "Stop."

She huffed and crossed her hands on her lap. "What now?"

"Let me open your car door and walk you inside. Please?"

After visible but silent argument with herself, she shrugged. "You're going to do it anyway."

Damn right I was. I opened her door and kept her on my weak side so I could draw on anyone stupid enough to approach. When we got inside the lobby, I demanded the keys.

"Stay in the hall."

"I hate you."

It wasn't said with venom, just frustration. I'd usually quip back that the feeling was mutual, but it wasn't. I was so far gone I couldn't even lie about it anymore. I slipped the key in, but before opening the door made her stand to the side where the wall would take the punch out of any bullets.

Nothing but darkness. Good.

I scanned the room for any unusual shadows or telltale smells or sounds that signaled danger. Something was in the air, but perhaps I imagined it.

Behind me, Ellie flicked on the light.

I blinked the temporary blindness away. "Warn me before you do that."

"Not everyone was born half cat like you were." Her sarcasm floated in the air behind her as she moved to the kitchen. I checked the corners, the spare bedroom, the bathroom with her little signs and tchotchkes, then opened her bedroom door.

The air was cold.

I slipped my gun out and hugged the wall. The shadows were all harmless. The broken window, not.

"Hey Ringo did you want a cup of— oh shit."

My heart rate damn near tripled. I tried my best to not yell at her. "Ellie, *please* stand in the hallway, and don't go near the windows. Please?"

She put her hand on my shoulder before doing as I asked.

I knew she wanted to argue, but probably took one look at the unmade bed, the broken window, and the general disorder of her room and understood why I was being so careful.

Her suitcases had been dumped onto the floor. Their contents mixed, searched, and trampled. The dresser where she kept her jewelry displayed like a decorating theme, ransacked. There was broken glass under the window.

I checked the frame for blood. None. That told me whoever had squeezed through the tiny frame was a pro, or at least wise enough to knock out all the glass and wear gloves on their hands before coming through.

Her nightstands were open. The contents strewn onto the bed. A photo of her and Allie was tossed carelessly amongst the covers.

A stain peeked out from the jumble of sheets.

I picked up the comforter to see if it was blood.

It wasn't. And that made things much worse.

While I was out hunting down the men who'd betrayed the Conti family, Johnny was doing more than hunting here.

"Is it okay to come in yet?"

I wanted to tell her no. I dropped the blanket so it would cover the evidence. "Yeah. Grab some things, check what's missing, and pack a bag."

Her eyes were wide as she flicked on the light and took in the disorder. They bounced from one disaster zone to another. "Was I robbed?"

Considering they didn't touch the rest of the house? Probably not. "Check your jewelry."

She shrugged. "Most of it is cheap. I don't keep the good stuff on display."

With that, she crouched down to pull the bottom drawer of her dresser out. She reached inside and pulled out two little canvas bags. After undoing the drawstrings, she dumped the contents onto a T-shirt that had been tossed to the floor. "Looks like it's all good. They didn't even get my wedding ring."

A growl threatened to spill out of my throat. I bit my lip so I wouldn't say something evil. She wore that damn thing the first two full days of the trip. It sat on her finger like a warning sign constantly reminding me why I shouldn't feel the things I felt.

But I did.

And she did.

Then I laid down the law. "Take that ring off. You're not married. And it makes you a target." It had. Carnival attracted all the tourists, and with them thieves of all varieties.

She put it in that little powder blue velvet box and tucked it into her suitcase. Thank goodness she'd moved it to her stash spot somewhere between landing and now.

Her eyes landed on the bed and they narrowed. "Tell me that son of bitch didn't—" she bounced to her feet and flipped the sheets to the floor.

The wet stain glistened in the overhead light. "That motherfucker."

"Pack your things, baby. We're not staying here."

She stared at the spot. The photo of her and her twin canted like an arrow pointing to the history of the event.

Ellie's mouth fell open to talk, but stayed quiet. She finally mastered herself and grabbed a suitcase.

As she picked through her things on the floor, I got a cloth from her cleaning closet and wiped off the photo frame before handing it to her. "Take this with you."

Her chin wobbled once, but she stiffened her expression until she'd mastered her emotions. "Thank you."

I handed her things she'd need, but soon discovered that it was a futile effort. If Johnny hadn't soiled her clothes with his shoes, he'd violated them other ways. After the third pair of sliced underwear, I gave up and directed Ellie to retrieve her shampoo and makeup. I was done wading through his filth. I dialed another number.

Conti-Messina answered.

I bypassed all the pleasantries we both knew were false. "Who do you have on payroll with expertise in setting up mistresses?"

Ellie bugged her eyes out at me. "Mistresses? Plural?" she mouthed, threatening me with her angry eyes.

As I got the reply, I wrote down the phone number he gave me.

"Excellent," I said to end the conversation. But he wasn't done.

"Do you have a mistress?"

That was none of Alfonzo's business. I hung up instead of replying. I dialed the number he gave me. A woman answered. "Alfonzo Conti-Messina recommended you. I have a woman who needs her life restored. How soon can you make that happen?"

I watched Ellie's anger fade to concern. It intensified as I packed what we could salvage into my trunk. "Are we going to a hotel? I can pay."

I slammed the lid a little too hard. "Get in the car."

"You didn't open the door for me."

Even upset, scared, and fleeing her home she had sass.

"Apologies, amòre miàu." The words spilled out unbidden. But I wasn't going to walk them back. Thankfully, she didn't understand what I said and settled into the passenger seat without calling out my slip.

When I pulled away from her place, she broke the silence. "You know what's weird?"

I braced myself for something guaranteed to knock me off balance. "What?"

"You know five languages, but only claim to be able spell correctly in four. Why is that?"

Not what I was expecting. "I'm sorry, what?"

"I mean, you slip into that really weird sounding Italian around Mario and the guys on the island. And I noticed that even Allie doesn't understand what you guys say. So, it has to be a separate language, right?"

When had we slipped up? It was forbidden to speak the language in front of outsiders. "It's just a dialect. Like Creole is to French or a Boston accent is to English. It's still Italian." The lie tasted wrong on my tongue. Technically, it was closer to the common Latin spoken before the Roman Empire. In the north, the language was further transformed by Corsican influence and inflections unique to that language.

She stared at me.

"What?"

"Have you ever learned how to write it?"

"No."

"See? Weird." She settled into her seat, smug in her assumptions.

"You don't write it down."

Her lips pursed. "One of those...things, huh?"

I smiled. "Yes."

Her eyes traced the scenery for a minute. "You know, if you take the Dan Ryan, you'll miss a lot of lights."

"Do you even know where we're going?"

"No, but I'd assume somewhere on par with your little hitman's hideaway that you showed off that one night."

This woman... "First, that *little* hideaway is eleven-hundred square meters. Second..." damn it she was brilliant. "Fine, where do you think we're going?"

"Lake Shore Drive. That's where all the fancy condos are."

"Where is this Dan Ryan street?"

"It's not a street, it's an interstate." The offense in her voice was clear.

"I'm supposed to know that?"

Ellie laughed at me. "I guess the internationally famous hitman doesn't know everything does he?"

"Ellie..."

"Turn left, follow the signs for 57."

I did as she directed.

"You drive like shit."

"I do not. I took lessons from Timo Bernard."

"Get your money back. You're going to get eaten alive during rush hour."

"Timo Bernard is one of the best drivers in the world."

She stared at me. "Then you didn't learn much. Exit."

I cut across two lanes to make the exit she pointed at so casually. It dumped me off under the expressway. The location was sketchier than the railway warehouse I'd visited earlier. "This isn't safe."

"Welcome to Chicago. Turn right at the KFC."

"The what?"

She groaned in frustration. "Kentucky Fried Chicken, surely you've had the truly American gourmet dining experience of chicken in a bucket, right?"

"Don't make fun of me." A memory flashed through my head. "If you do, I'll tell you the story about how Don Manca taught me how to make pollo al guazzetto from the coop to the table."

"I'll pass. What's the address for your current Hotel Continental."

"We're not staying at a hotel."

"Don't you watch—nevermind. Address?"

I rattled it off.

"Oh, we should have stayed on the Stevenson."

"I thought we were on the Dan Ryan?"

She let out a mighty sigh. "Pull over."

"No."

"Listen, you don't belong behind the wheel if you can't understand the freeway system here."

"Maybe if it made sense, I could."

She huffed.

Luckily, the streets took on familiarity, and I navigated to the high-rise building without her aid.

Ellie craned her head to peer at the facade just before I drove into the underground parking level. I flashed my card at the gate and wound through the levels to find my reserved space.

I warned her, "Don't touch that handle," then popped the trunk, grabbed her suitcase, and opened her door.

She affected an awful accent and spouted off something that sounded like, "Thank you, Jeeves. Lead on, my good man."

Crazy. Certifiably so.

And I wasn't referencing Ellie. I was talking about myself. The way things were going I'd have to check myself in somewhere. Or perhaps disappear for years in the mountains to get my head on straight again. That's how badly she'd tied me up in knots.

And as she slumped against me in the elevator, I knew I'd do it all again, a thousand times over.

11

ELLIE

The foyer of Ringo's suite had marble floors, fresh flowers, and expensive artwork. To the right, I glimpsed a formal dining room with an overlarge abstract sculpture taking center stage on top of an ebony-stained table.

Heck, maybe it was real ebony?

Ahead was a family room with fireplace, coordinated leather seating, and an entertainment shelf that doubled as a "small" library. That's if you compared it to the public one downtown on State Street. The room wrapped around a full-sized kitchen that took up the interior corner, and turned into a small dining area flanked on the exterior wall by floor to ceiling windows that framed Lake Michigan in glittery segments. Then the layout dumped into a fancier living space that had almost a two hundred and twenty degree vista of the lakefront starting from the due-north-facing view down to Navy Pier from its windows. The view was spectacular from this rarified strata.

It was like the morning I woke up at his home in Sestri Levante. I walked out of the bedroom onto the terrace and stared at the Mediterranean in awe. In this place, I'd be front row to the sunrise over the lake.

I'd kill for a place like this. Apparently, Ringo already did. That thought got shoved aside for more mundane needs. "Do you have a shower? I smell like beer." And sweat, but I'd never admit that.

He set my suitcase inside a bathroom more spacious than my condo's living room. With the attached walk-in closet, it might be bigger than my entire home. The shower was definitely larger than my bathroom. I fiddled with the nobs and such between sorting through Ringo's rushed attempt to grab my essentials.

He packed worse than I did. My loofa wasn't in the suitcase, my shampoo leaked onto my jeans, and there wasn't a piece of underwear in the damn bag anywhere. I could have sworn he picked up at least one from the mess of my room.

Maybe none survived Johnny's wrath?

I shuddered from the chill that swept over me. He seemed so harmless with that baby face of his. "Ringo?" I called out.

He peeked his head in the door without knocking. "Yes?"

Mental note: *lock the damn doors around him.* On the heels of that thought was another, *he'd just pick the lock.* This time my shudder wasn't as chilly.

"Did you find *any* underwear that wasn't ruined?"

His eyes swept down me and back. It wasn't sexual, more like clinical. "I'll see if I can find something for you to sleep in."

He slipped away before I could ask him what he meant. Did this place come stocked with clothing?

Or… did he have a girlfriend, wait, no… a mistress?

My stomach churned. I asked him once if he was dating anyone, and he denied it. But that conversation was before I found out he'd just been using me to get close to Mario during their falling out. "I need my head examined." I stripped out of my clothes, hung an oversized hotel-style bathrobe on the hook nearest the shower, and scrubbed the smells of the bar from my skin and hair.

I didn't hear him, but when I was done drying my skin and wrapping my hair with a towel, there was a pair of boxer shorts and a soft T-shirt on the marble counter.

They must be his. I picked up the shirt and inhaled. To my disappointment, it smelled like fresh laundry.

I wasn't perverted enough to smell his boxers and embraced the assumption they were clean, too. The folds were a little too crisp and the fabric just a little too stiff to indicate otherwise.

Then I wrapped in the monster-sized bathrobe and sighed a little. Its heavy weight felt like a hug. And the dense terrycloth absorbed any lingering dampness from my skin. My muscles were sore, and the day's rollercoaster that started with being startled out of bed caught up with me. I may have stumbled a little when I finally exited. Luckily, there was a bedroom directly across the hall. It had a king-sized bed and another impressive view of the lake.

Dawn would come too soon. I tugged at the curtains, but they wouldn't budge. I was just about to give up and find another room to crash in when Ringo entered.

"What are you doing?"

"Trying to close the curtains," I said.

He touched the panel beside the door, and the curtains slid into place, blocking out the lights of the city, the lake, and the peninsula that peeked up from the very bottom of the view. Now I felt like an idiot. Should I thank him?

"Sleep, Ellie."

I stared at the bed but didn't move.

"El?"

"I'm scared." Where did *that* come from? Frustrated with myself, I plopped onto the bed face-first. "And now I'm mortified. Leave." My words were muffled by the soft comforter.

I heard more than felt Ringo sit on the mattress opposite me. When I lifted my head, he didn't pretend he wasn't watching me.

"What?" My voice was slightly hoarse. I propped up on my elbows to study him.

He hesitated. "Remember Venice?"

"What part? The abduction, the trauma, or the murder?" I hadn't realized it at the time, but he'd slit my attacker's throat. I fainted at the first splash of blood.

His jaw shifted. "After."

The hotel. A dozen memories, not all of them bad, but

almost all of them highly uncomfortable, flashed through my mind. I'd exposed my Achilles Heel to him, then begged him not to leave me alone for fear I'd have nightmares. And he hadn't.

"I'm a big girl."

This time when his eyes dipped to the gap of the bathrobe, it was sexual. "No nightmares?"

There would be at least a dozen unless I was so exhausted I didn't dream. Defeated, I patted the bed. "When I wake you up, don't pull your gun, or your knife."

He stared through me. "I can't promise that. But you do know they won't be aimed at you, right?"

Yup. That was one line he hadn't crossed. Yet.

Casey was right, Ringo was a wolf. All teeth and cunning, but also the epitome of what my body craved to cuddle. Like that human touch could ever tame him enough to drive the killer instinct away? I knew better than that.

Then again, if Johnny came after me, I wanted a man like Ringo at my side to scare the piss out of him. Maybe even eat him like those creatures in old fairy tales did. One big bite and voila! Problem not only solved, but eliminated from existence.

As if it were that easy?

I stared at the sculptural vase that perched on my side's nightstand. The flowers in it were just as fresh as the ones in the lobby. That meant someone was employed to come in and change them. Perhaps they cleaned the place as well? This maintenance would happen every day for the length of Ringo's stay. What kind of money afforded that?

Even winning the lottery didn't give me that kind of perk.

Ringo was a wolf. One that solved problems. Rich, connected people hired him to eliminate their complications. Permanently.

That's what hit me hardest. The permanence of it all. His whole adopted family had done this same trade for well over a thousand generations. The family business was not going to go away no matter how much I wished for it to disappear. As long as there were people with problems there would be people like Ringo who'd solve them.

Could I accept that? I thought I couldn't. And before that, I naively thought I could.

Now, I didn't know.

I must have stared at the flowers for longer than I should have. Ringo walked around the bed to my side. Gently, he offered an arm for me to lean on as he pulled me up and tore the covers down so I wasn't on top of them. I let the robe fall to the floor and climbed in, handing him the duty of tucking me in.

He did without complaint.

Then he circled the bed, removed his clothes and crawled in next to me.

I'd barely registered his body wrapping around mine before nodding out.

Hours later, I woke with a start. My breathing was too fast and my skin clammy with sweat that had broken out.

In my dreams I'd been running. The backyard of the house I grew up in was too long. It became a dark forest. The men pursuing me called out all sorts of promissory comforts. "Come home, Ellie. It's too cold out here. You're not safe. Come on, little girl, you can't stay in the woods all night. There are wild animals out here, Ellie Jacobs. Come back."

I feared them more than the dark, more than the cold, and certainly more than the animals.

I couldn't breathe.

Ringo's arms wrapped around me. "I got you. You're safe."

I couldn't breathe. They were everywhere. At the windows, lurking in the shadows, and even inside my home.

"Ellie!" Ringo shook me.

I stared at his face. It was familiar, but also not. The concern was new. If I could, I'd lie to him and tell him it would be all right. I gasped for air, panting in the darkness.

"It's okay."

Was it?

My mind cataloged the surroundings. The bed, Ringo, the fancy vases on the nightstands, the gun hanging off the headboard within easy reach. The hilt of a dagger that had slid out from under Ringo's pillow.

I was in the woods. Deep in his realm where it was anything but safe.

My breathing calmed. I drifted a bit, leaning on him as the rush from hyperventilating sent tingles through my body that bordered on pain. "Thank you."

He exhaled and the warmth of his breath caressed my scalp as his lips brushed against my hairline.

"You're not kidding about those nightmares. Venice wasn't like this."

No, it hadn't been. I'd only had the beginning of one that night. It startled me awake like a bullet. And in the aftermath, the adrenaline rush made me cling to his body for more than just comfort. I needed an outlet or validation that I was alive. Flight or fuck, Kat called it. She had her own trauma growing up. We clung together and learned unorthodox coping mechanisms to deny admitting our childhoods had broken us.

One was spitting in the world's face. When life hands you lemons, put 'em in a bazooka to blast them back at their owners.

"I'm okay now." While I spoke the right words, I didn't push him away like I should have.

Part of me wondered why I didn't.

Ringo rubbed my back in little soothing circles. "That's good. Can I ask what was chasing you?"

"The FBI."

His reaction was about as I expected. He shifted to hold me at arm's length to check whether I was joking or not.

The trouble was I wasn't joking.

"From your childhood?"

He knew about that because Allie talked. I never did. Or tried not to. My make-believe had gone on so long that I'd almost managed to block it all out. Along with big gaps of memory that may or may not have occurred like Allie claimed it did. Those experiences and stories were hers. Mine were a black void. It wasn't until I met Kat and started getting in trouble that my actual memories started. It was like I hadn't existed before that point.

Except for the dreams. Ones Allie swore didn't happen.

I was never lost in the woods. I never was chased by agents in the middle of the night. And I certainly wasn't abducted from the house in a black panel van one winter night. But those things played on repeat in my nightmares.

Sometimes I even wondered if the nightmare in Venice was real.

"Tell me I'm not crazy. Please?"

His hand cupped my face and then burrowed into my hair in such a tantalizing caress I leaned into it. Ringo shook his head and uttered one word. "Babe."

"I remember things that aren't real. And I don't know if some things *are* real. Like Venice. There were pictures, so it had to be real, right?"

His fingers tightened. "Tell me what you think you remember."

"We spent that first day doing touristy stuff like the gondola ride, where you knocked my phone into the water." I was never going to let that one go.

He grimaced. "And?"

"And then you had to leave. So, I went to the hotel and had room service. The next morning, I had coffee and those funky fried donuts that tasted like oranges with raisins in the dough. I like the chocolate-filled ones better."

"They're called *frittelle*. They're special."

"One word, raisins. The tiramisu was far superior."

"Heathen," he muttered.

I shot him a glare. "Anyway, I went to the museum Allie had on the schedule, boring. Then the costume shop. That was fun."

"That dress was scandalous."

"You loved it." I smiled, remembering how it came off. He didn't argue.

"Then drinking in the square and dinner… but I don't remember you finding me. Just—" I drew my finger across my neck. A carnival scammer tried to take my picture as I drank the lemony aperitif. I told him to fuck off, creatively, of course. Then, one of the costumed harlequins shoved between us, sending the guy packing. He seemed charming. I thought it would be fun to stroll through the square because our costumes matched in color. It was a bit of a blur, the music, the laughter, the tourists snapping photos of everyone partying like it was the day before we'd all drop dead.

He grabbed my arm to steer me. I'd gotten used to this and let him lead.

Until the music dimmed and the lights were far away in the streets, not this dark place.

And just a few seconds later, a shadow moved across his throat, and a line of red blood spilled.

Then things went black.

Ringo's jaw was tense. "You didn't feel the knife he held to your ribs?"

I shook my head. "Maybe the corset was too thick."

He nodded, hesitantly. "That's probably right."

"How'd you know?"

He shifted, straightening the sheets I'd tangled in my attempt to escape my nightmares.

"Tell me, please?"

"I knew because it would be what I'd do on a job." His face was grim.

A noise escaped me. Whether it was acknowledgement or grief, I couldn't tell.

I felt the urge to be completely, utterly honest with him. After all, he'd been honest with me. "I liked you better when you lied to me."

12

RINGO

Saturday

Ellie paced the full length of the windows that wrapped around the eastern and southern sides of the building. Her call to Allie started calmly enough with catching up on her sister's welfare, the extended vacation, her marriage to Mario, and then it shifted to her life, and Ellie's replies grew shorter.

She was lying by omission. "There's a gathering at the bar tonight." The topic change was on the heels of mentioning she could see the lake from my rented flat. Nowhere in the conversation did she mention the break-in at the house or the horrific nightmares she suffered. Instead, she painted a rosy scene of her usual routine, now infected with my presence, because, and I quote, "He thinks he's Firenze."

I did not. Firenze couldn't match my worst on his best day. And despite the little crush he nursed for Ellie, he still couldn't tell the difference between her or her sister. That was a key detail. You can't love someone and not be able to tell instantly whether they are their sister or not. It's unnatural.

Except I didn't love Ellie. I couldn't. I was simply an excellent observer.

And I couldn't stand getting woken at odd hours in the night and traversing the entirety of this apartment to console Ellie. That meant the expedient solution was to sleep next to her. It saved time and my sanity.

Maybe not the latter. Her scent was distracting. The way she swayed as she walked was distracting. Her smiles were as well.

And the little way her eyes narrowed? Amusing, but also concerning.

I was learning that expression meant I was in trouble. But for the life of me, I didn't know why.

Her eyes did that now.

I'd done nothing wrong. I'd been a perfect gentleman. She wore new clothes, her apartment was being cleaned, the window fixed. And she went to the bar to work.

"Remember how you complained Loppa wouldn't let you go on the terrace?"

Ellie was looking at me, but this question was directed at her sister. She'd spoken loud enough I overheard, an unfortunate byproduct of being in the same room.

"Yeah, well he's insisting on watching me as I work."

I didn't watch her work. I watched everyone else watching her.

"And he thinks my apartment is unsafe."

It was. A ground-floor unit with a sliding door was too vulnerable. Especially for an attractive woman living alone. There were more lunatics out there than just Johnny Pornstach.

"And he's got a grudge against my ex."

Duh.

The man touched her. Then he terrorized her.

He simply could not live another day. If I could find him, he'd be dead already. I'd rattled cages, shook trees, dug deep into the dealings of not only the Conti faction but all of the major players in the region. What I'd learned is that Johnny was a minor blip. At least he'd been until about six months ago. Then he began dating Ellie. And people took notice.

Especially when he began trading on her family's history.

Despite that, only one family reached out. And it wasn't even official. Dianora had dangled legitimacy in front of Johnny to suck him in. And he fell for it.

If it were any other twit, I'd almost feel sorry for him.

Ellie laughed at something Allie said. "I know."

Knew what? I logged that moment so I could ask Mario what his wife said about me.

"You think I should?"

I braced myself. That overly sweet tone spelled doom.

And since I was the topic of conversation that meant Ellie and her twin were devising a torture aimed at me.

Another laugh.

If evil didn't cackle, it would have that silvery cadence. In fact, it likely did disguise itself in angelic tones. All the better to murder you with.

"Oh. I'm sorry, I haven't. I forgot."

I couldn't help myself. "Forgot what?" I asked.

Ellie covered the mouth microphone. "To go check on her place. She told the neighbor she'd only be gone a week. It's been almost a month."

"We'll go there before your 'event' tonight."

Her eyes narrowed again. This time I knew why. My reluctance to an unnecessary exposure was well-voiced in both tone and argument.

"You don't have to go," she told me.

We'd hashed this out already. I was going. And if we weren't going together, I'd go separately. Johnny's friends weren't helpful because they'd ditched him once he began hanging out with the wrong crowd. And his new acquaintances were equally unhelpful because he was hiding from them. Someone had to know where he was, but if they did, they'd successfully lied to no fewer than three crime families, and the cops.

The latter was a surprise.

Once the hit on Mario's head was lifted, so was the ban on outside involvement. Two weeks after the hit-and-run shooting, an investigation was opened. Johnny was the primary suspect as the photos from the crime scene quickly identified him, but not his dark-haired "accomplice."

That was buried in lies. No one wanted the Conti name dragged into this fiasco.

And everyone was hoping Johnny would remain a person of interest... permanently. As in, never located, never charged, and certainly never able to talk about the crime. That put pressure on me to find his ass and eliminate any trace of it.

"Love you. Stay safe, and keep me updated about the... you-know-what present."

"Present?" I asked as she lowered her phone.

"None of your business. Do you own a tux, or at least one of those super-sexy designer suits?"

A man could get whiplash from her topic changes. "I—"

"Never mind. It was a stupid idea. No one gets that dressed up for the bar."

I squinted at her. "Are you talking about tonight?"

"Duh."

"I'll wear what I usually wear." The sports team jacket I wore concealed my weapons well. It had an added benefit of making me look like I belonged in this town.

Her face fell a little.

"I could wear a suit jacket."

Her smile came back.

"And what will you be wearing?"

Ellie tilted her head. "Nothing special."

That was an outright lie.

∼

The thigh-high stiletto boots should have been the first clue. But the tops of said boots were concealed under an oversized coat that covered almost every inch of her that wasn't boot.

"Are you wearing anything under there?"

Her grin went wicked. "I bet you'd love to find out, wouldn't you?"

I adjusted the lay of my tailored jacket. The sleeves had gotten a little too tight and the cuffs rode up to reveal the trigger mechanism for my wrist blade. "How long will it take at your sister's?"

"Just a few minutes."

That meant at least a half hour, maybe more. "We'd better leave soon."

Ellie slipped her hand under my jacket and slid it over my chest. "You clean up nicely."

If she moved her fingers two inches to the right, she'd touch my shoulder harness. I tugged her hand loose. "Try not to distract me."

Her lower lip pushed out in a pout. "You're no fun."

"Is that what tonight is about? Fun?"

"Of course." Her wink wasn't reassuring.

Nor was the untended state of her sister's mailbox. Ellie waved at the neighbor. "Hey, Hank."

He stared at Ellie and waved back. "Are you back from your trip?"

She replied by tapping her chest. "Ellie. Allie's going to be at least another two weeks before she gets back. She got married!"

Hank's jaw went slack. "Allie?"

"I know! Freaked me right out," Ellie confided.

"Fifteen minutes," I reminded her so she wouldn't get side-tracked.

I got an eye-roll in reply and she shoved her way into the house. "Damn door always sticks." She dumped the mail on the coffee table and checked on the refrigerator. "Huh. She must have been in a hurry. I better throw this out." She pulled out a pizza box and tossed it in the trash. Then, because that was filled, she tugged the bag out and tied it off. I took it from her because tottering up the front steps had been an ordeal, but I wasn't going to waste any more time waiting for her to take the bag to the back.

"Where are your bins?"

"They're called trash cans. And they're behind the garage. Don't move them to the curb, though. I don't remember which date is pickup."

Then she did something unexpected. Ellie tipped higher onto her toes, a mean feat in those heels, and kissed my cheek. "I appreciate you."

Funny how three little words can be so…powerful. I was still pondering them when I got back.

"We're good. Let's blow this popsicle stand and celebrate my very merry un-wedding."

"Your what?"

"You know…" She sang a few stanzas of a repetitive song I'd never heard. At my confusion, she asked, "Don't you watch cartoons?"

"None recently."

"Oh my God. We're renting *every* animated movie when we get home."

My wince leaked out before I could control it. "Every one?"

She tossed her head in a gesture that could be closest to negative, but it probably meant she couldn't believe my naiveté.

"I can't with you. Let's go. Ticktock, right?"

I checked my watch. We still had eight minutes to make it to the car. That was probably enough time.

It almost wasn't. She waved at another neighbor, who mistakenly thought she was her sister. Before she got in the car with me, she yelled out, "Hey, Mrs. Carpello, watch this." Then she kissed me.

With tongue.

The older woman gasped. "Ellie Jacobs, I'm telling your sister when she gets home!"

Ellie laughed and climbed in the car.

When I pulled away, she confided, "That woman can't tell us apart unless I do something outrageous."

Which may have been the theme for the party. Yes, my black suit and black shirt fit in well with the color scheme, but it was sedate compared to the leather and sequins, and… was that a gimp suit? Club music pounded against the low ceiling and Ellie didn't waste a second of her entry to drop her coat into my hands and scream, "Check it out, I'm FREE!"

And wearing something…short with fishnet.

A black woman walked past me and halted just long enough to nudge my jaw shut and declare, "Get used to it. I'm Kat by the way."

Since my hands were full, I couldn't shake her hand, or do more than nod and say, "Ellie's mentioned you." A lot.

"What are you drinking?"

"Jameson, neat." It was *that* kind of night. There would be no way to guard Ellie in this madhouse.

Except, as I scanned for exits and threats, the former was limited to the back stairs, which we'd come down. The stairs to the main bar upstairs were closed off. Only people who knew about the back door to this place could enter the basement tonight.

And Ellie knew each face. The numerous hugs that followed were harmless. And whoever outfitted her with a tiara and a feather boa wasn't threatening either.

I recognized Tall Bob and Casey. After delivering my drink, Kat flitted behind the bar occasionally to serve others. I swirled the alcohol in my glass, and settled near the cluster of small couches and overstuffed chairs that created conversation centers and a place to park her coat. Ellie took center stage on a leather bar stool and bounced between talking and toasts.

"Hey, Ellie, who's your next victim over there?"

I was *not* a victim.

"That's Ringo, you know… like the guy in that western. *He's an educated man.*"

I knew that movie at least. It was one of my mother's favorites and one of the few memorable things we had in common.

Kat joined the group and stood in the space next to me. "That movie's a classic."

Someone from her group asked, "Hey Ringo, can you spin a gun around like that?"

The devil on my shoulder tapped once and took over. "Naw, but I can spin a knife." With that declaration, I flicked out the blade hidden under my cuff and showed off…just a small amount.

When I tucked the knife back into its spring-loaded sheath, I laughed. Her friends laughed, too. Except for Casey. He stared at me like I'd just proven myself to be a threat. The knowledge in his eyes reached back decades. I extracted myself from a lame conversation to approach.

"Ringo Devlin." He spat my name like a warning shot.

"Did you look me up?" I'd done a thorough background on him. He was ex-cop with a black mark on his record—one bold enough to make his benefits disappear with a pen stroke. The sale of the bar to Ellie and Kat eliminated his debts. Since that time, he'd been unremarkable.

He leaned in. "Scuttle is, you ain't Irish."

"My mother would slap you for saying that." That was no joke. She wouldn't care if he was an ex-cop or a real one. Neither did I, if the truth needed to be told. But if the streets were whispering already, that meant someone in the families talked. "Who whispered that in your ear?"

"Wouldn't you like to know?"

Fucker. Since he was Ellie's former boss and a good friend, I couldn't kill him. Yet.

13

ELLIE

"You're fooling yourself," Kat whispered in my ear.

I paused, mid sip of the virgin cosmo I asked her to make for me. "What?"

"Don't make me repeat myself. That man." Her head tilted toward Ringo.

She didn't have to say the rest. My brain was already screaming it. Or maybe it was my pussy, or my stupid, stupid heart. I was putting up a good fight, and that's about all I had going right now. "I'm tired of fighting it."

Her eyes went a little wide. "It?"

"You know…"

The glance she shot to the chair where Ringo sat by the door was obvious. Her voice lowered. "It?"

"Yes, *it*. I had sex with him in Italy and it was good. No. Not good. Cosmically altering."

Her jaw canted a little to the side as she absorbed my words. "For six months you strung the baby-faced guy with the barely legal mustache along and never once mentioned anything cosmically related. You were a veritable saint—which I know you ain't—and then you know Mr. Dangerously Sexy over there what, one day…two?"

She was fishing.

"One day was on the plane. We sat together."

Her eyebrow went up. "Together? In those first-class reclining seat bed things you showed me you booked?"

I bit my lip. "I sold him Johnny's ticket."

"You *sneaky dog*." Kat held up her hand for a high-five.

"There was a barricade between the seats so we really couldn't do much more than talk." Sexual banter was more accurate of a description. We both pondered the logistics of mile-high sex. I picked up a coaster and fanned my over-warm face because thinking about it made me remember other things.

"And then?"

"We landed in Venice. He did the touristy stuff with me for the first part of the day. Then he had 'business' so had to leave. That's it."

Kat was really confused. "I could have sworn you implied that you had sex with him."

"I did. *Later*."

Realization dawned on her face. "He came back for you."

I nodded, trying to tamp down the flutter that my started somewhere between my stomach and my heart. Even after finding out he killed people for a living, that memory sent tingles through me.

"And he came *here* for you."

"No, this is just business."

She held up a hand. "Flag on the play. Let me clarify something for you. If he were only here on business, he'd have stayed in whatever hotel room he was holed up in and not come here." She pointed at the rug under her swirly Keeyahri heels.

That flutter? It went south to my stomach. The discomfort didn't stop my heart from doing a little dance.

"Okay, what if his business here, in this room, is to keep me safe?"

Kat's face took on a little gray. "From? I need you to elaborate here."

I glanced around. The party had wound down. Only a dozen people remained. Some of the usual regulars and a few of the girl posse Kat and I cultivated chatted in little groups. Some of them had even paired off. Which had been the point of all this. I mean, just because I was single didn't mean that my friends couldn't find love, right? And because the focus was no longer on me, I could admit a little to Kat.

"Allie's husband is kind of a—um…" I tried to gesture my meaning.

"Italian? Duh. I spotted that a mile away."

"Sardinian, actually."

She blew out a raspberry. "And that's a crime?"

I let my eyes go a little wide to indicate that yes, very much yes it was. "And Ringo is his best friend," I finished.

Her head tilted, and she used a tone I was certain to interpret correctly. "Girl?" Her hand wiggled as she tried to imitate Ringo's earlier knife juggling act.

"Yeah."

My breath was shaky. Even admitting that much out loud was dangerous.

She lowered her volume and deliberately did not look anywhere incriminating. "Does Casey know?"

"It's likely. He's probably run at least three deep searches on him."

"Do you think he'll find anything?"

I shrugged. "Rumors probably. I don't know. It's better for him if he doesn't find out, if you know what I mean?" I winced. That was too bold of me.

She took a longer look at Ringo this time. "And yet, he came back, twice."

I took a delicate sip of my drink. "He came a hell of a lot *more* than that."

Her cheeks turned a little pink. "Does he have any friends? I'll take a little danger if it can tear your big sister out of her sphincter and knock you right into a rebound fling with all the zing. Especially after you tried so damn hard to keep things with the bow-chicka-bow-wow man virginal."

We'd been huddled with our heads together, so there was no warning.

"Virginal? Not me, I hope?" Ringo grinned like he'd invented a cure for that. While he certainly wasn't the first panty-melting badass to crack a killer smile, he owned it.

Every inch of it.

I flushed red.

Kat, the traitor, jumped into the breach. "Obviously. Why aren't you two going at it like rabbits? Or are you and Ellie's just pretending to fight the good fight?"

Ringo stared at me. Something dark was in his thoughts because I'd seen that piercing hyperfocus at least once, likely twice before. The first time was too quick, so it didn't register. He was lining up a killer in his gun sights. The second time was when he carried me out of a gun battle. That time I woke in his arms, jostled seven ways to Sunday, and he glanced down.

I didn't know *that* man, and it scared me. So, I did what I always do. Lied. "I'm saving myself again."

"Bullshit." Kat was quick to call me out.

Ringo, on the other hand, wasn't as versed in my twisted quagmires of illogical blurtations. "Saving yourself?"

He was right to speak with such caution. This was my version of a mined zone which was one of the first bastions of protection I'd erected around my heart.

"For marriage. Like she did with Johnny Pornstach."

Too late, I realized what Kat had inadvertently confessed.

Ringo's left eyebrow went up. He valiantly rallied. "That's a lie."

"This is the Blarney Zone, and lies hold as much truth, and maybe more weight when they happen here. What is your best swagger? Lay it on us." Kat swung her arm around as she faked an Irish accent. Her antics distracted Ringo from the gaffe she made.

I laughed and played it off like this was exactly what she said, not a deeply personal secret I'd confessed to her one drunken night before I left for Las Vegas.

Ringo played along. "Oh, that's an easy one, lass. I am the gentlest man in all of Chicago at this moment. I'll kiss you so sweetly, your Christmas candy will pale in comparison." His accent was much more convincing.

She laughed hard. "I'll wager we can find at least one man gentler than you."

"Never. The truth is, I'm just plain impotent. Isn't that right, Ellie?"

Asshole. He knew how this game was played. I hadn't counted on that.

But I had the key to his undoing. I shot a hand out and brushed it across his groin, intending to make a joke about his flaccidity, or the lack of any evidence of a maleness at all, and met the hard ridge of his cock instead.

He trapped my hand against it, practically daring me to measure his length extending the full span of my hand from wrist to finger-tip with another inch to spare. "Now, now, you wouldn't want to make me break my gentlemanly vows, would you?"

I squeezed. "A gentleman, you say? I'd not make anything occur that wasn't possibly there in the first place."

His laughter was good-natured, but the light growl that rumbled against my ear held an edge as he whispered, "It's getting late. We need to leave soon." Then, his lips brushed against my cheek.

A zing of awareness shot through me. His teasing ignited a fire in my soul that flared outward, consuming with a sharp longing for more. Memories of his lips, of his skin, and of those too-few nights flashed through my body leaving a buzzing trail of arousal I struggled to contain.

On the outside, I laughed. I fired off one-liners and solid ripostes that kept both Kat and Ringo on their toes and off my ass. But inside? I was a horny bundle of need that wanted one thing.

Funny how you always seem to want what you shouldn't.

The shadows were deep as I walked Kat to her car parked in the alley behind the bar. Ringo lurked on the perimeter like a phantom. Even with my back to him, I was hyper-aware of exactly where he was. There was a compass tuned to him, not true north, and my heart wanted to follow it.

The taillights of her car faded into the distance. I was rooted to the spot, knowing if I took a step, it would be straight toward him. Would that be awful?

Of course it would. He was everything I shouldn't want. A killer, a criminal, a man who'd never be content to stay here in Chicago, and one who'd eventually bring the wrath of law down on me.

And if, God forbid, we had children in this little fantasy of mine? What then? Would they be stalked and monitored like I was?

I shivered a little.

The soft scuff of Ringo's shoes on the pavement sounded behind me. I may have leaned a little when I felt his heat near my back. "Are you ready to go home?"

A gloved hand brushed my shoulder.

"I've been waiting for you to ask."

The voice was too high. I turned just as Johnny grabbed

my hair and yanked hard. His other hand covered my mouth as he dragged me deeper into the alley.

I kicked, twisted, tried to smack his balls with my fists, but nothing worked.

"Quiet. Just come with me and you won't get hurt."

My muffled, "why" was plainly written on my face.

He twisted my head and looked me in the eyes. "You left me at that wedding chapel."

Technically, Allie had. I tried to tell him that but there was no way with his mitt acting as a muzzle. I kicked his shin instead to get my point across.

"Ow!"

He let go of me to hobble back a couple of paces and rub at his abused bone.

"You son of a bitch."

"Language, Ellie."

"Fuck you, Johnny. Fuck you, and your stupid cheating on me— your fucking stupid mobster-wanna-be antics with shooting Adelmo Conti, and fuck your ugly mustache!"

He pulled a gun from his coat.

I may have went a little too far with the mustache comment. I did what anyone normal does. I froze.

"You're coming with me. I need that money."

That's what this was about? "Money? That's all I am to you?"

"Of course."

Despite suspecting that admission was coming, hearing it knocked me for a loop. "You lied to me." My voice was weak.

"Like you don't lie to everyone you meet? Hell, you lied

to your friends, your sister, your parents… You even lied to me."

"What? How?" I hadn't caught up yet. I was stuck with the emotional aftermath of being betrayed. I'd had weeks to deal with that, but somehow it had just become real.

"You are anything but pure."

Gun or not, I was going to *murder* him. "I was going to marry you."

I'd have said more, but a car came to a screeching halt in the alley, mere feet from where I stood. I jumped back and flattened myself against the brick wall of the bar, stupidly thinking that it wouldn't hurt as bad if I melted into the brick. My feet slid on the little bank of snow that hadn't thawed, and I ass-planted into the icy slush.

Johnny took flight.

A car door slammed and Ringo shouted something at me. But my brain was in fuzzed-out mode where hearing and thinking, heck, even digging my soggy keister out of the numbingly cold snow was more than I could handle.

But I did note one thing. Ringo left me.

I was going to die in an alley, and he left me.

That made my insides turn frigid. No one loved me. My compass was completely wrong, and Johnny was right. My lies were burying me.

"Are you okay?"

Ringo panted, and his face was flushed. I'd never seen him that way. Even under gunfire, he was calm and deadly competent. But this?

If I didn't know better, I'd say he was upset. "Where's

Johnny?" I accepted the hand Ringo held out so I could stand.

Water dripped off my dress. It was ruined. Was my whole life cursed? Every time I got something nice, it was destroyed, ruined, or tainted by tragedy.

"He took off. I should have ran him down and killed him, but…"

I brushed the grayish-black sludge off my ass.

Ringo's words registered. "Killed him?"

"He had a gun on you. Didn't you notice?"

I had. Funny how that little detail had shrunk in my memories. It was as if I knew it wasn't the biggest danger to me. "You want to kill him?"

Ringo's eyes narrowed on me. "Babe. I don't just want to kill him, I'm going to."

There was a pause that lingered a beat or ten too long.

"You got a problem with that?" he asked.

For the first time in my life, I couldn't dig up a lie. I didn't want to. "Ringo? I… I wish you didn't do that. But I'd be fooling myself if I said I didn't feel the same way."

His jaw shifted, as if he were making room for something too big to clamp down. "Not everyone acts on their emotions. Especially the ones that result in such… permanent solutions."

I laughed. "That's a funny way to phrase it."

He blinked once. The words he wanted to speak rolled around his face in a jumble of emotions. "I'm used it. You're not." He held out the crook of his arm, as if expecting me to take it so he could guide me to the car he'd left running in the alley.

But I needed him to know the truth. "A long time ago, I thought being bad was my only choice. I mean, if was going to be blamed and stalked for something I didn't do, I wanted to actually *deserve* it. But the first time I got in trouble, real trouble, I realized I'm not cut out for prison." I shrugged.

"No one is. It goes against human nature to crave confinement."

I studied him. "Then why?" Why do you do what you do? Why do you take the risk? Why can't you stop?

"Because it is also in human nature to crave order. Without the will to commit to that path, you get lost. There's no purpose. That makes you prey to the people who embrace order." He paused to laugh bitterly. "Cops and killers aren't that much different. Once you realize that, it makes a lot more sense."

There was one question burning in my soul. The flame had been there for as long as I could remember. But I'd never had anyone explain this to me. "How do you stop being prey?"

Ringo didn't smile. He took my left hand and held it in both of his with my palm facing the sky. His fingers touched my thumb. He spoke quickly in his strangely accented Italian, then translated. "This part of your hand grips. It makes you able to cling to life. Therefore, it represents life. It gives purpose, promise, and strength. It's the code." He paused to clear his throat and look around. "We shouldn't be doing this here."

No, we shouldn't.

"Take me home. Your home. Please?"

14

RINGO

Trouble. I was in it deep. I should have ran Johnny over. It would have been messy, and difficult to coverup, but the job would be done. I could hear Don Manca's voice in my head berating me for the missed shot. Just like he'd yelled at me when I missed the first time we went hunting. That was so long ago. The lesson imparted, he made me try again. It took me two days to run down my quarry, but I killed it on the second try.

For that, I got one word. "Good." You'd think I was a fool for taking that single word of praise and making a career out of it. But that was more than any parent, teacher, or authority had given me before. It was validation. I wasn't a waste. I wasn't a fuckup. I had purpose.

Ellie was lost, too.

Cold, frightened, alone… she was all the things I'd shoved away. Which meant I was the world's worst choice to give advice. I fell back on what I knew. Those words Don

Manca spoke to me over cold nights on rooftops when the world waited to find a pattern to exploit. I learned that, too. Find the pattern. See the gap. Work your way into the cracks and wait.

I hated waiting. I hated being small.

And worst? I hated being alone. That's why Mario and I worked together. Alone I'd eventually implode. He kept me sane. His dedication to method and order created a safe space I could depend upon when the chaos I attracted became overwhelming.

Ellie's sister was that for her.

It's no wonder Mario and Allie found each other. They were magnets. Attracting the pattern and honing it into perfect symmetry.

Which begged the question, what would happen if two chaotic, lost souls clung to each other? Would they find a perfect fit, or would they repel the other with such force that they'd both shatter?

That's what I was afraid of. It's why I sat in the darkened living room of the penthouse, staring at the flames from the artificial fireplace. The night sky was bright and cold. The reflection of it shimmered on the lake. It reminded me of camping on the bluffs in winter. Although, I doubted Sardinia ever got this cold.

"I think I used all your hot water."

Ellie had a towel wrapped around her hair, and the rest of her body was engulfed by one of the universally sized bathrobes supplied by the staff.

I motioned to the couch next to me and pulled the blanket from its folded perch on one arm of the sofa. "Sit here. You're probably still cold." An adrenaline dump and crash would do that.

She slid into the spot I indicated and didn't stop until she had plastered herself at my side.

Carefully, I shook out the blanket so it could cover us both. Then I tucked the edges in around her to trap the heat.

She squirmed a little to pull out her left hand. Once free, she held it out, palm-side up. "Teach me."

"It took me ten years."

"Teach me," she insisted.

"Are you sure?"

Her eyes met mine. "I want to understand. And, I want something to grab onto. Something that won't let me down."

Funny. That's exactly what I'd been thinking.

I stroked her hand. "Did you know that before man invented sextants and astrolabes, they used their hands and the stars to navigate?"

"You're making that up."

"No. I was told this by a really old fisherman in Isola Rossa. He must have been ninety."

"He made it up then."

I shook my head. "The way he told it, his ancestors were one of the original sea people in the Mediterranean. They navigated by luck, wind, and stars." I held out my hand, placing it behind hers.

"You find Orion's belt. That's one of the easiest star clusters to find. And you put it right here." I pointed at the mount under my ring finger. "Line up your thumb with

Betelgeuse. That's the really bright star. Sometimes you have to twist your whole arm to get it just right. Once you get in position, look at the angle of your arm to the horizon. You know exactly what month it is by that angle. When you're turned all the way around like this," I paused to position it just right, "it's time to sail home so you're not caught in winter storms. Your pinkie finger disappears under the horizon."

"How does that help you navigate?"

"Easy. The angle, plus the direction you're facing, against the line of the horizon works to tell date, and compass. But each day the compass moves a little east or west. Sailors learn how to do this with their left hand so they can steer with their right. Both hands work together to guide your travel."

"That doesn't make sense. Why not used something fixed?"

"Because you can't always see it. Like the North Star? It gets lost in the sky if you go too far south. Too far north and you lose the Southern Cross."

She pondered that for a bit. "I suppose that's important."

"Each hand works together." I wove my fingers between hers. "Your fingers each represent a truth. The thumb is life. The index finger, it's honor. Clarity you might say. The middle finger—"

"That's the 'fuck you' finger."

I laughed. "Discipline."

She frowned. "You mean, it's the 'I can fuck you up' finger?"

"That's right." I moved to the next digit and stroked it, thinking about its meaning.

"Love?" she guessed.

"Respect. Love is fleeting. Respect lasts longer, but demands work and effort to keep."

"Kind of like love."

I had to know. "Did you love him?"

She tugged her hand away, closing it on itself. "To be honest? No. I thought I found someone who was just bad enough to match my desires and not nearly awful enough to be unsafe. I was wrong. Just…wrong."

"You wanted to respect him?"

Her eyes shot to mine. "Yes."

It was easy to raise my final finger and ask, "Do you know what this one means?"

She shook her head.

"The thumb is life, the pinkie is death. It's small, final, opposite of the first. But it is also not weak. It's necessary for a strong grip. I didn't believe it at first, but Don Manca made me hold my pinkie out and try to squeeze his hand. I couldn't do it. Not until I folded that finger down. It is the force that makes or breaks us. And it will always be there whether you want it or not. Kind of like it follows the other fingers when they move. It's like a shadow."

I was lost in thought and memories.

She shifted closer, holding me in her arms.

"Everyone has that shadow, Ellie. Everyone."

"My sister doesn't."

Bullshit. "If she didn't, she would have sent Mario packing the first hour she knew him." Allie most definitely had a shadow. She may have been as innocent as Ellie thought she was before she met Mario, but death recognizes itself in odd ways.

"So, you're saying it's Mario's fault?"

I should discourage that kind of thinking. Mario wasn't a man to be toyed with. And he certainly wouldn't like his secrets known to his wife's sister. Yet my love for him surfaced in odd ways. "Next time you see him, you try telling him that."

"I value my sanity, thank you very much."

Odd. Most people value their lives around Mario. "Your sanity?"

"Yeah. He's… he's like Allie. You tease him, and he'll find twenty-five reasons you're inaccurate, then lob a zinger at you that explodes like a shit balloon, making you look like an ass for saying anything at all."

I smiled. That was an accurate observation. I'd made it my life's calling to find ways to needle him. Some had been successful. Most had not. It might be fun to see how well Ellie fared. "I dare you."

"You left sanity on the short bus you rode to school in."

My chest twitched at her insult. I kept my face stoic. "Tell me, how quickly do your parents change the subject when they're asked about you?"

Her mouth fell open. "I'm not as dumb as you look."

Ouch. "You talk a big game for someone with a 9 o'clock curfew."

That one made her eyes narrow. "Oh lovely. A battle of wits against an unarmed opponent."

"I envy people who have never met you."

Ellie leaned back, studying me from head to toe. "You wanna know the best thing about you?"

This ought to be good. "Sure."

"You're biodegradable."

While losing the battle by laughing, I logged that one to use against Mario. He'd appreciate it. "You win."

I leaned back on the couch and stretched my arm over the back, encircling Ellie under it. "You know, if you weren't still rebounding from that asshole—" I cut my words short. Ellie didn't need to know where my thoughts veered off course.

"I'm not rebounding."

The sex we had in Venice said different. Hell, she told me herself that I was only a substitute for her disappointment. "Remember what you said to me on that gondola ride?" I didn't let her chime in. "You said, 'Ringo, this isn't permanent. It's a blip because I don't adjust well.'"

"Oh, I get it now. I bruised your ego, and you took it out on my phone, right?"

That was part of it. The other part was cutting Mario out of her sister's conversation before I could gracefully exit Ellie's life. I'd gotten what I needed. Confirmation of where Mario holed up. I didn't need Ellie anymore. And she certainly didn't need me.

Except she did.

Pornstach was still a problem. One I should have eliminated tonight, messy or not. He needed to die. I stood up, tucked the blanket around Ellie. "I'm going out."

Ellie tossed off the blanket I'd tucked around her. "No!"

Her bathrobe gaped open just a little. My eyes fixed on the glimpse of flesh, that sensuously enticing curved shape.

"I mean, please? It's late and— Are you staring at my boobs?"

I quickly looked away.

"You were, weren't you?"

"I'm a guy. Sue me."

"You still *like* me, don't you?"

The way she drew that word out irritated me. "Don't be juvenile."

"You're the one staring at my boobs."

To prove her wrong, I looked her in the eye. "Are you done?"

Her mouth opened, but she hesitated. "I… I'm scared."

Yeah. I could see why. But that didn't change the fact that she was using me to not be scared, or to get over her obsession with that— a thousand words flashed through my mind. Almost all of them tied to the ways I hated that man.

The quickest way to failure is to let your emotions cloud your mind. Mario's voice echoed in my head. Until he met Ellie's sister, that man lived by those words.

Funny how one blond-headed menace and her twin could change things so quickly.

"El, I know you're scared. I also know I'm tired of being your punching bag."

Her eyebrows pushed together in the center. "I'm not punching you."

No? The urge to fire back a string of reasons clogged in my throat. I pushed them aside and struggled to be logical and cold. "I'm your rebound guy. The guy you latch onto when you're scared. I'm nothing." That was wrong. "I'm nothing more than that."

Her face went blank. She didn't argue with me.

"Thought so." I turned to grab my coat. I had no clue where I'd go, or what I'd do. But it would start at the bar. I'd stand in that alley and reconstruct the scene. Then, I'd search for footprints, or a trail in the snow. I'd run Johnny Pornstach down like a fucking deer to slaughter.

"Ringo?" Ellie's voice cut through the murderous rage in my head. I froze in front of the coat closet.

"In that alley, I thought you abandoned me."

"You were with Kat. I was getting the car so you wouldn't have to walk through the snow." I stared at my wool coat.

"That is very sweet."

"I'm *not* sweet."

Her sharp intake of breath was audible. The shaky gust she exhaled was quieter, but heavier. "You're a killer."

I tilted my head, as if to acknowledge that fact. Then I reached for my coat.

"But you're also a nice man. I'm having a lot of trouble putting those two things together. And that's why you probably feel like a human yo-yo."

My hand fell from the fabric. It was dragged down by a desire to become something better. Or maybe more. But that type of shift in a world like mine was a death sentence. "I hear what you're saying."

"What you aren't is a rebound guy. I never slept with

Johnny. I made him wait until we were married. I think that's why he was with Dianora."

Was she serious? I scanned her face to detect the bullshit she was shoveling. "Never?"

"Never."

"What about kissing him?"

Her eyebrow went up. "Are you jealous?"

A common trait weeded out good assassins from bad ones—the ability to recognize emotion and the courage to name it. "Yes. I'm jealous." I stepped away from the closet and paced the length of the condo until I stood in the fishbowl-shaped formal living room and practically plastered my face to the floor-to-ceiling windows overlooking the empty lakefront highway and the even emptier lake spreading out like some northern ocean. Ellie padded up behind me. Her reflection was a blur of white and softer shades from her blond hair and tanned skin. She stood behind me, but far enough away that I couldn't feel her presence.

I spoke to that cold, blurry image. "Every man who's touched you, kissed you. Every person you smile at, or let inside that wall of protection you built up, I envy them. They get you. And I don't."

I turned so I could face her. "I'm goddamned jealous."

She studied me for a long moment. "That's not healthy."

"Neither is having nightmares every night."

She blinked. "I know. And you're right. I'm scared. I've been scared since I was five years old. Allie and my parents think I'm making those nightmares up. But they're real. I know they are. I know at one point or another I slipped out of the house and those men chased me. I know they did. But no one believes me." The blinking grew faster as she struggled to keep her eyes dry.

"Grown-ass men chasing a child." They deserved to die. I made a mental note to hunt them down, too.

"I'm always going to be scared. That is something I can't change. But you weren't the rebound guy. If you were, I wouldn't be so conflicted right now."

My back itched, exposed as it was. I led Ellie back to the couch where we started the night, but didn't sit. "I'm always going to be who I am. Some men say it's because I owe Don Manca or Mario. But I know that I was born to this life. If I hadn't found them, I would be doing this for someone else. Some organization without as many rules, or morals. Then I'd be much darker, and you really wouldn't think I'm a nice man at all."

Her gaze peeked at me through the light wisps of her long bangs. "Allie trusts them."

I nodded. "It goes both ways. She took care of Mario when he was injured. She didn't have to, but she did. That proved her worth."

Ellie's eyes fell. "And I'm worthless."

That kind of thinking wouldn't fly. I grabbed her arms and pulled her close so she'd listen to me. "You are not worthless. You are a smart-ass, but also smart. You're sharp, witty, business-savvy, tough—oh my God, so tough—soft, beautiful…" I got distracted by the texture of her cheeks under my thumbs. I was careful to catch her falling tears and push them into her hair where they'd remain hidden. "I think you are amazing."

"You're just saying that to get into my pants."

"You're not wearing pants."

15

ELLIE

Ringo's low rumble sent shivers through me. The way his eyes hungered as he scanned my face and body thrilled me. But it was the faith he had in those lies he used to describe me which undid me. "I'm not smart."

"You are. Street smarts count. You have that in abundance."

"I blame Kat for that."

He shrugged, ceding the point. "You can't blame Kat for you how pretty you are."

Rogue. "May I kiss you? I promise to be careful and not pull your yo-yo string if you don't want me to."

Instead of replying, he swept me close, and his mouth met mine almost instantly. His kisses were starved and overpowering. I wanted sweet, so I met his force and took control of the kiss, allowing a moment of ravaging insanity, then drew back just a little and softened the kiss until only our lips pressed together. But in that movement I poured my heart.

Everything I felt for him, the insecurities and the longing, the wonder and the fear, was softened and rolled into something so big it dragged me toward the center of the earth, but also made me fly. When the kiss broke, his expressive eyes reflected my fear.

"I promise," I repeated.

He drew a breath. "I want you."

With deliberate caution, I loosened my grip on his shoulder. But only with one hand. Once free, I slid it down his arm and found his fingers. With only a little tug, I stepped back once. He followed my lead. His eyes traveled to the arch behind me. Immediately beyond the transition from family room to foyer was a door on the right wall. It opened to the room we'd spent every night in since Johnny destroyed my bedroom. Ringo's eyes fixed on that opening.

"Only if you're sure." I'd sleep somewhere else and deal with the nightmares. I'd managed that by myself for over two decades.

He bent and slipped a hand behind my back, and another under my knees. Barely a second later, I was in his arms and he was moving fast. He kicked the door wider with his foot and cleared the hallway and turn with ease. I clung to his neck afraid my weight was too much.

But he'd carried me before. Hell, full-on ran with me tossed carelessly over one shoulder, uphill. He was strong.

Another piece of my heart stripped free of the cage I'd put around it and soared toward the promise that I'd finally found a man who could protect me. I tried like hell to tug it back, caution it, and cajole it to return to its guarded fortress, but it wouldn't listen. I was losing.

Worse? I would hurt Ringo if I let the rest of my heart follow. Then again, I suspected it was already in mutiny and had found the keys to the prison. It was only lingering behind to wait for my brain to catch up.

And that traitorous organ whispered, *you love him*. It knew. My heart knew.

Heck, my soul knew him the first moment we met in line at the airport in Vegas. He'd overheard my argument with the airline staff and offered me cash to use Johnny's ticket to Italy. Since they'd informed me the window to get a refund was closed, I jumped on it. And for the next twenty hours Ringo entertained me with stories, jokes, and even better, was a bulwark the outside world had to crash against to get at me. And nothing did.

He was a seasoned traveler. That made the transfers, customs, and other hoops breeze by. Not even Allie could have arranged things better.

In hindsight, the trip went almost too smoothly.

He waited at the edge of the bed. "You still with me?"

"How did you get through the gate with Johnny's name on the ticket?"

His cheek grooved with a smile that quirked up only on one side. "Trade secret."

I sighed.

He let me down. "And…I've lost you."

"No. It's…I'm still processing, but I *do* want you. I was thinking about how we met." He deserved more honesty from me than that. "About how I recognized a kindred spirit almost instantly." I met his eyes, so he'd see through the walls and know I was telling the truth.

"I was using you."

His confession made me laugh. "I knew that."

"You did?"

I nodded. "You said I'm street smart." I let that dangle a little so he'd catch up. "Duh."

An uncharacteristic blush crept up his skin. He licked his lips and tried to study me while also trying to hide the act. Eventually, he gave up and stared at the carpet. "Kindred spirits…"

I tugged on his shirt so he'd pay attention. "Yes. My soul knows yours. Deal with it."

His mouth opened a little. I longed to kiss him again.

"Ringo?"

Something cleared on his face. "We're even."

It took me a moment to catch up. "Yes, we're even. You used me, I might have used you to get over the wound of my ego getting bruised by Johnny's bad behavior. We've even. Now, where do we go from here?"

His eyes drifted to the bed.

With a tug, I pounced onto the mattress, dragging him with me. The robe's knot worked loose, and I snuck a hand up his shirt. We were both kissing the other deeply. His tongue twisted with mine, vying for control. It was messy and perfect.

I got one of his arms released from the sleeve, but the rest of his shirt tangled on his chest.

My robe pooled at my waist, and he wrapped his freed

hand around my left tit. I glanced down, realizing this was moving fast.

Our eyes met.

Ringo tipped his head, as if to ask, are we going to talk or …not?

I shook my head and slipped my hands free from the fabric and stripped his shirt off. I tossed it on the floor before attacking the fastening of his pants.

But I couldn't finish the job because he picked me up again and tipped me to my back. His body wedged between my legs and his shoulders kept them spread wide. I protested until his mouth met my pussy.

There were much better things to do than complain. I gripped his hair. Control or desperation drove my fingers to tangle there and dig in.

He growled against my clit. A shiver of ecstasy shot through my body, and I couldn't stop the cry of delight that broke free. That sound made him double his efforts to drive me insane. His tongue flicked in maddening erratic circles, and he'd shifted his grip on my legs to press against the soft hinge of my hips. His thumbs were free to caress my slick skin under his chin.

I squirmed as one thumb rimmed the opening. "Ringo, please." I needed him inside me. I needed release. Hell. I needed him desperately.

His reply was muffled by his lips and tongue working me toward the edge. It buzzed against my skin. That made my eyes cross. "Do that again."

His half stifled laugh blew across my skin. I moaned

because I missed his mouth terribly. A second later he hummed and flattened his tongue on my clit.

I shot out of my head as my pussy clamped down on the finger he'd slipped inside me. My cries panted free as my body both came alive and shut out the world. It focused on the sensations shooting through my system, and tightened around his head.

He licked me again, and my back arched. A moan, unladylike and guttural escaped. I couldn't even form his name as I panted in its wake.

"There you are," he said as my eyes refocused.

His chin was wet and his eyes sharp. *He's a wolf.* I thought. Casey's warning almost made me giggle. "Get up here. Let me taste you."

Ringo grinned. "You mean, taste yourself."

Whatever. I dragged him by the hair so I could latch onto his mouth. My legs wrapped around his waist to fit his covered dick against my sensitized pussy. It felt good, but not nearly good enough. I broke free and shoved him to his knees so I could finally unbutton those damn slacks and strip him bare.

"Ellie."

I ignored him, getting the button free and attacking the zipper.

His voice sharpened. "Ellie."

I froze, barely daring to meet his eyes. "I want you."

A smile washed over his face. Sure, a little devious, and naughty, but also lighter than any I'd seen on his face before. "Let's not pretend we don't like each other, okay?"

He was a piece of work. "What do you think I've been doing for the last few minutes?"

His grin deepened. "Hopefully enjoying the shit out of yourself."

"Yeah. And now I want you to enjoy the shit out of yourself. Take. Your. Pants. Off!" I tugged the fabric with each word.

He leaned away from me. The smile morphing into something else. It wasn't a frown, but it had changed. The glint in his eyes held fire.

My heart went all in. "I dare you."

His nostrils flared. The colder, deadlier side leaked through his expression. "I told you, I'm a jealous man."

"And?"

The expression on his face settled into that wall of determination and control I'd witnessed once. It was right before he pulled the trigger of a wicked-looking rifle. Barely a second later, up the slope, against the wind, and masked by a bank of scrubby trees, a man fell out of his blind. Shot directly between the eyes. This was the assassin staring at me.

It thrilled me. I must be sick to want him so, but maybe that was my shadow? Or maybe it was the shadow I created to laugh in the face of authority. It grew inside me to protect me from the monsters that lurked in the dark. I leaned into that villain they created. "And?"

The devil he joked about grinned at me. "And you will never leave me. Understand?"

"Like I want to?" I reached for his pants to slip the garment down his hips.

He trapped my fingers. "Do you? Do you want to be free of me?"

Never. "I'll let you know if that surfaces again, okay? And I'll be nice about it."

"Fair enough." He lifted one knee, then the other and wiggled free from his clothing. His cock hung heavy and stiff. The tip glistened with precum. I licked my lips, imagining how good that would taste.

Or better yet, feel between my legs.

He held it in place with one hand. "Ladies' choice, Ellie. Which set of lips are going to kiss this first?"

Damn. I felt those words in my pussy. But I crawled to him and licked the tip, torturing myself for a few minutes longer.

His fingers tangled in my hair. "Babe."

That groan was all the encouragement I needed to suck him deep and curl my tongue against his flesh. I traced the nuances of him from tip to root and back. He tried to hold in place, but his hips rocked toward me every time I took him deep.

"Ellie." There was a note in his voice. It begged me to stop. Or maybe it begged me to finish him.

I did neither immediately. Instead, I worked him, played with him, toyed with him at the edge of danger. I could do no less because it was who I was.

When his fingers tightened their grip, I let him pop free.

My breath came in gasps and I yearned for him to fill me up.

He released my hair and dragged my lips to his for an echo of our previous kiss.

The next thing I knew I was on my back. He'd flipped me there without hurting me, and before I could register that I'd been man-handled expertly.

His cock fitted against me. He gave me a breath, maybe two as he dragged the tip between my lower lips. Then found home and sank deep.

This. This was where heaven started. I groaned his name. "Yes. That's exactly what I want."

My encouragement made him smile. "Say it again. Say my name. Tell me who owns you."

I panted. "Ringo." It was a warning, but also a plea. "You fucker."

He planted deep. So deep, I pulsed around him once. It wasn't an orgasm, but it might have been a warning. "My name, baby."

I met his eyes. "Say mine."

"Ellie." He stroked out and then resumed his deep penetration and held there. "I l—"

His eyes were hooded. Even as we hung there, listening to the echoes of his near mistake, I knew.

"Ringo? I love you. I have since you left me in Venice. Remember? You were such a gentleman that you told me to enjoy my vacation. And you left."

His eyes closed, but his grip on my hips tightened. "I remember."

"And then, you came back." My voice quivered a little. "And I loved you a little more. Each time you come back, it happens whether I want it to or not. I love you."

The anguish on his face was real. "You shouldn't."

I grabbed his hair. "Shut up and fuck me."

"Baby…" His body curled into mine and he whispered my name against my skin. "Ellie, you own me. I don't know—"

"Shhh…" I arched so he'd move and he did. Each stroke held promise, lies, and the intriguing sharpness of two souls who knew the other intimately, thoroughly, and completely. While the memories weren't there, the recognition was. We fit.

He pumped harder, digging for that light we both knew once but had lost. I clung to him, tearing at him to plead silently for help to rip down the walls we'd built. Tears threatened to spill from my eyes as I said his name over and over.

Ringo dug deep, a cry on his lips and his heart in those echoes. And I followed him with a final mental swing like a sledgehammer crashing inside and bursting forth with agony.

As the flutters quieted, he kissed my shoulder. His voice was barely a whisper. Maybe even softer than that. A breath. A secret?

"I love you."

Why did his whispered confession make me want to cry?

16

RINGO

The hard case of my phone rattled on the nightstand. Ellie was wrapped around me so tightly, I could barely move.

Luckily, she was a sound sleeper after the nightmares wore her out. I slipped an arm free and stretched to grab the buzzing annoyance before it rattled right off the edge. The screen displayed a familiar number.

"I'm up." My raspy voice and the whisper I used so I wouldn't wake Ellie told the caller that I was lying.

"Are you alone?" Mario's sharp question jarred me because I'd been expecting the gruff and heavily-accented tones of the family's shot-caller who always observed social niceties before talking business.

"Hang on."

I could practically see the expression on my friend's face. He hated my obsession with Ellie, thinking it distracted me. It did. Last night's failure being immediate proof. I moved to the laundry room which was in an obscure offshoot of the flat.

"I'm clear. Whatcha got?"

I must be on speakerphone because Don Manca spoke next. "What are your intentions with my granddaughter's sister?"

Shit. I thought he was on board with this. "What do you mean, my intentions? You're the one who sent me here."

"I did not tell you to set her up as your mistress."

I wasn't doing *that*. Mario had to be fuming right now, which explained his brusque greeting. This needed to be nipped in the bud. "Where are you getting that idea from?"

Mario's low curse rumbled in the background.

"Who are you with this morning?" Don Manca demanded.

Busted. "Ellie."

That cursing wasn't as quiet now.

"I can explain—"

"Taci!"

The urge to continue talking and ignore Don Manca's command was strong, but I was still very much their pawn.

"Alfonzo Conti-Messina tells us his favorite piece of ass is in the hospital. She was at Ellie's home early to drop off clothing you purchased for her."

In the background, Mario uttered the word, "lingerie" as if it were a filthy word.

I held the smile from my response. "Sì, I replaced what was damaged. You said hospital?"

"Damaged?" Mario must have approached the microphone because his voice was clearer.

"Yeah, Pornstach broke into her house last week and cut up her underwear among other things. And since your wife kept the stuff she bought for the trip—"

"Leave my wife and her clothes out of this."

I laughed. He had it bad for Ellie's sister. I addressed Don Manca because Mario had his head up his ass. "Will the *giga* pull through? And more importantly, why didn't Alfonzo call me first?"

"You're sleeping with Ellie?" Mario was uncharacteristically unfocused.

Don Manca overrode his question with one of his own. "The woman was badly injured, but is not dead. You can guess why he did not contact you. I'm certain you are smart enough for that. Do you know for certain it was Porciello who broke in?"

"Oh yeah. The dick left his juicy calling card all over her mattress. I moved her here with me the same day. Tell Mario, he owes me for four nights of interrupted sleep because she gets nightmares every damn night."

"That doesn't mean you have to sleep with her!"

Mario shoved that stick back up his— "Excuse me? Who was it who married a woman he stole from less than an hour before the wedding?"

"Ragazzi!" Don Manca's dressing down shut us both up. "Porciello is a problem. One you were sent to Chicago to correct. Why haven't you done so?"

The long answer was that I was distracted, foolish, and sidetracked by one very beautiful, very frightened woman who owned my heart. The shorter answer was even more embarrassing. "He is slippery."

Silence.

I filled the void. "I believe the cops are looking for him. That's not on record, but there is an agent watching the bar every night. She thinks he's going to try make contact with Ellie."

"Which he did. Twice, as of this morning."

Don Manca didn't know this, but technically, it was three times. At least this morning, Ellie wasn't home. "That's why she's with me."

"That's the only reason?" Mario asked.

"Nipote, cease." Don Manca was a wise old bird. He could have sent any of his men here. Or sent more than one man with me, so I could deal with the Conti issues without distraction. But like the wicked Filonzàna, he spun a larger web. "This agent has a name, no?"

If this call was monitored, saying it might trigger an investigation. "I'll pass it on, along with any information I have about our problems." There were many. Ellie's ex was an annoyance, but fixable with the right circumstances. The other issues were much more headache-inducing. Starting with the fact that Alfonzo cut me out. I hadn't even been in town one week and he'd dismissed me. And that was on top of cleaning up the betrayal in the organization's ranks. Surely, he'd heard a rumor about that by now. I needed to teach him how to respect the Left Hand. "Then, I'll find out where Porciello is holed up."

So much for spending a fine morning in bed with Ellie.

"Have you even looked?"

Mario was not being helpful. I couldn't help but needle

him. "I had your list. Perhaps you got something wrong? Maybe ask your wife—"

That was all it took. I smiled as Don Manca reined Mario back. Then he addressed me, "Have you asked your woman if she knows where that pig is?"

"I doubt she knows." If she did, she'd probably steal one of my guns and hunt him down.

"Did you ask?"

While obvious, it wasn't the right question. "With all due respect, Don Manca, she doesn't need anymore nightmares."

He measured his next words carefully. "You must take care of those."

Oh yeah, I would. "It's at the top of the list."

"Good. Call Alfonzo. Remind him you are not only trained to be left-handed, but you are also right-handed by birth."

That would be a mean trick. Reminding anyone that I was Don Conti's blow-by was a matter for lab technicians and lawyers. Convincing them I'd inherited his ruthlessness? I didn't even want to acknowledge that let alone broadcast it.

Moreover, failing to kill Johnny Porciello was undermining my reputation. He had to have friends helping him, or a safe place to cower in. Somewhere, someone in his background held the key to his downfall. Too bad I killed all those men. One might have talked.

But they were a good place to start. They had associates, friends, neighbors.

And I had bait.

Lovely, sensuous, delicious bait.

"You're insane." Ellie squared off against me with the kitchen island as a battlement.

"It's one bet." And I'd be there as her backup.

Her eyes narrowed. "Do you have any idea how much that man lost on me last time?"

I snatched a slice of bacon from a plate she'd set on the counter. While I chewed, I calculated where Vincent's demarcation between business and problem would lie. "Forty-grand? Sixty?" That would put a dent in the monthly profit.

"I hate you."

"No, you don't. You just hate that I know you, the real you." I couldn't help it my eyes dipped to her chest. Those delectable treats were encased in lingerie I'd bought, then covered with a thin steel gray sweater knitted from the finest cashmere money could buy. The garments hugged her, shaped her, and drove me absolutely rabid with envy.

"Has anyone ever explained to you how much oxygen trees *waste* on you?"

That was a good one. I stared into her eyes. "You love me."

Her face turned pink. "I'm never gambling again. Think of a different way."

"You won't like the other way." I didn't like it. She'd hate it.

Her eyes spoke of my death. "Don't underestimate me."

I shifted in my seat. "Okay, it involves going door to

door and begging his friends for information on where he is. Your cover story is that you're desperate to find out why he dumped you, and you want him back."

Her upper lip curled.

"Told you. You hate it."

"It's a good plan, but not me. I'd go door to door asking where he is so I could murder his ass for being a dumb shit and cheating on me before the wedding."

"We're trying to avoid getting associated with his demise, remember?"

She deflated. "Fuck."

"How much did Vincent lose?"

My question was ignored so she could pour the beaten eggs into the pan. Once they were secured and heating, she kept her back to me. "The odds were five to one. I made three hundred thousand. Do the math."

Jesus. "And you walked away?"

"Yes. Losing that much is stupid."

"But you didn't lose."

"Eventually, everyone loses."

True.

I studied her. Despite her projected recklessness, she had a solid center. It was strange. Her twin projected that competence as her personality. It was one of the main reasons Mario noticed her because they were so alike in that way. Ellie hid hers.

I moved the glass of orange juice she'd poured for me. It sat between us. Once she'd turned to face me again, I pointed at it. "Is that half full or half empty?"

"Don't try to psychoanalyze me. It doesn't work."

"You sure?"

She picked up the glass and chugged down the contents, then set the glass between us again. "Are you happy now?"

I stared at the residue collecting on the bottom. "It can be filled up again."

Her finger poked at me. "You are an optimist."

"No, I'm not."

"You're definitely not a pessimist."

I smiled. "I think outside the box."

"I destroy boxes. How's that for a head trip?"

She was being argumentative for a reason. It made for a good distraction while I worked out a plan that wouldn't involve gambling or groveling. "Does Johnny owe you any money?"

She blinked. "I—"

This was going to get interesting. But pressing her on an answer was delicate. The change in her demeanor was abrupt. A twinge of jealousy clouded my mind for a second. It whispered, she still loves him.

Or she hated him. But there was passion there that had caused that mood shift.

"I spoke to Don Manca this morning."

Her eyebrow went up at the subject change. Quickly she masked it and turned to address the eggs. "How's Allie doing?"

"I didn't ask, but Mario's being a distracted shithead, so I'm guessing he's not getting much sleep."

"Good for her."

I snagged a belt loop on her jeans as she tried to slip past me to get the orange juice from the refrigerator. With a tug, her body plastered against mine. "I didn't get much sleep either."

"Whose fault is that? Not mine."

"Bullshit." I kissed her because her delicious lips were so close.

She leaned away. "You don't fight fair."

"Fuck fair. Kiss me again."

"The eggs are burning."

I released her so she could stir the contents of the pan and turn down the heat. Then she avoided my reach as she refilled my glass. It must have been all the years of bartending that taught her that dance. "You're beautiful."

She set the carton down slowly. "Do you mean that?"

With my entire soul. And yet, I wasn't talking about her face or her body. "My mom—" the frown on my face came automatically. I straightened it and continued. "She's pretty. But, she's also empty. You're not. That makes you better." God, that was lame. Usually, I was much more well-spoken with flattery.

She turned the knob on the burner all the way off and circled the island to get close to me. Once she was between my legs, I couldn't resist holding her there. It was as if I was afraid she'd slip through my fingers, and I had the urge to cling tightly. I met her gaze with mine. "Babe?"

"I love you."

I forgot to breathe. How could she? My mouth opened, but words were too elusive. Instead, I pulled her closer. So close our bodies aligned. My dick yearned to be against her skin, not sandwiched against layers of clothing.

"Are you mistress or wife material?" I asked.

She shoved distance between us. My stool rocked with the force. "God damn you!"

"What did I say?"

She picked up the carton of juice and cocked her arm back. It hung in position while she debated her next move.

"The maid comes two days from now. You'll have to clean that up."

Ellie slammed the carton on the countertop. Her back was turned as she contemplated the eggs. "You know what? Feed your fucking self."

I caught her as she tried to escape and held her close despite her struggles. She glared at me even after her body stopped resisting.

"I wanted to make sure. Marry me."

Her chin went up. "Listen up, buddy—"

"No." I put a finger on her lips. "Please? I love you. But I'm not a good guy. I'm not Mario with a stick up his ass and a long ass list of do's and do not's. I'm a rule-breaker, a bastard, and probably a bad bet for marriage. That's why I gave you the option. Okay?"

"I don't—" her breath overrode her words. It shook as she inhaled. "Would you cheat on me?"

I swallowed. My heart screamed, "Never!" But my gut and my brain threw out all sorts of situations where I'd be tempted, or perhaps even ordered to entertain the betrayal. "I'm not my own man."

Her face fell. This time she extracted herself with more grace and less force. "Will you ever be?"

I sighed. My head shook once.

"How do people like Mario and Loppa and Don Manca do it then? They get married, you can't?"

Don Manca went through three wives. Loppa wasn't active as more than a very dangerous bodyguard, and Mario? Well, he was always the exception. Unlike me, he created rules to live by. He knew how to work through any crack or obstacle with precision. He applied force only when necessary, and when he did, it was surgical and final. I didn't have that kind of skill. Nor did I have the grace of being born into the family to protect me. "I'm not family."

Her face hardened. "You're also Don Conti's heir. Doesn't that count?"

It did, but only slightly. "That's a delicate situation."

Ellie crossed her arms. Her mood was decidedly darker.

I rallied. "I should talk to Don Manca. If only to make him aware I can't— I won't do work that entails women." I swallowed. Despite being the twin sister of one of the most treasured wives our family had in this generation, I shouldn't have said that. It would topple us all if word got out I was telling her our secrets.

"Have you ever…done that?"

"No."

She relaxed a little. "Do you have women in your family who…?"

"I can't tell you that."

Her face shifted through several sarcastic thoughts.

"Can we talk about this after I ask Don Manca?"

Ellie's shoulders dropped. "What if he says no?"

A muscle in my jaw twitched. If he said no, I'd disobey

him and marry her anyway. Then I'd be dead. The last thing I wanted to do was tell her that.

"About Johnny…"

Her eyes narrowed on me. "I'll make a list. You can pretend you're the insurance adjuster for the Mustang. It's in my name, but his name was on the title."

"You bought him a car?"

"What? Do you want one?" she shot back.

"No. I can afford my own cars, thank you very much."

Her jaw stiffened as she shot me a look. "I made you eggs. I hope you choke on them."

With that, she disappeared into the bedroom. As she slammed the door, she yelled out, "I'm going to change clothes, then I'll be at the bar. Don't bother following me."

At least I knew where she'd be. "I'll drop you off!" I yelled through the walls.

"Fine!"

"Fine." I muttered under my breath. Then I smiled. My life, even it if was a short one, wouldn't be boring with her as my wife.

I dialed Don Manca to tell him I was going to need help. A lot of it.

17

ELLIE

Kat walked in the door, keys in hand and froze in place when she saw me behind the bar. "Not to sound like a cliché, but are you even supposed to be here today?"

I shrugged. The bar was a good reason to be out of the lakefront condo. If I stayed, Ringo would kiss me senseless again, and we'd end up in bed, and…

Well, none of that helped either of us.

Kat moved closer. "Are you hungover?"

"No." Last night I quit at three drinks like usual.

"Then why so quiet? Usually, you would have hit me with at least two smart comebacks by now. Is your coffee machine broke?"

Until she mentioned it, I had blocked out the trouble at my place. Ringo wouldn't let me go in this morning, but he'd parked across from the broken slider now boarded up with plywood and crime tape.

"Ellie?" She waved a hand in front of my face.

"He asked me to marry him."

Both of her eyebrows went up. She blinked at least twice, opened and shut her mouth, then finally got her synapses online and working enough to ask, "Which he are we talking? Ringo?"

I nodded. "Well, first he gave me a choice. Mistress or wife, but— Shit, come to think of it he only gave me the choice. He didn't ask."

"That bastard." She delivered the words with all the enthusiasm of cardboard.

"What?"

Her face. The one that said, "you know better" while also saying, "you are one dumb white chick, you know that?" I squinted at her because I honestly didn't know why she was singling me out on this.

"When's the wedding?"

My shoulders went up at her sharp tone. "I don't know."

"Valentine's Day next year, or—?"

"No." That was Allie's day now— her and her husband's. I couldn't take that date from them. Although waiting a year to see if Ringo was serious or not was probably a good idea.

"So, when?"

The futility of loving him hit me. "Maybe never?"

She took the stool across from me and watched me prep lime wedges. "You know your problem?"

"I have a bitch-ass friend with a big mouth and an attitude?"

Kat snorted. "No. You don't know how to be happy."

I protested. "Oh, that I know how to do. You've been with me many of the times when I've been happy."

"I mean with a guy."

My mind went blank. I didn't have a smart comeback for that. "I was happy with Johnny."

"No, you weren't."

Was she serious?

Kat ignored my glare and pushed on. "You were unsure when you were dating. So much so, you made a pact to not sleep with him until the ink dried. Then, you got all caught up in wedding plans—I think that did make you happy. I swear you were more like your sister in those moments than I've ever seen you. Anyways, once the plans were made you opened your eyes and immediately knew he wasn't all he was cracked up to be, and you suspected he was cheating on you. You told your lawyer to find out, and went on fooling yourself."

I regretted ever confiding in her. Although, that regret wasn't as deep as the remorse I felt about dating Johnny. I'd wasted a ton of time and money on him. "I'm not fooling myself."

"No? Then why do you think Ringo is the one?"

"Oh, he's the one. If there ever was a man perfect for me, he's it."

Her eyes focused on me. The scrutiny was so sharp, I felt it cutting through the layers of my bullshit. "What?"

Kat sighed. "You have always been the kind of person who brags about herself but does it in a way everyone knows you're joking. Which makes me think you don't value yourself. And if someone is perfect for you, then they aren't worth the risk. So, you pick the most awful choices possible."

She had a point. A terrible one. But she was wrong about Ringo. "Let me list some things. One, he's good-looking. He's athletic…" *He can cut a man's throat in under three seconds.* "He's got a good smile." *A totally disarming one that is lethal in the right circumstances.* "And, he's got money, or at least a lot of friends with money and doesn't need or want me to buy a car."

"Fucking Pornstach."

I narrowed my eyes at her for her interruption.

"Go on… extol the bonafides of your latest conquest."

Something in her tone warned me. "I thought you were okay with him?"

Her hesitation was telling.

"Oh, geesh. Tell me now before I go off and marry him, spend a lot of money on bullshit, or something dumb like I did with Johnny."

"I never said anything about Johnny because… well, you seemed happy and it all happened so quickly that I didn't really get a chance to talk to you about it. And then you were off to Vegas and I offered to watch the bar, but you know what? That fucking hurt. We've been best friends since second grade, and you cut me out like that." She snapped her fingers.

She was right, I had. "In second grade you tried to wax the floor with my face."

"See? Friends. If you were an enemy, I'd have accomplished that feat."

"What did you dislike about Johnny?"

Kat hesitated again. "Do you promise to let me tell you everything and not interrupt?"

I couldn't.

"Okay, you'll interrupt, but don't you *dare* defend that baby-faced bastard."

Considering he held me at gunpoint last night? He could rot in Hell. "I'm ready. Hit me."

Her eyebrow went up as if contemplating my turn of phrase.

"Not for real, 'kay?"

Kat held up her first finger. "That mustache."

I rolled my eyes. It was on the tip of my tongue to defend him. I mean, genetics isn't a character flaw.

A second finger went up. "He dressed flashy, but trashy."

That didn't make sense. "What?"

"Walmart shoes and Armani? Please."

Okay. "…But Armani—"

"He shopped his father's closet or a thrift store for that suit."

"Next."

She lowered her hand. "The way his eyes roved when he was with you."

The morning Dianora left his apartment flashed through my thoughts. "That witch stole my hoodie."

Kat pushed up each sleeve. "Where is she? Imma gonna get it back."

I laughed. "In lockup somewhere in Italy. She tried to kill her father, wait, succeeded in killing him. And she killed her brother here. Well convinced—" I cut my words off because the FBI agent who'd been shadowing the bar walked in.

"FBI Agent Perkins. You're visiting us early."

Kat stiffened but managed to plaster on a wide grin. "One of Chicago's finest of the finest. Wow. I didn't know we were *that* popular."

Her gaze took in the two of us. "I'm not here on business. Vodka grapefruit if you have it."

It was barely two in the afternoon. "One Salty Dog coming up." I pulled a monster-sized grapefruit out, sliced off a nice wedge, and then juiced the rest. At least Agent Perkins was getting her vitamin C with her booze.

Meanwhile, Kat asked, "What's wrong?"

Perkins shook her head. "I need that drink first."

I strained it into her glass and set the garnish. Then, I poured a shot each for Kat and I from our special stock under the bar. It was iced tea with just a splash of premium lemon vodka to taste. I lifted my glass and quickly toasted, "A bird never flew on one wing."

She sucked down half of her glass. When she set it down, she sighed. "You can just call me Bridget now."

Kat shot a question at me.

"Not agent, or special agent?" I asked.

"I've been terminated. They told me to go home."

A likely story. One crafted to get me to sympathize with her. But I wasn't going to. "Where's home?" My words were a little too sharp.

To answer, she pulled out her wallet and flashed her ID and the contents at me. "I can tell you won't believe me, so I'll show you. I came here from Boston. I haven't even gotten my license updated. And see, no badge. Are you satisfied now?"

"Boston. Funny, I never pegged your accent," Kat interjected.

"I spent most of my childhood in finishing schools. They wiped that shit right out the first semester." She tucked the wallet back into her purse. "They took my badge and gun this morning."

"What did you do?" Kat asked.

Bridget gave her a side-eye. "It's what *wouldn't* do. That's the problem. And don't ask." She stared at her glass and sighed. "Fucking politics."

Even though she scared the hell out of me, and even though this could be a trap, I was angry on her behalf if she was telling the truth. I leaned in and divulged one secret. "In the Blarney Zone, you're free to embellish the shit out of your life."

"Ellie's an expert on that."

I glared at Kat.

"What? Like your lying is a secret?"

Bridget Perkins followed the conversation with curiosity. More than I was comfortable with.

"Heck, it's almost as notorious as your bad taste in men."

"Here now. Let's not, and say we did." She was treading on dangerous ground.

Kat, however, didn't listen. Instead, she looped Perkins

in on the conversation we had earlier. "Bridget, a hypothetical for you, if your best friend was dating a—"

"Careful." I poured myself another shot because this was not going to go well. Maybe after five or more of these I'd have just enough alcohol in my system to kick her ass.

"—someone who's bad for her. Okay?" She shot me a look before continuing. "And they know this fact, but *they* don't want to hear it. How would you spill the beans?"

Perkins blinked. "Up until thirty minutes ago, I would have run a full background check on him and handed off the results. But now? Jesus." She stared off into space. The musing went on for only a few seconds, then her attention snapped to me. "Johnny Porciello?"

Fuck the kindergarten booze. I needed fortification. I tugged down the Jameson and filled my shot glass to the brim. Kat noticed and bit her lip.

"I guess that's no secret," Perkins continued, oblivious. "I ran him, his friends, and you and your family. Sorry."

I slammed the shot. It went down with a roar and kept fighting when it hit my guts. I breathed through the battle until I won. "You wouldn't be the first agent digging into my life."

"Nor the last, I'm sure of that."

Kat was *not* being helpful.

Perkins frowned. "Did you know your sister's file is only this thick?" She held up her fingers barely two millimeters apart. "And yours?" She laughed.

I mixed her another drink and waited for the fallout.

Her hands set somewhere between two and three inches apart. "You kept the department busy for a *long* time." She sobered. "Not so much in the past four years until six months ago."

This time her gaze was clear when she stared at me.

"Johnny Porciello was a nobody until he started dating you."

"He should have stayed that way," Kat mumbled.

I reached across the bar and slugged her in the arm.

"Hey!"

"Traitor."

"I'm just stating facts," she shot back.

Perkins took a small sip of her second drink. "Facts. Ha. Johnny's new friends are, or perhaps I might say, were? I don't know. Either way, they're connected to the D'Antonio family. But not Johnny." She fiddled with her straw for a silent moment. "When he turned up on the radar, a lot of folks were asking questions." Her scrutiny shifted to me. "And the only link we had was *you*."

I gave her my best unemotional bartender stare. "Do I need to cut you off already?"

Perkins shrugged. "If you do, I'll just walk next door to your competition."

"And I'll call them and tell them not to serve you." She hadn't said anything that made me want to hug her, even though I sympathized with her jobless situation.

"February twelfth. Adelmo Conti died in an automobile accident."

My fingers began to tingle. They did that before I fainted. I gripped the bar so I wouldn't go down. There were photos from the accident. I'd seen them. So much blood. Poor Adelmo was still alive when the airbags went off and saved his life. But seconds later either Johnny or his lover, Dianora, shot him. And simply for knowing all of that, I could go down as an accessory. It would be a difficult fight to clear my name simply because of my family's connection to organized crime. My grandfather fucked up by cultivating his nefarious reputation.

Perkins stared at me. "The very next day, your files, Johnny's files, and the accident's files were sealed." She frowned. "Not only sealed, deep-sixed. Why?"

My head was light. The tingling was well past my fingers now. It was in my cheeks. I stared at the heavy polish on the bar surface. It was an ancient piece of wood. It had been harvested from an ancient oak in the late 1800s after the Second Great Chicago Fire.

It was used for the bar at a brothel-slash-bar in the notorious Levee District. In the 1920s the establishment was shut down. The bar was torn out to make room for apartments when the place became a boarding house.

Casey found it in a barn where it had been stored for sixty years.

He sanded the scars, refinished it, and set it here to remind everyone that survival isn't pretty. I traced a particularly nasty gouge. He claimed it was likely a knife jabbed into the surface.

"I run a bar, Bridget. I wouldn't know."

The tingling subsided a bit.

She frowned and turned to Kat. "I'd tell your friend exactly what I think, and not hold back. She has a right to know."

Kat's gaze was soft as she studied me. "I'm so glad you

dumped that asshole before you married him. He was bad news."

"And?" If she didn't like Ringo, I wanted to know why.

"Well, I hope you see the similarities in whoever you date next before it's too late."

We seriously needed to talk, alone. But that wasn't going to happen any time soon because the afternoon regulars shuffled in and the pace picked up. I retreated to the back room to hide from everyone.

At seven, Kat put a slice of pizza in front of me.

I'd been reviewing the rents and balance sheets from my two other businesses. The landscaping firm was between winter and spring seasons. There was no snow left to plow, and lots of outflows for hiring workers to plant flowers and re-mulch the green spaces encircling the suburbs like so many taxidermied trophies.

"Thanks."

She took a seat across from me. "Bridget left. I poured her into a cab."

My foot tapped against the desk leg.

"She's not that bad of a person."

Since I wasn't losing money I couldn't afford, I lifted my eyes to hers. "I called my lawyer."

"Which one, the business attorney or the family one?"

"The Family one. He needs to know."

"What did he say?" she asked.

My shoulder went up. "Not to worry about it." It was a little stronger than that. His exact words were, "It's taken care of."

Kat leaned back in her chair. She picked at a loose thread near the seam. "Did you ask him about Ringo?"

"Why should I?"

Her reaction was to mutter incomprehensibly to herself sarcastically. Finally, she finished with, "Oh, I don't know, maybe because he strikes me as a hood?"

I gave her my full attention and mimicked her nonchalant pose. "*Why?*"

"Aside from your admission last night, the knife thing. Why does he carry?"

I couldn't tell her that. "What else do you have?"

"Ellie. Don't you get the hint? Even Pornstach didn't carry a knife."

"How do you know that?" He obviously had a gun. Maybe more than one. My gut twisted.

"Are you saying he did?"

That shot of Jameson had worn off hours ago. I contemplated what I could drink that would be stronger. "I'm saying that he—"

A knock stopped my lie.

"You better be bearing Thin Mints and Vodka, otherwise I'm tossing your ass to the curb!"

Molly peeked her head around the door. "Uh, I don't have candy, but your boyfriend is out front."

Kat's face puckered.

"Is he drinking?" I asked.

Molly stuttered an affirmative. "Is that bad?"

No, I preferred him off guard. And I was done torturing the staff. Molly hadn't done anything wrong. "Make sure he gets top shelf, and ring it up under my code."

Kat groaned. "Eco-boost Mustang," she muttered reminding me of the sports car I bought Johnny.

Molly's eyes went a little wide. "Are you sure?"

"Yes." I motioned for her to get moving and shut the door behind her. Only after I heard the click did I address Kat's issues. "He's buying Conti Commercial, Inc. I don't have a problem tossing a hundred bucks at that."

"He's buying it? The whole company?" Kat's disbelief was palpable.

"The company he works for is. It's the same one Allie's husband works for."

Kat sat back. A little, "oh" squeaked out. "It's legit?"

She said it as if Allie could do no wrong. Kat needed a good knock on the head. I stared at the room, remembering something my lawyer once said about my grandfather. "While it is legit, monopolies and money sometimes have ways of getting muddy."

Her jaw gaped. "Ellie!"

"Johnny was a dick. He used me to try to claw his way in. I don't have to worry about that with Ringo."

Her eyes grew a little wider.

Her mouth moved but nothing came out.

"So, yeah. That's why he carries a knife." I shuffled the pages in front of me. "What do you think about pansies? Personally, I hate them, but the landscaper says they're cheap."

"You're serious?"

"Yeah. Pansies suck. You see them everywhere."

"You're fucking serious?"

I frowned at her and set the page of numbers down. "At

first, I was just trying to get over Johnny. Now? I'm screwed, Kat. I shouldn't have anything to do with him or that family, but Allie is all in."

"Just because Allie lost her mind doesn't mean you have to jump after her. Damn. I *never* thought I'd say that."

"Which goes to show maybe things aren't going to turn out as bad as you think."

What a bunch of bullshit.

18

RINGO

Ellie was here, but not where I was allowed to enter. For a little thing, Molly had the ferocity of a chihuahua on steroids. I sipped the premium whiskey and studied the bar. I'd spent at least an hour in the alley behind the bar trying to find any sign of where Pornstach ran off to. Then I visited Ellie's condo again.

Alfonzo Conti-Messina himself met me there. His girl was going to pull through. But he had to remind me of what I owed him.

"He knifed her."

More proof that Johnny Porciello wasn't and never would be a professional. She'd be dead if it was one of ours. "Did you reach out to Vincent?"

"He's still sore you took out all five of his men. You couldn't let one live?"

That didn't deserve a reply. "Did the sale go through?" I'd given him the information for the family's lawyer.

"It's going through. I spoke with my cousin."

Which one?

He read my face. "You know. He'd be your third cousin, I guess."

"How is Remo?" I knew of him. He wasn't a bad person—a banker by trade. He'd only been scorched by Don Conti's failures. I'm certain his sudden rise to power was giving him nightmares, though. Not a single male heir in the Conti family lived long. Don Conti being the exception of the past three generations.

Messina studied the pavement. "He's on board. What did you do? Threaten him?"

Didn't have to. Dianora and Leandro followed in their fathers' footsteps well, eliminating or tyrannizing the competition. "I don't *threaten* people."

His chin tucked closer to his neck, as if avoiding the garrote prepared for it.

I switched to the subject he came here for. "The company Adelmo created, it's too legit. I'll need a business manager who is squeaky clean and knows their shit. *Not* family. I think for all of our sakes, letting it continue as-is might turn down the heat on us."

Alfonzo licked his lips. He'd have come to the same conclusion, but I also knew he was eyeing the vacuum and calculating just how far he could shove his toes in before they got cut off.

"Did you talk to your uncle from Sicily?" Mario visited him last week.

"Yeah."

He certainly didn't sound happy about that. Which spoke volumes.

"Listen, the Left Hand doesn't like the fancy shit. We're only interested in Adelmo's portion. We'll stay out of your business, I promise."

"After *you* decimate it like you did with Vincent's boys?"

"Do you have problems like he did?"

His reply was short. "No."

"Then there's no need to fix them. Is there?"

His eyes traveled to the boarded-up slider and the crime tape. "I think you need to fix your own house first. Then I'll have more confidence in your ideas. Until then, you owe me."

He strode away, turning his back on me. That cut me to the bone.

"Can I get you another?"

Molly's offer snapped me back to the present. "I'm good."

"Ellie says it's on the house."

All the more reason to turn it down. I laid a banknote on the bar. "Make sure the staff, not the management, splits this."

Her eyes widened just a little.

It was a large enough denomination to warrant the shock. And, it could buy that bottle of Ellie's premium Irish whiskey. "I'm not Porciello. I don't need her charity."

Molly snatched the money up. She tucked it into a bundle of singles, then stuffed it into the pitcher behind the bar. Her guilty glance at me turned into a blush. I ignored it and studied the rest of the bar. In particular, the back hallway Molly ran off to when I asked about Ellie.

Soon enough, she and Kat emerged. I picked up my drink and met them at the far end of the bar.

"Ringo." Kat's greeting was cold.

Ellie's wasn't much better. "You're not going to stay here all night, are you?"

"Only until you leave. Then, I'll go with you." She would not be left alone again if I could help it.

"You know, this whole jealous Jedi vibe you got? It's kind of suffocating."

That was cute. "Do you want me to back off?" I'd also called Don Manca and Mario and filled them in. Don Manca had expected my change of heart. Mario?

He didn't take it well. He threatened my life at least a half-dozen times.

Kat, who'd only been eavesdropping until that point, spoke up. "Would you? Would you leave her?"

Never. "That isn't on the table." I'd gotten the green light from Don Manca. He *wanted* this union. If only to ease the tension between his grandson and me. But Mario was dead-set against it. He feared I'd break Ellie's heart.

Judging by the hope in her eyes, I'd say leaving her would do that. "I can ease up a little. But you need to be safe. And I don't want to see any of your friends hurt while you're doing that." I slid a glance at Kat to convey the message.

Ellie frowned. "He's right, Kat. Johnny showed up last night after you drove away."

"What?!" She glared at me. "Where were you?"

"Getting the car."

"You fucking moron!" Kat took two steps away, then circled back around to yell at me. "Tell me you killed him."

"I didn't." Couldn't. I was too busy worrying about Ellie.

"Why the fuck not?" She swore loudly, and the outburst got attention. One glare and the nearest patrons sipping their drinks shifted to empty seats farther away. She quieted and asked Ellie, "You're okay, right?"

Ellie nodded at her question. "He pulled a gun on me. Ringo almost hit him with the car which made him run."

I wished I'd done it.

"Where do you think he went?" Kat asked.

That was the billion-dollar question. Alfonzo didn't know. Vincent might, but he wasn't talking to me. I'd checked Johnny's old haunts to no avail.

"If I knew where he was, he'd be dead already," Ellie said.

"Say that a little louder, why don't you?" I muttered and glanced around to see who was still listening.

"Oh, get over yourself, Ringo. Just because you had one bad night doesn't mean you suck."

Only two people understood what she'd said.

Kat stared at me, realization dawning. I raised a brow as if to ask, "Are you going to say anything?"

Her obvious avoidance answered for her. "You have an MBA, don't you?" I'd done some background work on Ellie before coming to Chicago. I knew all about her former boss getting drummed off the police force. I also knew that Kat worked hard to obtain scholarships for college, but remained here with Ellie.

"Yeah."

"That's why she's my business partner." Ellie swung an arm around her waist, giving her friend a squeeze. "There are no secrets between us." Her steady gaze sent a warning at me.

"I suppose you're too busy to look at an acquisition?"

"What kind of acquisition?"

"Shipping and logistics. CCI. Did Ellie mention them?"

Kat blinked as she nodded.

"I need a competent business manager. Not family, but close. Someone loyal and honest but sharp. I think you fit the bill."

"Working for *you*?" Kat's tone indicated her distrust.

"For the parent company once the sale goes through. It's legit." I scanned the bar they'd built. "It's not as fun as this place, but…"

"My starting salary as Chief Operating Officer needs to be at least fifteen percent higher than the base average for Chicago, not the region. I expect profit-sharing, full benefits package, and a minimum of 40 days leave."

"You're leaving me?" Ellie piped up.

"Please. I can juggle your books and a shipping conglomerate. Ye of little faith."

Ellie's face fell.

"Besides, I have a feeling we'll be seeing each other a lot if this one sticks around. Are you going to stick around, Ringo? Or are you playing with my girl?"

They'd talked. "I proposed."

"Badly."

They definitely talked. "I apologized for that. She knows why I said it that way."

"I don't see no ring on her finger. That means, you have to step up your game. If you got any game, that is."

Did she know who she was talking to? I glanced at Ellie, confused.

She sent me a look that called my bluff and doubled down on it.

"I've got game."

Ellie ran behind the bar and flipped a switch. In an instant the mirrored sign with gold lettering turned into a glaring lightbox of green and flashing yellow. The word, "Blarney" was outlined in glowing red.

The regulars seated the bar slapped the surface, and the ones at the tables picked up their tattoo with glee. "Blarney!" They chanted.

Kat climbed onto the rungs of a stool and like a sideshow barker shouted over the crowd as she called their attention. "This liar here says he's got game."

The shouts of "Blarney" increased.

"What say ye?" she shouted.

My ears rang from the din.

Ellie lined up a row of shots.

"No…" I couldn't afford to get drunk. Ellie's safety relied on it.

"Then admit it, you are full of shite." Kat picked up the first glass.

Was she going to go shot for shot with me? I calculated half of the row. I should be able to manage that.

I reached for the next in line.

Ellie stopped me. She placed a tumbler on the bar-top. Next, she set four bottles down next to it. "We call this the Four Horsemen. You drink two while Kate drinks her row."

I eyed her pour. "One."

"Then you admit it, you've got no game."

If I were to stay on top of Ellie's safety, I had to remain sober. "Woman," I warned.

Ellie grinned evilly. "You come to our bar, you play by our rules."

I picked up the tumbler. "Remind me to bring you some of Loppa's special reserve mirto." I slammed the concoction, ignoring its assault on my senses. Irish whiskey should never be gang-banged with that combo of corn mash, scotch, and tequila. The drink was an abomination.

Which was likely the point.

I set the glass down and indicated she should refill it.

Kat drank four shots.

The sign above their heads must be on a timer because it began to flash.

I braced for the second drink. The first hit my system like a freight train. And it was only going to get worse. "This reminds me of that night Mario and I stole Signora Verina's home made berry brandy."

"Did you get caught?"

I slammed the drink before answering Ellie's question. The alcohol burned, but not half as badly as before. My head swam a little. "I puked on her prized ram. But Mario was the one who had to bathe it." The liquor was purple.

Even after it mixed with the contents of my stomach. The berries in it stained the wool. I laughed at the memory.

I set the glass down. Kat offered me one of her shots. I declined. She started to finish them off, holding the last one under my nose to smell.

Lemons and tea.

The bottle label claimed it was bourbon. "Wait a minute."

"Too late." She laughed and finished the final shot to a cheer from the bar.

I'd been duped. I pointed at Ellie. "You."

"I get to drive your car home. Keys." She wiggled her fingers at me.

I held them back with one demand. "Don't wreck it."

Tall Bob signaled for a drink as the sign's lights went out and the bar resumed its normal din. I breathed through the fumes muddling my head.

Kat led me to a table near the restrooms, just in case. "Are you serious about that job offer?"

"I am. I need to run it past the—" Even as drunk as I was, I stopped before telling secrets. "—the board."

"Is it really legit?"

I nodded. "Adelmo, the former owner, late owner. Shit. My brother—half, he tried to get out of… well, you know. It cost a lot of money and wasn't very fruitful." I blinked. "So yeah."

There was more she needed to know. I tapped the table to get her attention. "Edward."

"Who?"

"You'll meet him. He's putting up one hundred and sixty million. That will get you on your feet with it."

"Is he a silent partner or?"

"Full. He likes his American investments. And…" I scanned my memories for anything incriminating. There wasn't. Edward ran a tight operation. "… his buy-in allows the other investors a degree of certainty everything will be profitable." I rested my head on a hand. "They don't trust me."

"Why?"

I stared at Kat. She'd not asked "who" which was wise. "Because, I'm just the messenger. Not the brains."

"What kind of messages do you send?"

I grinned lopsidedly. "You don't want to know."

"Are you serious about marrying Ellie?"

My nod wobbled a bit. I tipped off balance but caught myself. "I am." My desire to quit was the one thing Don Manca disagreed with. But it would go a long way toward appeasing Mario. "I'm getting out."

"Out? Really? Does Ellie know?"

I shook my head. "I need air." I walked through the back door and stood in the alley where I'd skidded to a stop. The apartments fronting the opposite side of the block had tight fences which kept the noise and the riff-raff from disturbing them. Except for the gap between two fences that Porciello sprinted through. I stared at that space for a long time.

Ellie joined me. "Are you doing okay?"

"You shouldn't be out here."

"I'm worried about you."

The drinks were wearing off, thank goodness. "Remind me never to bet against your friend."

"You'd lose."

Confirmation aside, I had other things to think about. "How many times did Johnny visit you here?"

"Are you getting jealous again?"

"No." Surprisingly, that was the truth. I was looking at this like I would a job. Wide open to the street on the north. A sharp turn to exit into the quieter street to the south and west. There was a sister pub next door which was directly linked to the Blarney Zone by an open beer garden, and hemming in the other side, residential buildings. Some of them had to have security cameras pointed at the alley. There was no way to murder someone here and get away with it.

"He came here maybe twice. He usually took me to the clubs downtown and near the university."

He wanted to be seen with her. "He was using you."

"I know."

I slanted a look in her direction.

"I'm sorry?"

"Don't be. I'll find him."

Ellie hooked her arm with mine. "About that, can you let someone else to do it?"

"What are you saying?"

Her cheek flinched. "Can you ever retire?"

I cupped her cheeks. "I'm trying."

The smile on her face was worth the trouble it would cause.

19

ELLIE

The crime scene tape on my apartment was tattered. I stared at it wondering why Ringo hadn't told me anything. Two reasons came to mind. The most obvious was that he was protecting me. But that didn't make sense because the police had to know whose building this was, and who lived in that unit. Right? Which also meant that this was somehow connected to him and the organizations he worked with. A.K.A., point two.

"Hey Ellie, everything okay?" My neighbor gestured toward the tape barricading my former home.

I smiled and waved at him. "Just evicting a honey badger who took up residence. No big."

"I hear those things are vicious."

"They'll tear your face off if you get too close." I shot back, keeping the banter going. He probably thought I was the weirdest chick on the planet. Which was just fine. "You didn't hear the commotion, did you?"

"Naw, I've been working doubles lately. I was doing an overnight at the hospital, came home and saw the tape. Sorry about your window."

Window, right. The boarded-up plywood covered my entire sliding glass door opening. "Thanks."

He toddled off, clueless.

I stepped over the little wrought-iron fence and examined the damage. Someone had swept up the glass, but there were little glittery pebbles stuck in the crack between the building foundation and the concrete slab I called a patio. My home would be a tomb without the light coming in.

"Hey, Ellie."

I turned to see which nosy neighbor was hailing me now and stopped short.

Bridget Perkins, former FBI agent—my ass she was a former one—stood in the parking lot. "Did you get reinstated?"

Her face darkened. "Bastards." She followed that with a cheerier, "What happened here?"

She knew where I lived. I made a mental note to pack all my shit and move it into Ringo's condo on the lakefront. At least that building had a guard in the lobby. "Squirrels."

Bridget stared at the plywood behind me. "Awfully big squirrels."

I shrugged. "Yup. About the size of a small dog. Jumped off the second balcony, saw its reflection and wanted a piece of that, then hit the glass with his dick angled just right and shattered the whole thing."

She chewed on that for a beat. "I've read your file."

Shit. She'd know about the tall tales then. "What do you think happened?"

With a scan of the lot and the building she spoke. "Johnny Porciello got angry you dumped him at the altar and is stalking you. He's escalating, isn't he?"

I bit my lip. The pain voided out the little jitters that had started working their way from my spine to my knees. "I wouldn't know."

Her approach stopped short of the little fence, giving me the illusion of safety. But in reality, I was trapped. "You've been staying with one Ringo Devlin."

"You make him sound like a perp." I laughed, trying to make light of it.

"Isn't he one?"

"Why did they fire you again?"

The calculating look on her face froze. "Invite me in, I'll tell you all about it. You won't even have to get me drunk this time."

"Ah, a cheap date. Gotta love that."

"I'm serious, Ellie. You may think you know what's going on, but it is a lot bigger than you realize."

There was an art to smiling without artifice when your entire body wanted to run. I'd perfected it by the time I was ten. "Invite you in… I don't know. Don't you need a warrant?"

"I'm jobless. That doesn't mean I can't warn you. In fact, I'd say I'm in a unique position to warn you about the mistake you're making. Your call." She motioned to the door.

Reluctantly, I stepped over the fence, swiped my card

over the reader and entered the lobby with Bridget on my heels. I stopped at the door. That had crime tape on it, too. "Is it even legal to go in?"

"For the owner of the building and the tenant, yes."

Well. Both of those peeps were me. "Fair warning, I don't even know what I'm facing here. I bet the house is a mess."

Bridget put a hand in the space between me and the door. "Hang on." She pulled a small revolver out of a concealed holster.

I took two steps back. My hands shook, and my knees threatened to buckle. The memory of Johnny pulling a gun on me overrode all the other times I'd seen one. Ringo's friends thought they were must-have fashion accessories. That didn't make me like them any better. At least they never pointed them at me.

"Relax, this is my personal firearm. I'm licensed."

My hands were in the air. "I don't like guns." Or knives, or garrotes, or anything else Ringo and his friends carried. Even flame throwers.

"Just wait here until I clear the unit, okay? Trust me."

There was too much gibbering in my head to reply. I handed her the key and let her do her schtick. She returned a few minutes later.

"Well?" I didn't want to look. My home had been violated, not once, but twice.

"Looks fine. Other than the window, I don't see a thing wrong.

It took an act of will to step over the threshold. No

wonder Ringo hadn't told me about any of this. He must have figured out I would freak.

Inside, I took a breath. A lot was out of place. It looked more like a show home than the place I'd adopted, nurtured, and smeared my thumbprints all over. My non-PG cross-stitched pillows were gone. Someone replaced them with artfully coordinated teal pillows.

Teal.

I wanted to puke.

My mug collection?

At least some of them were still on the shelves. But there were books strategically placed between the more mundane pieces.

As if I read books that color-coordinated with the furniture? "This isn't my home."

"What?" Bridget asked. She looked around. "What's wrong with it? I think you have a nice house."

I'd see about that. I stomped into the bedroom, the scene of Johnny's scissor tantrum and sludge fest.

A brand-new Wayfair bed with padded headboard dominated the space. The sheets were slightly rumpled, as if someone had lain on top of the piece, but otherwise, it was a study in beige. Allie would love this. I made a mental note to have it moved to her place and replace her utilitarian twin mattress that she'd kept since Mom got rid of the bunk beds.

Bridget followed me in.

"See this? Does it look like me?"

Her caution was understandable. "What looks like you?"

"Up until about a week ago, I had three pillows with the word 'fuck' embroidered on them."

Oh shit.

I ran to the kitchen.

My little sugar bowl had been turned around so only the white side faced outward. A nice little bouquet of flowers should have graced the table, but they were wilting something fierce. The petals fell off as I moved it to the sink. I set the vase down and turned the bowl around so Bridget could see the word on it.

"Cocaine?" She picked up the bowl, dipped a finger in and tasted. "Cute."

"See? That's me. The rest of this? Nope."

"What happened?"

"Johnny Pornstach."

It took her all of two seconds to work out the nickname in her head. "Man, if I were still on payroll, the guys wouldn't believe that you call him that. Not a single one of them would be able to say 'Porciello' again. Damn."

"My sister thought of it."

"Allie? I thought she was the nice one."

I laughed. "Wow. You realize that's an act, right?" I rummaged through the cabinets, finding all my worst mugs hidden on the top shelf, and brand-new packages of food everywhere.

Not a single pantry item was missing, but it was all new. Ringo's connection was thorough. I appreciated the thoughtfulness of it. I rinsed the coffee maker carafe and measured the water. "You drink coffee?"

"I might have lost my badge but I didn't lose my mind. Double up on caffeine if you can. Please?"

"Firehouse brew coming up."

While I wanted for the carafe to fill, I rearranged the artful cups with my staples. In the process, I found a T-rex mug that made me laugh. Kat got me that one. Allie got me an orange and white mug that looked like a prescription bottle. The large text on it said "coffee." I handed that one to Bridget.

Even the refrigerator had been restocked. "I love being a kept woman."

And I forgot I had company.

"Who's your sugar daddy?"

I set the cream down next to Bridget. She could open it and smell to see if it was off or not. "Ringo Devlin."

Her reaction wasn't as shocked as I expected. "About him."

"Let's not, we're not girlfriends."

"Out of former professional courtesy, you do realize he has dubious friends, right?"

"You mean Mario, my sister's husband?"

Bridget made a noise. "Let's start there. Mario Valentini. Son of Italy's trade minister, Nicolo Valentini. His mother was the daughter of Graziano Manca, one of the most notorious crime figures in Sardinia."

"And your friend, Ringo, spends a *lot* of time there."

"How thick is the file on my grandfather?"

Bridget raised an eyebrow.

"I mean, is it as thick, or thicker than the files you have on Mario and his family? I'm curious."

She clammed up.

"Because I would guess my grandfather's file, or files have to be at least five, six-seven binders full. Probably more.

And yet, he never served any time in prison, never was brought up on charges. He filed his taxes religiously, and even after seventeen lawsuits, I'm a still getting my trust monies. Why is that?"

I didn't let her talk. "I'll tell you. Because the mob? It's gone legit. They got tired of going to jail. And people like my grandfather helped them do that. And now? You don't have shit on any of them."

"Why did five members of the Conti crime organization go missing four days ago?"

"Who?"

"Never mind. What I'm saying is that Mario, his family, and his *friends*, are rumored to be elite hitmen. The kind they make movies out of. And within a couple of days of Ringo Devlin arriving in Chicago, five criminals disappear."

I was going to strangle that bastard.

"And, we can't seem to find your ex." She tipped her head as if to convey some pointed message.

And, yes, I got the words loud and clear. I had a newly decorated apartment, brand new bed so fresh it still smelled like the warehouse, and an assassin boyfriend who was the jealous sort. Of course, Bridget didn't know that part.

"Let's talk about my ex. Why can't you find him, and what did he do that you *want* to find him?" I asked.

She didn't mince words. "He killed Adelmo Conti. His accomplice in that murder was Adelmo's sister, Dianora Conti. She's being held in Italy for the murder of her father. It appears she attempted a coup. But then, as her father lingered on his deathbed, he changes his will and names one…I kid you not on this…one Ringo Devlin as his illegitimate son and orders the American holdings transferred to his name.

"You're in this thick, Ellie. I wish I knew why."

That would make two of us. "I get it, I'm some criminal mastermind using the bar as a front. Right?"

"No, the bar is legit. Either that, or you've built up a hell of a cover story. I mean, winning the lottery, that's hard to fake."

Because it wasn't faked. I'd been so frightened of losing Jaja's money that I tried to lose it myself. That way I wouldn't miss it and could only blame myself. "What's your angle?"

Bridget sighed and stared at her coffee. "At first, I wanted to break open a case so tied up it had stymied whole departments for decades. Then they started changing things." She frowned.

"Like what?"

"Don't ask. Long story short, you can't think for yourself, you can't have friends who are themselves, and you certainly can't have any loyalty to the mission anymore. There *is* no mission. It's close your eyes, toe the line, and cross your fingers that you're not going to be swept up in a fraud case. Or made an 'example' of as they kick your ass to the curb with barely a compensatory settlement."

"You should talk to Casey. He's got stories about stuff like that."

"Interesting that you bring him up. You collect washed up anti-establishment types."

"Just call me Robin Hood."

Bridget shook her head. "You're not. What you are is

someone with a good beef against the kind of assholes with badges who think kids are fair game to target."

"Huh, you actually did read my file."

"One of the last things I did before getting fired."

Yikes. "I hope that wasn't the trigger."

"It might have been. I was digging into a money laundering scheme that pointed at Adelmo Conti and his company. When he abruptly died, my case was dead. But I visited the impound lot to look at the car that got mangled in the accident. And what do I discover? Bullet holes in the seat."

Her eyes went a little wide.

"You had a shitty job. I couldn't do it."

"Adelmo was murdered. Johnny is being sought for a hit and run, but *not* murder. That means, someone on the police force and in the media buried details. It's kind of… scary that in this day and age of cameras everywhere, and social media conspiracies that a crime like murder simply vanishes. Worse? Anyone with connection to Johnny Porn—Porciello vanishes, too. Except you. Even your sister is out of the country and beyond reach."

Bridget was treading on dangerous ground. If she only knew how dangerous, she'd… I had second thoughts about what she'd do. Because once an agent, always an agent. I'd learned that lesson early enough. "Your point?"

"Your grandfather had over seventy binders on him. Those were the ones the task force *could* read. You know, the ones not locked up for national security reasons. It's like… someone is protecting you from beyond the grave."

A chill rattled me. The familiar tingle of a fainting spell

concentrated at my hands, but luckily didn't creep any farther. I needed to find Ringo and tell him everything about this conversation. Too late, I realized that Bridget hadn't just "happened" upon me at the apartment. She was stalking me.

 Just like Johnny.

20

RINGO

Saturday morning my phone rang almost at the same hour as the sun rose. The first rays of light peeked through the curtains. Ellie, being a night owl, insisted they stay closed. I took the call in the formal living space so I could watch the sky shift and the lake glisten. "What's up?"

"What Ellie says about her new friend is true. The woman was forcibly dismissed." Mario's voice was an unwelcome rumble before coffee. He had the advantage of being awake hours before me, and his unwavering logic ran circles around me on my best days.

"So, we don't worry about her?"

"Did I say that?"

Fuck. I looked at the ceiling so I could stretch the tense muscles of my neck. "What happened to the days of clarity?"

"You stabbed me."

"Nicked you. If I'd have stabbed you, you'd be dead."

"Semantics."

"Important ones," I reminded him.

"Don Manca wants her handled internally."

That would go over well with Ellie. Not. "Are you asking me, or telling me?"

"You're smarter than this."

"Thank you."

Mario's insult didn't sound any better in Italian than it would in English. I ignored it. He needed to get it out of his system. Finally, he asked, "How is my wife's sister?"

"Sleeping." Finally. The nightmares were getting worse. It took forever to coax her into bed, and even longer to massage the knots out of her shoulders.

"When she isn't sleeping, have her call my wife. Allie misses her."

I'd bet. Ellie voiced the same opinion last night as she cried on my shoulder. "Did your wife once mention she was in therapy?"

Mario hesitated before replying, likely scanning his database brain for the answer. "She's mentioned it. May I add, not fondly."

Which would explain why Ellie was resisting getting help. "This new situation is a lot like when they were kids."

"I'll remind you that when they were children, they weren't exposed to anything that could endanger them. But you insist on—"

"I'm not the only one putting their woman in danger. You are, parading your wife around to all the families."

"If I recall, the only danger she's been in was your fault."

"She was perfectly fine on the boat." Perfectly fine out of the boat, too. Until Dianora's cousin went looking for me. Which, again, wasn't exactly my fault. He wouldn't have been looking at all except I had to rescue Mario from his stupidity. That left his wife exposed. "No one put a gun to your head and said 'go stick your ass in a noose.'"

"And I explicitly told you to watch my wife."

"I don't take orders well."

"Obviously."

It was funny that we ever became friends. "You're going to be my best man, right?"

His soft expletive told me he was surprised I asked. "Do you have date set?"

No, that was Ellie's job. Except she wasn't doing it. "Maybe your wife can make a suggestion?"

"She'd plan the whole thing."

That would be great, except… "I was kind of looking forward to wearing a costume. What do you think, would I be a vampire or a phantom like you were?"

He laughed once. "Allie liked the mask."

"You kinky bastard." I chuckled. Despite being so far apart, he was still my brother.

"Can you wait nine months?"

I froze. "No shit?"

"Perhaps. We are— hopeful."

I let out a breath. A kid would change everything. My smile fell. "We need to get you out."

Mario was silent.

"Brother?"

"If I leave, Don Manca will be short-handed. Where does that leave you and your plans?"

It was on the tip of my tongue to quip, "I'll be better off without you." But that wasn't true at all. We were a great team. Take one of us out of the equation and the whole thing crumbled. "What does your grandfather say?"

"He doesn't know yet."

Well. There was that. "He's not getting any younger."

Mario snorted. "We have enough time with him yet."

True. "Congrats."

"Hold onto that for at least two months, yes?"

I could do that. "Has she talked to Ellie about it?"

"She knows."

How? She lived right under my thumb for the last week plus. Surely, I'd have suspected something. "Wait, twin talk." They had a whole vocabulary of weird phrases and inside jokes to rely on. One they'd built their entire lives. Kind of like the family language. Except only those two understood it. Maybe Kat did, too, being one of the rare people in that circle.

"Sì."

We were fools, outwitted by double trouble.

"Edward is coming to Chicago. Today. He wants to meet the staff at the office and interview your pick for his new operating officer."

Although it was Saturday, CCI had a perfect view of the river. I'd planned on going there with Ellie to show the place off a little. The staff made an event out of St. Patrick's Day weekend every year. "When? Traffic is going to be a nightmare. Does he know that?"

"I doubt he does."

Fuck. It was likely too late to arrange a helicopter. "It's a holiday weekend here. They party harder than Budapest on a regular night. Today, though? Ellie claims it will be epic, and a nightmare for driving. The ride from any airport to downtown will take at least an hour at best. What are the logistics?" Knowing Mario like I did, he had plans created already.

"Eight your time. The airport is Midway. We need to hire a car. He's traveling with two bodyguards."

I did some quick thinking. "If I can get Kat to pick him up, she can drive them in." Being a native, she'd know which routes to avoid.

"The business manager? Good choice."

"They dye the river at ten. It's quite the spectacle from what I'm told." I couldn't fathom it. The photos I'd seen had to be doctored.

"Make it happen, confirm the car is suitable, and call me back."

The call disconnected abruptly. Mario would hate retirement. I dialed Kat.

"Do you have any idea what hour it is?"

"Hey, Kat. Did you close the bar last night?"

She grunted. "Why are you calling me, Ringo?"

"You have an interview today. And the CEO is landing at Midway Airport in one and half hours. What kind of car do you drive and is it clean?"

"Mercedes, and what?"

"Clean, as in pristine. Edward is exacting." A Mercedes was acceptable, unless, "it's not a coupe is it?"

"Duh, do I look like a sedan driver?"

"That's no good. I'll rent a car for you. It will be waiting when you arrive at the private plane terminal."

"Wait one second, dick. One hour?"

"One and a half. You can do this, right?"

Her swearing didn't exactly inspire confidence. "I have to. I want this job. This Edward, is he a leg man or all business?"

"Legs."

"Fine. That car service? Have them pick me up. I ain't walking all over the place in high heels. And, where is this interview?"

I explained the event at CCI.

"You realize Ellie and I have a bar to run, right?"

"And you've both hired competent people to do that. Unless you don't want the job?"

"You bastard."

She hung up on me instead of answering. I took that as a yes and arranged for the car service to pick her up. Ellie wandered into the room as I finalized the call. As usual, she blinked at the sunrise streaming through the windows. Her quiet perusal of the lake was different today. Less angry and more accepting.

"Good morning."

She made a vocalized response, barely acknowledging me.

I handed her a coffee doctored to her preference for the current time of day. Then I wrapped an arm around her and studied the view. It was peaceful. Despite being in the middle of one of the largest cities in the country, we faced away from all of it. Only the traffic below us betrayed the breadth of civilization at our backs.

"The sale is going through today."

That got her attention. "Does that mean you're leaving?"

I shook my head. "No. I might make this a permanent move." That depended on her. "If that's what you want?"

She studied me for a long time. "You need to think about what you want."

"I want you."

My quick reply made the corners of her mouth go up. "How often will we go to Sardinia?"

"As often as we can? Did your sister mention she's pregnant?"

Ellie sucked in her breath. "It's too early. A bunch of stuff could go wrong so don't tell anyone."

"Who would I tell?"

"Me."

She was finally awake, and her sarcasm with it. "I know we talked about his in Venice—"

"No. No kids until I'm ready."

She'd gotten an implant and testing done before her wedding. There was a supply of condoms in her suitcase, but that had ended up with Allie. Apparently, Mario ignored those. "What do you think they'll have?"

"A boy."

"You sound certain."

Ellie shook her head. "Allie wants it, boy then girl. Big brother, little sister. And Allie is just perfect enough it'll happen that way."

Speaking of perfect, I pulled her closer. "I love you." The words didn't trip in my throat anymore.

She leaned against me. "I know."

I kissed her cheek. "We have a lot to do today."

Ellie groaned. "River, crowds, bar. I know."

Her scent tempted me. "Shower first?"

"I think we'll need to share."

My fiancée was brilliant. I kissed her neck to show her how much I appreciated that.

"You're going to make me spill my coffee."

"You have twelve seconds to set the cup down. Go."

I released her and stalked her to the island where she set the mug down. Then she dropped the robe, and I followed the sway of her naked ass.

She turned the water on while I stripped off the pajama bottoms I'd pulled on to take Mario's call. Ellie's body was reflected in the large vanity mirror. I watched it, rather than her. It gave me an opportunity to see us together without artifice. In the frame, we were just a man and a woman. Sure, I had scars that told the stories I couldn't utter to anyone but other than that, I was normal. It was a life that I didn't know I wanted. She fit against me and ran her hands down my chest.

My distraction didn't go unnoticed. "Do we need to install a mirror above the bed?"

"Look."

She studied the scene. "I don't get it. What am I looking for?"

"It's what you don't see."

Her head tilted. "We look normal."

"Yeah. Like life isn't as shitty as it was." My brow wrinkled, and I had to look away. The lie faded in the light of truth. I was not that man, and Ellie's nightmares were unknown to that reflected lie.

"Life and death." Ellie looped her pinky around mine.

I mirrored her motion, capturing the other hand with mine. "Death is your gift, Life is the reward." Sure, I said that in backward order. But the mantra made more sense that way. At least for me.

She squeezed my fingers with hers. A small gesture, but one of importance because we were finally on the same page. Life would be our reward. I'd gifted enough death.

I'd done enough, right?

She kissed me and pulled me up the single step that separated the giant shower stall from the rest of the room. I followed like a lamb.

Under the spray, I took my time kissing her, caressing her skin, and marveling how well our bodies aligned. The walls were cold, but the water was warm. Ellie didn't complain as I lifted her in my arms to align my cock at her opening.

Her legs wrapped around me, slipping slightly, but that only made the first thrust slide in quicker. I braced against the wall and rocked into her over and over. This was mine. Ours. Us. I was hers. My life was upended, a truth that hadn't quite stopped being a lie, and a life ahead full of unknowns. Except for one thing, it wouldn't be any kind of life without her in it. I couldn't tell her enough how much that meant to me. I finally had something of my own.

Someone. And eventually, we'd be ready to follow Mario and Allie into parenthood.

I wanted a girl. A little spitfire like the beautiful woman I fucked hard.

My thoughts locked onto that wish as I poured into her.

Ellie's gasps and the soft clench of her inner walls told me she was with me as we clung to each other.

My life wasn't even close to normal, but I'd learn how for her. "I love you." I whispered into her ear. I doubted she heard me over the water, but that didn't matter. We had a lifetime to whisper those words to each other.

Or so I thought.

21

ELLIE

Kat was in her element. The goon Ringo made her pick up from the airport wasn't what I expected. In fact, he wasn't a goon at all, but a polished business type with just a hint of distinguished gray edges kissing each ear. What he wasn't was jovial. The last-minute changes, and the forced trip to Chicago from his base in Las Vegas irritated him. But Kat handled him, his two bodyguards, and the staff of CCI with the grace of a professional executive. So well, he was in deep discussion with her about her vision for the company. Even without the formalities, she was in. I was happy for her.

But I couldn't help feeling like part of my childhood was being erased. I mean this was the woman I played hooky from school with. And now she was explaining not only her new role, but all the ways the business could be improved. And from what I could see, she had everyone eating out of her hands. This was her dream career. One she had worked her ass off for. I wasn't going to do anything to mess it up.

That's why I was crowd watching rather than trying to squeeze my way against the west-facing windows to watch the boats work their way up and down the green river. I'd seen it often enough on TV and a couple of times in real life to know the ritual by heart.

Ringo, however, had never seen it. He was in danger of falling out the window with how hard he pressed against the glass to watch the spectacle. "All this because of a holiday?"

"Your holiday," I reminded him. "You're part Irish."

His mouth hung open. "I never felt Irish, but…" His eyes danced with excitement.

I bit my lip. He'd never known his heritage because of his fucked-up mother.

The urge to change that rose from my chest. I wanted to get married in Ireland. A Catholic church or a castle… or maybe even a pub like my own. I also wanted everyone there from both the bar and Mario's family, just in case he needed a distraction from the weight of discovering what he missed. And then we'd go to Sardinia and party with the centenarians. We'd drink mirto at midnight and skinny dip in the ocean.

That meant the date was going to be summer. Maybe late fall so we could avoid tourists? I'd have to ask Allie what was the right time. Of course, it also would be at least a year from now because I wanted her as my bridesmaid. Kat, too.

"You are now. Everyone's Irish this weekend, so… learn."

He sent me a smile of gratitude.

I liked that look.

His eyes shifted to the crowds below. Something had caught his attention. What I didn't know, but Kat picked that moment to extract herself from the crowd and snag my arm. "Bathroom. Girl talk. Now."

What could I do? I followed her into the lush powder room that created a transition between the office and the utilitarian portion of the space. "What?"

Kat was breathless, her professional mask set aside for me. "That man owns eight luxury hotels. One of them is a flagship they modeled the Burj Al Arab after. Not just that, but the industrial holdings and synergistic assets are immense. You know what this means, right?"

"Not a clue. What is a Berg Al-whatever?"

Her face went blank as she tried to figure out a way to explain it to me. "Fine. One man… just one…" she took a deep breath and recalibrated, "I need to go a bit more basic than that. Here goes, the cake out there. It's cut into 24 pieces. One man holds a whole piece. The rest of this entire country gets the remaining pieces. That's how much that guy is worth out there."

Now I wanted cake.

"On a scale of one to ten."

"Definitely an eleven."

Well, shit. Now, I was really happy for her. "You mean Ringo knows someone with more money than—" I didn't say God because what would he need money for? "The Catholic Church?"

Kat thought about it. "Maybe?"

Wow. "Can he buy the Sears Tower?" I still called it

that. You can't change decades of indoctrination. Willis didn't roll off the tongue nearly as well.

"He probably owns a part of it."

"Cool. Is that what has you freaked out?"

"No, it's the fantasy. That's the problem."

I studied her. Out there she'd been the picture of classy executive. In here she was my bestie from Beverly. And she was scared shitless. "You worked your butt off for this fantasy."

"Yes…"

She certainly didn't sound sure of herself. "That scares you?"

"No, it's the suddenness. I mean, last weekend I was just needling your boyfriend, making him walk on tip toe, and he just casually buys a company and knows—" Kat lost words for a moment. "—him!"

I tried the truth on for size. "He also murders people for fun."

Her jaw dropped open, then she laughed at me. "Good one."

So much for honesty. "He knows people. Is that wrong?"

Kat's eyes got a little bigger. "It doesn't happen. It's not natural. Girls like you and I we work hard, fight our way to what we think is the top, get a half-decent life, but it's still crap compared to… this." Her arms waved around to indicate the posh bathroom and the accompanying posher office.

I raised an eyebrow. "It's almost as if you won the lottery. Congratulations." I wasn't joking. I was serious.

She stared at me. "That's it. You're lucky. You are a walking, talking good luck charm."

I crossed my fingers in front of her. "You're going to jinx me. Stop."

Kat sucked in her breath. "Right. We don't talk about that sort of thing. Just enjoy it, right?"

I shook my head. "No. You *own* it. That's what you need to do. You've worked hard, you know your shit. Now go out there before someone wonders if you flaked on them."

With a quick check of her eyeliner, Kat did just that. "You're the best," she shot at me before exiting.

Remember that when I put you behind my sister in the bridesmaid order.

I blew out a breath. I hadn't told her about my Irish plans. There was time. I checked my makeup and slipped back into the crowd. This time I elbowed my way to the windows. It was much easier since the boats with the green dye cannons had all left. Now the river was dotted with pleasure cruise boats and tourist regattas giving them an up close and personal view of downtown.

Boring.

Even the crowds thought so. They'd left the park below and were making their way east for the parade set to start in an hour.

Ringo must be around here somewhere. I searched for him in the cluster by "Edward." For a man with one name, everyone wanted a piece of him. Maybe that was a thing. Drop your last name and refer to yourself in third person and suddenly you're famous.

It was probably the other way around. Like some big

cosmic in-joke. If you didn't know them well enough to call them by their first name only, then you weren't worthy.

Ringo wasn't in any of the conference rooms, or by the food, or even in the lobby where I could monitor the exit to the men's room discreetly without looking like a perv.

The bartender exited, and I took the moment to ask him if he'd seen my boyfriend in there.

"Nope, it's empty."

Huh.

People really shouldn't leave me unsupervised. That never ended well. I was bound to blurt out something and ruin Kat's chances forever.

An hour passed as I sat on the western-facing sofa watching the reflections in the windows of the hotel across the street. Ringo was still a no-show.

Kat plopped down next to me. "Hey, having fun?"

"No."

That got her attention, because she knew that tone meant one of two things. Someone was going to get socked in the eye, or something was going to be set on fire. "What's wrong?"

"I can't find Ringo."

She shot me a side-eye. "For real."

I nodded. If I crossed my arms and legs any tighter they'd be permanently attached to the wrong sides. "I think he left."

One nervous glance toward the crowd by Edward later, she asked, "Should I ask *him*?"

My groan was closer to a growl.

"I'll ask."

"Don't get yourself in trouble for me."

She shrugged. "What are besties for?"

"Be discreet. It's not a big deal." The lie sat crooked in my throat.

Jinxed. Just by mentioning my luck, she'd undone the juju. That's how it worked. You couldn't have nice things once you realized you shouldn't.

Instead of imagining him cheating on me, I imagined much worse scenarios. He'd gotten a call. Don Manca wanted him to chase down someone and drown him in the green river. He'd do it, too.

That made me second-guess my Irish plans.

Could I be the woman who waited at home for him to waltz in hours…days…maybe even weeks later? Could I handle this life? I wasn't afraid of the Edwards, or the glitz, or the caviar. I was afraid of losing Ringo's smile. What if each contract made him lose pieces of his soul?

I shook my head to clear out the foolishness. He probably…

Fuck. There was no probably about it. He would have waited to tell me if it was something innocent. The business deal was done. The new owners of Conti, Inc., were all here. The old owners were mostly here, enjoying one last hurrah with their staff. Even some of the more dubious types had shown their faces.

One in particular reminded me of the late patriarch. I'd had the misfortune to meet Don Conti one horrible morning that ended in a bloodbath. Of course, I passed out for that part. But I'd seen his daughter shoot him. Both had that hooked nose. Both of them stood with an arrogant chin wedged outward as if daring a fist to punch it.

I stood up and brushed the wrinkles out of my green dress pants and approached.

"Hi, I'm Ellie Jacobs. You can call me, 'El.'" I stuck a hand out, waiting.

He turned his beak toward me and raised a bushy eyebrow. "Jacobs? As in the granddaughter of Alfred Pulaski?" He took my hand and didn't shake it, only held it in place.

I didn't like the way his grip heated my hand to the point of sweat. "The one and only. Did you know him?" *A.K.A., are you a mobster?*

"I didn't have the good fortune. Alfonzo Conti-Messina, at your service. But please, call me Al, all my friends do."

Ah, I was right about that nose. "Are you related to my… uh… friend, Ringo?"

His eyes narrowed slightly. "Just recently."

I feigned interest long enough that he let my hand go.

Thankfully, it slid out of his hand without leaving a slimy trail.

"How do you like the renovations on your condo?"

He knew about that? *Aw shit. He was the mistress guy.* "I could do without the crime tape garland. I mean, it's not Christmas anymore. And the yellow clashes with my St. Patrick's Day decorations."

His face lit up with amusement. "Now I see it."

Fuck. "See what?"

He sobered. "What attracted Mr. Devlin to you." The scrutiny in his gaze was unsettling.

"Oh goodie. It must be my charming personality, or my extreme brilliance. Perhaps even my dazzling portfolio." The blarney was coming fast and thick. I needed to curb it before I got my ass in trouble.

His eyes dipped to my mouth.

I took a step back.

A quirk of his mouth broke his scrutiny. "You're wasted on a man like him."

I faked a glance at my bare wrist. "Would you look at the time. I have a bar to open." If I took the Red Line south and called a rideshare to take me the rest of the way, I'd make it with plenty of time to open.

Surprisingly, my phone buzzed just as I finished talking. "Damn it. Sorry, I got to take this. It's my sister."

Alfonzo dipped his head. "The woman who married Mario Valentini?"

Now I knew he was a bad guy. "Married? She's his queen. 'Got the whole family crest ring and everything. Don't underestimate her."

With that, I turned my back to him and took the call with just enough volume he could eavesdrop. Because I knew he was the type who would. Ringo did it all the fucking time. "Big sis, what's up?"

"Did you tease Mrs. Carpello when you left my place last week?"

I thought back to the day, and smirked. "Duh." Nosy old bat. "Lemme guess, she found her address book and called you."

"Well, yes, but not about that. She thinks someone broke into my house."

"Today?" Of all days... it was the city's St. Patrick's Day Saturday celebration, and the bar was going to be a madhouse. I had a shit-ton of prep to do. I almost tried to talk Ringo out of coming here. Which reminded me that he ditched me, stole Kat out from under me for the whole day, and made me dress up for the business crowd. I spun to pace and almost ran into Alfonzo Conti-Messina.

"Trouble?"

I crossed my eyes. "She wants me to check on her place before I go to the bar." I switched focus to my sister. "I'll be there in about an hour and a half. I got stranded downtown."

"Okay, be careful. If someone did break in, I don't want you hurt. Do you have anyone who can go with you?"

Right now? No. But I couldn't tell her that. Mario would get involved. And while I teased him a lot, I still had the brains to figure out he wasn't the kind of man who liked complications. He and my sister were perfect for each other that way. Life was one big itinerary to plan out contingencies for with them. Me?

I was the contingency. "Sure thing. I'll call you tomorrow. The bar is going to be packed and with the stop, I won't have time. Did you need anything else?"

"No, that's it. Love you."

"Love you, too. Tell 'It's-a-me-Mario' I send my best."

Alfonzo's eyebrow went up with the nickname. His face shifted as he tried and failed to keep his expression neutral and failed. "Wasted. Completely wasted," he muttered.

I hoped not.

22

RINGO

That mustache needed its own criminal code. I'd stared at it in photos long enough I thought I was hallucinating when I caught the upturned face in the crowd. But a trained eye looks not at the details, but what stands out. Like one upturned head when the main attraction was playing out in the river below.

Or that thick-as-fuck mustache on a baby-soft face.

Ellie had disappeared with Kat somewhere, so it was easy to slip out of the party. I was only leaving so I could cross the bridge and drive a knife between his ribs. Then I'd dump his body into the river and return before anyone noticed I was gone. The crowd would only see the body fall, nothing else. It was the perfect crime with a million suspects and none of them would be me because I was in the building across the street, right?

I ran the deed through my head, trying to analyze it like Mario would. I timed my walk to the crowds vying for an empty ledge along the river. There was constant motion but none of it focused on going far. Just pushing and shoving and anonymous faces.

Johnny stood out because he wasn't watching the boats. He stared up at CCI like he could burn it down with his eyes.

The seeds I'd planted this week bore fruit.

I'd worked multiple angles. The bar patrons who knew Ellie was going to watch from CCI while the Journeymen Plumbers Union dyed the river green.

Alfonzo was at CCI because I'd arranged the event through him. He'd provide a bullet-proof cover story for me. Edward would, too.

Vincent knew I was at CCI because I'd dropped the legal documents off with his team for their signature and mentioned it, knowing they weren't invited. That was sure to irritate them enough to seek out Porciello and "ask" him for one more hit. It was subtle, and a long shot, but apparently, it had paid off.

Killing Pornstach was the only way I could ensure Ellie's friends were safe. And with Kat along, Ellie was safe. This was my chance.

Johnny glanced around.

I slipped between a moving cluster of parents and children who were complaining loudly enough that one more adult not making eye contact with others was a common sight. With a step to the side where a light post blocked Johnny's view, I re-checked his location.

Shit. He was on the move. Something must have spooked

him. It wasn't me because the urgent glances he shot over his shoulder were in the wrong direction.

I doubled my pace, which was too damn slow because the crowds were insane. Americans thought swimming upstream on dry land was fun? It was a nightmare. Pickpockets, or assassins could have a field day with this hunting ground. In fact... I blocked the thief's hand just as he reached for the open purse of a distracted mother. He frowned, but I slid into the crowd so quickly the crime was thwarted in an instant.

Johnny checked over his shoulder again. I spared a quick moment to scan the street. Nothing stood out. *Odd.* A tingle went up my spine.

I glanced at CCI which was beginning to fade into the skyline. I should get back before I was missed.

But Porciello was a meager thirty meters away.

It might as well have been a hundred because the crowds blocked my path forward. The next bridge span across the river was packed with bodies. I dodged left to use the street's gutter instead of the sidewalk. Porciello headed south, opting to cross the multi-lane street against traffic.

Cars honked. Heads turned.

The chase was on.

I scanned for a group I could blend in with as the traffic resumed its struggle to escape the mob of green. It was the color of the day. Everyone wore something with an emerald hue. A hat, a scarf— whole outfits of bright green. For the unfortunate, vendors sold lighted bands with blinking shamrocks that bounced on springs over the wearer's head like alien antennae.

It was all too commercial for me.

Ellie had the foresight to buy me a green tie. With it, I blended in as one of the slightly better-dressed festival-goers.

Even the dogs wore the color. *Damn.*

I made it across traffic and hustled down the side street Johnny dipped into. The block was bisected by an overhead train. The "L" as it was called here. When Ellie pointed it out, I thought she was pulling my leg and naming it after herself. Then I looked it up. Chicago was a strange city. A street ran under the tracks. It was barely wide enough for a car, and yet trucks zipped down the path at top speed.

They drove worse than my woman did.

I scanned for Johnny.

If he hadn't looked back at that moment, I'd have missed him. But he did. I ran under the elevated tracks, dodging traffic and nearly getting run over. He'd spotted me and turned into an alley.

Perfect.

I ran after him, heedless of the puddles and trash. He turned north again as the block ended.

There was a moment he was out of my sight. That cost me.

By the time I emerged from the alley, Johnny had disappeared.

I halted under a movie theater's marquee and looked for likely avenues of escape. A metro entrance was barely yards away. The rumbling of the platform informed me I had little time.

I ran up the steps, jumped the gates, and scanned the crowds for his dark hoodie.

There. He slipped into a train car just as the warning bell rang. I ran to intercept him and was foiled by the doors sliding shut.

My hands hit the glass where his face mocked me.

He mouthed, "Fuck you!"

I pointed at him and mouthed, "You're dead."

He had the gall to laugh and flash a middle finger at me as the train began to move.

I backed off, not willing to get dragged under the wheels and glared at him until he was out of sight.

The train was heading south. I made a mental note to check the map and determine if it would land him near the bar. If it did, it meant he had a base near Ellie's condo. Which made a lot of sense.

"Ringo Devlin. I see your quarry escaped."

A gun poked me in the ribs. I turned my head to note one of Vincent's men as the bearer.

"George." I'd made a point to know the remaining faces and names.

"Boss wants to talk to you."

I'd bet he did. "You do realize who you're holding a gun on?"

Another man joined him from my left, boxing me in.

"Hey, Phil."

"Don't make this difficult," Phil commented. His head turned and I noted two others waiting at the steps.

A transit police officer watched from the safe distance of

the security alcove. He dipped his head at the blatant display of force and turned away.

That's how it was going to go down, huh?

"Where is Vincent?"

"Not far. Walk." George indicated the stairs with his head and poked his gun into my flesh a little harder.

I sent another glance toward the police officer. Another had joined him. Both deliberately ignored our group. I knew the Outfit and the Organization worked together, but I hadn't realized how closely until this point. "Lead the way." If I was going to kill these bastards, I'd like to at least not get shot by police while doing so. *Divide and conquer*, Don Manca whispered in my memories.

We hit the street, and they steered me toward a stairwell door next to a tourist attraction. The circus-style signage promised torture, courtesy of the Medieval era.

I glanced at the grotesque image of a man in a bright red executioner's hood as we walked past that entrance. Too bad we weren't going in there. I knew at least a hundred ways to use the tools and devices behind that door to kill these bastards.

Two flights of stairs later, my guards were winded, and I saw an opening. Phil was the first to fall. I elbowed George, putting my weight into the shove so I could pin him against the wall. With my body so close, Phil hesitated to take the shot. I squeezed the trigger twice, taking him out with a bullet to the chest and another to the head.

George struggled, stumbling down a step and teetering on the edge of his balance. I spun, using the momentum to swing my gun into his face and ending his chance with a single shot. He fell backward, and I let him go.

As he fell, he took out one of the men behind him. I shot the other as he raised his weapon. It took three bullets to take him down.

The other rolled with George's bulky form down the entire double span of stairs, only losing a small amount of momentum as they hit the landing between the first floor and the second.

Above me, a shot rang out and the bullet gouged the plaster by my head. I went to a knee, returning fire and ending the threat. As he slid down the steps face-first, I tapped him a second time.

The man at the bottom groaned and shoved George off him. I fired down the slope and missed. My bullet hit the glass door, but the heavy glass absorbed the brunt of it.

Bulletproof. Figured.

I fired again, then an itch made me pay attention to the top of the stairs. Two more men opened fire on the stairs. I rolled, only breaking my momentum to snatch at the door frame of the second floor and flatten my body in the recess. Using it to block the bullets from above, I timed my return fire. But they were well-concealed by the framed opening above. A third joined them and chewed up the wood with his automatic.

I shot the door behind me to break a hole in the heavy wood. Chancing it, I kicked the knob and slipped inside as the frame splintered from a bullet that landed too close to my head.

A piece wedged into my shoulder. I pulled it out and rolled into the narrow hallway. At the end was a window.

I hoped like hell it had a fire escape because my welcome was definitely revoked. I fired, shattering the glass and praying the fall wouldn't be hard as I dove out the opening.

Luckily, the cross bars stopped me from dropping to the pavement below. I kicked at the rusty drop ladder to escape, but it wouldn't budge.

A shot pinged off the iron frame and I pushed my back against the brick.

As I waited for Vincent's goons to find their balls, I checked and replaced the clip of my Glock. The familiar waffled hand guard of an ArmaLite poked out. I rolled and fired into the body of the idiot who'd been stupid enough to broadcast his presence. Then I took out the two behind him as well. One of them didn't get up, but the other crawled toward a door probably hoping to get away.

Before I killed him, I shot the man still in my grip.

The pieces of his head splattered against the wall, painting it red.

That made the one still moving scramble. I chewed up the frame trying to end him, but didn't get the right angle to take him out.

The guy who fell down the stairs with George emerged at the end of the hall and fired at me as I tried to correct that situation. His bullet caught my jacket, leaving a trail of heat and the familiar sting of a graze.

That was too close and it pissed me off. I fired on him until my gun ran out. Then I tugged the rifle away from the dead body hanging out the window and let the hallway feel my wrath.

The echoes of the rapid fire made my ears ring.

That's how I missed the guy coming down the fire escape.

Instead of killing me, he hit me on the head once. That hurt, but I was still standing.

Which just wouldn't do.

The second blow took me down.

I woke tied to a chair.

The angle of light coming in from the windows told me I'd lost an hour.

Ellie was going to be pissed at me for ditching her.

I cursed my stupidity and focused on the room.

Vincent sat in a chair across from me. He cleaned under his fingernails with a stiletto.

Poser.

Other than the grazed shoulder, the splinter puncture, and a throbbing head, I was functional. He should have stabbed me with that blade while I was out.

Apparently, he needed to talk first. Yippie, just what I needed.

"You are a particular menace, Mr. Devlin."

"I take after my mother that way." Maybe even my father.

Vincent wasn't in a joking mood. His jaw clenched and he paused his fascination with his fingernails as he probably contemplated driving that knife into me. "I want something from you."

"Name it." If it got me out of here, I'd promise just

about anything. Hell, I'd lie and promise him whatever his little black heart desired if it got me out of here. Then I'd return and kill him.

"I want Chicago."

As if I could deliver that?

On consideration, I likely could. All it would take is Don Manca's approval, the combined yeses from the ruling council, and me stepping down as the Conti heir. No big, right? Except, there was at least one more person in his way.

"Alfonzo will have a problem with that."

"He won't. He's weak."

If this were a different place and a different time, I'd truly consider stepping down. In fact, if he'd approached me last night, unarmed, I'd have made his little fantasy happen.

But that was before getting hit on the head.

Twice.

I slipped the zip ties they'd wrapped around my wrists over the large joint of my thumb. They should have duct-taped them in place. That would have made this take at least two minutes longer while I worked up the sweat it took to make the adhesive loosen.

He had three men left. The guy who'd rolled down the steps with George and two others. Each had an AR-15 in hand. The one farthest back would be the hardest. I needed a shield.

And I knew just the right body to use. "Conti-Messina is connected, not weak."

That observation was met with narrowed eyes. "I'm connected, too. You can make *that* change happen."

Ah, a contract. "Seven million, a day."

Vincent shook his head, disagreeing with me. "You'll do it for free, or you'll die right here."

I smiled as the last plastic cuff slipped free. "I don't think so."

I led with my head, pulling the chair with me and using the proximity of his body to stave off immediate retribution.

Dropping the chair, I wrapped around my prey and took his knife.

It took maybe three seconds. Mario really needed to get me training new recruits in the gym sooner rather than later. I held the blade to his neck. "If any of you move, he's dead. Got it?"

They held position as I dragged Vincent toward the window. I glanced out and picked the one with a fire escape. This time I'd use the damn thing and jump to the ground at the end. Fuck waiting.

The guards clustered as they moved closer.

Even better.

Using his body like a bowling ball, I lifted just enough to keep Vincent from dragging his feet and rushed the group.

They scattered, but not nearly fast enough.

I caught one of them as I dropped their boss. The butt end of my borrowed knife hit him at the base of his skull, repaying him with a fucking headache, or maybe even a concussion that would kill him. I didn't care at this point.

I stabbed a second guard who stepped into the fray. His gun popped off twice, tearing at the ceiling. I wrested it from his grip and leveled it at the room. "Move. I dare you."

Vincent raised both hands.

His guards, however, didn't. The one at my feet groaned. I danced away, knowing it was deadly to remain too close as he got his bearings. "Here's how it's going down. You'll answer to Alfonzo, just like we arranged. If I hear any complaints, all four of you are on the list. Not *my* list, the Left Hand's list. One wrong move and you won't see it coming. Death is the reward, boys. Life is your gift… for now."

I slowly edged my way to the door.

"This isn't over, Devlin," Vincent warned.

I paused. "Why's that?"

"You're an upstart. A bastard. You haven't proven yourself. You don't even have the family name."

"What do I need to do? Kiss your ass? I think not."

"You can't even kill Porciello. Do that, and maybe I'll reconsider."

"I'm working on it."

"Work faster," he got to his feet and brushed his suit off. "Or I'll let everyone know the Left Hand can't be counted on."

As insults go, that one was worthy of death. I crushed the urge to pull the trigger and waste all of them. They'd be better use to me alive.

Maybe.

Emboldened by his boss's bravado, the one on the floor pulled his handgun. I let my baser instincts run free.

When the smoke cleared, all four were dead.

And I was in a world of shit for killing family.

23

ELLIE

None of Allie's neighbors were present when I got dropped off by the rideshare. I made sure I had all my things and got out to scan the block.

Nothing seemed out of place, except that newer model sedan. My gaze zeroed in on it.

Of course. Bridget Perkins was up to her same old shit. It was likely her who broke in.

Would it be breaking in? I decided it was because she wasn't employed anymore. Unless she was reinstated? Then the bitch was tromping all over our Fourth Amendment rights.

With that and the shit sandwich of the hassle of public transportation and Ringo being a dick, I wasn't in the greatest of moods when I unlocked the front door and called out, "Yo, Perkins? You've got a lot of nerve breaking into my sister's house. Get your ass out here so I can kick it."

Silence.

Huh. Maybe I was wrong and that wasn't her car?

I pulled a knife from the butcher block in the kitchen just to be on the safe side. "Ollie-ollie-oxen-free. Show your face, Bridget." I checked the hallway that ran down the center of the house. The living room had a wide arch that connected to it, but I'd been in that room and no one was in it.

The bathroom door was open, so she wasn't hiding there. Nor was she in the middle bedroom.

Call it a premonition, or just my weird luck, but I'd skipped the spare bedroom to my left.

Before I walked all the way down the hall to Allie's room, I decided to check it out.

The door squeaked as I opened it.

Usually, Allie kept this room empty. I'd have used it for storage, but my tight-ass sister did things the normal way and either shoved her shit in the attic, or down in the basement depending on whether she wanted to chance it getting wet or not. And while the middle bedroom was all done up as a guest bedroom, this one was simply empty.

Except it wasn't.

Perkins was tied to a chair that was smack dab in the middle of the room.

The shock of it froze me in place.

Then I started noticing things.

Her wide eyes and the struggles as she tried to get my attention.

But that wasn't what made my fingers tingle.

Nope. It was the blood.

I don't know why, but I noticed the little trail of drips on the carpet first. My vision narrowed in on them, making them fifty times larger than they really were. That trail led to the legs of the chair. Then to her pants. There was a scuff mark on the knee that was almost invisible because she'd worn a dark, utilitarian canvas. But her white shirt had more red stains on it. Courtesy of that head wound which was still bleedi—

I woke up in the same predicament as Bridget. Tied to a chair and placed just out of arm's reach of her. Of course, since both my arms were bound to my torso and the chair back, I couldn't reach if I wanted to.

Johnny Porciello paced the room.

It was such a small bedroom that it took him four steps. Then he'd turn and take four more steps, turn, and—

"You're awake, fucking finally."

I wiggled my fingers. They were tingling because he'd zip-tied them together too tightly, not because I was going to pass out again. Of course, all bets were off if I turned my head toward Bridget. Which I didn't because…

What was I going to do? No one except Allie knew I was here. I didn't even have a car outside to tip someone off that I was in the vicinity. "What the fuck do you want, Johnny?"

"Seventy grand."

I blinked. "It was fifty."

"Yeah? It was fifty before half of fucking Chicago's underworld wanted to wax my ass. Did you know there's a bounty on my head?"

"How much?" If Ringo was going to get paid, I wanted to know.

"A hundred grand!"

He said it like it was a lot of money. "That's it? Who put the hit on you? I'll pitch in another half mil just to see it done properly."

"You bitch." He swept a hand out and backhanded me.

My cheek stung. A trickle of warm liquid tickled my chin and dripped onto my shirt.

I made the mistake of looking down.

Funny, I felt detached rather than overwhelmed at the sight of my own blood. "That's all you got? I'm bumping that up to a fucking million."

While that would hurt my lifestyle a lot, getting rid of Johnny Porciello was worth it.

"Why aren't you fainting? Were you faking it?"

He rounded me, and pulled out the kitchen knife I'd pilfered.

Unlike a few moments ago, that sight triggered a whole slew of emotional and chemical reactions inside. "Flame thrower." Odd that I thought about Ringo.

Or maybe not so odd. I wanted to tell him that he was foremost in my thoughts as I faced death. Sure, he hadn't been the one time, wait… make that two times before when I'd faced down my demise. The first was so quick I hadn't had time to think beyond looking for an escape from the dark alley I'd been lured into. The second time I had to keep up with Mario's quick thinking. That took all my attention. I didn't realize I was in trouble that time until Don Conti was on the floor bleeding from the gunshot wound.

But this time all I could do was think. My reflection glinted in the blade. It was too small to be more than a dark blur against the backdrop of light streaming in from the window, but that told me the time of day. This window faced west. Because of the angle of the roof and the proximity to the neighbor's two story, the sunlight only came in this room during early to mid-afternoon.

I was supposed to be opening the bar right now. Someone would miss me.

And if Ringo gave two shits about me, maybe he'd know that.

How? I had no clue, but I wanted to put some hope into that wish.

"How did Bridget get mixed up in this?" I tipped my head and shot a quick glance at my silent partner. She'd slumped in the chair and looked much worse than I remembered.

"She was creeping around the house when I got back. I had to knock her out, but your nosy neighbor saw me. So, I dragged her inside. Who is she?"

It gave me great pleasure to tell Johnny exactly who he'd abused. "She's an FBI agent. So… not only do you have the mob on your ass, but the Feds too." I giggled. It was all I could do not to scream out loud, "How does it feel, asshole?"

"FBI? Wait, she was watching *you*."

I nodded. "That's right. Courtesy of dear old granddad. Bet you didn't know Alfred Pulaski's granddaughter was so interesting, did you?"

His face went a little paler than normal. "You mean…?"

"Yeah, the entire time. Your little excursion with

Dianora Conti? All documented. They know you offed Adelmo."

His nostrils flared a little. "Ninety grand."

I blinked. "Haven't you been paying attention? I want you dead."

"But it will cost you less if I just leave. Pay me and I'm out."

As tempting as that was, I knew he'd be back as soon as the money ran out. "Was that all I was to you? Money?"

"No." He sounded offended. Good.

"Enlighten me."

"You were connected. I just didn't know how connected. The FBI? Jesus."

As if they were the worst thing he should be worried about? "Did you know Allie married a member of the mob's assassin squad? Think movie-level or video game level. And you are on their list." I relished telling him that. "There's nowhere you can hide. They're everywhere."

"Please, Ellie. A hundred grand, I'm gone."

"Where will you go, Canada? That would be Firenze. He speaks French really well. His favorite weapon is a Berretta Tanfoglio. Would you run to Alaska…beyond? I'm pretty sure Loppa knows Russian. He's good at strangling people."

"Ellie." He lifted his hand, warning me to shut up.

I couldn't. Something drove me to pester him until he broke. I don't know why I did it, maybe I just wanted to know he wasn't as tough as he thought he was, or that I was tougher. "Mexico would be Don Manca's grandnephew. He likes to fish with the Spaniards off the western coast. Sure, his Castilian would stand out, but not as badly as a gringo with a funky mustache."

He uttered a growl that bordered on a scream. He came down with the knife and stabbed my leg.

It hurt, burned, and oddly only enraged me. He left the knife in place and pulled out a gun.

"What are you going to do? Shoot me? You won't get a dime then."

He turned the gun on Bridget's slumped form, going as far as to hold it against her head.

"What are you doing, Johnny?"

He glared at me. "I know you. You talk a big game, but as soon as someone else is threatened, you jump right in. Both feet. Washed up cops, friends from grade school, drunks. You're a softie. And you're going to give me a hundred and twenty K. Right?"

Damn him. I stared at the blood on her shirt, hoping to have it trigger a fainting spell, but it did nothing. Not even a tingle.

"Sure. One twenty. Get my checkbook and a pen." I didn't carry a checkbook. He'd find out soon enough.

"How can I be sure you're not lying?"

Double damn him. The trouble with dating an asshole was they knew everything about you. "I promise. You'll get that money."

His face screwed up in disgust. "Just like you promised to marry me? You kept lying to me, pushing me away. Telling me to 'wait for our honeymoon.' You had no intention of fucking me, did you?"

Put that way, no. "I dumped four grand on lingerie.

Eight grand on plane tickets. Not to mention the twelve grand for the costumed Valentine's Day extravaganza in Las Vegas complete with calling in a favor from the local justice of the peace! You don't think I'm serious? Who the fuck do you think you are?" If my hands weren't bound behind my back, I'd've taken the knife out of my leg and stabbed his worthless ass with it.

The gun he had at Bridget's head dipped as he jumped into a rant. "You're a bitch. That's what you are. A cock-teasing bi—"

His words were cut off when Agent Perkins shot from her chair and disarmed him. The move was seamless, as was the quick way she whipped the pistol around and aimed it at him.

Johnny fell to the floor and crawled to the wall to shake. "D-don't shoot me." His hands went into the air.

"I should," Bridget stated. She seemed perfectly fine, rather than comatose. Apparently, she could fake a faint more believably than one of my very real spells. I twisted in my seat to witness Johnny piss his pants.

"Please?" His hands met over his head and he let them settle on his hair.

"Bridget? Shoot him for me, please?"

She heaved a breath. Her feet were still bound to the chair and the scuffle had twisted it to the floor. She was on one knee, keeping her eyes locked on Johnny. "Sorry, Ellie. As much as he deserves it, I can't. He's my ticket back into the agency's good graces. I want my job back."

"Your job? The one chasing little kids down? Doing the government's dirty work? That job?"

As much as I shouldn't, I kind of hated Bridget.

"Ellie, I've tried to do the right thing for a long time. Just… give me this, will you?"

My breathing was too fast. I wanted revenge.

With a clarity I hadn't had in a long time, I remembered why I had nightmares. "Did you know the FBI hid a child predator in their ranks? He was lead on my family's task force."

"Ellie, stop." Bridget tightened her grip on the gun.

Johnny's eyes darted between us. "Is that why you hate cops so much?"

I didn't hate cops.

One saved me.

I remembered everything now. It wasn't a forest. It was a public park. And it wasn't night, but the middle of the day. Mom took us to play at the playground.

The agent lured me away from the swings.

A Chicago cop saw it and followed.

He's the one who knocked the agent out and took me back.

I remembered the blood coming from the cut on his head.

All the blood.

"Casey's partner caught him. He was a rookie at the time, but he was about to get a promotion. It was his word against the entire FBI's. They busted him back down to the base rank and it took him years of scraping the bottom to dig his way back." And while he did that, he made friends with all the drug dealers and gangland thugs. Eventually that got him killed and Casey framed for the murder. All because he did his job one afternoon in the park. He didn't even ask for credit for it.

Bridget swallowed. Something in her expression conveyed guilt.

"That was in my file, wasn't it?"

She nodded with a very small dip of the chin. "I'm sorry. But I promise, I'll do better by you."

I scoffed. "By going back? How? They aren't going to let you back. The Outfit and the Agency and the Organization, they all work together. You might as well go straight to the head of the mob and beg for a job. Because that's the only person who's going to approve your way back in."

Sometimes I really should shut up. It was distracting Bridget. Her attention wavered as her certainty failed.

Johnny's face twisted into a grin.

I expected him to leap up and wrestle Bridget for the gun.

What I didn't expect was Ringo reaching over Bridget's shoulder and gripping her gun and hands so hard she winced. "I'll take that. You won't be needing it."

My white knight had arrived.

But I highly doubted he'd leave witnesses.

24

RINGO

When I'd returned to CCI, Ellie was gone. I'd cornered Kat who hadn't a clue as to when she'd left. She quickly called the bar to find out Ellie had been a no-show. As the shit storm Kat fanned grew, Alfonzo Conti-Messina approached.

I practically took him out.

Edward had to tear me off him.

"This is your fault." I spat out.

"How? I've been here the entire time. Unlike you." Alfonzo fired back.

"Gentlemen, please." Edward squeezed my shoulder, which was a mistake. It made the skinning I caught ooze blood that trickled down my sleeve and onto the floor.

A woman screamed. Edward's bodyguards closed in, and we were whisked into a conference room. Kat left to obtain a first aid kit.

Quickly, I outlined what happened.

"He gave *you* the slip?" Edward asked.

That wasn't helping.

"That isn't the only thing that's slipping," Alfonzo commented.

"Maybe if you took care your house, I wouldn't have to clean it up!" I came off my chair ready to pound his face in. Vincent's aspirations might have been warranted.

"That's not how we do it here. This isn't some heathen backwater like Sardinia."

He really wanted to die, didn't he?

Edward squeezed my wounded arm again. I almost hit him. "Knock it off."

"Think, I hope you're capable of that, or was it only Mario who propped you up?"

"Fuck you."

Kat knocked on the door and entered with the kit.

I stewed as she managed to clean off both wounds and kept her mouth shut.

It was Edward who ordered, "Leave us and stay away from the door."

As she slipped out, she sent me a worried look. "I'll find Ellie." I promised her that much.

No sooner than the door snicked shut, Alfonzo asked, "What is her location worth to me?"

I cracked my neck with a twist, preparing to fight both Edward and my cousin to the death.

"By that movement, at least three hundred million."

"You think you're funny?" Edward wasn't a comedian by a long shot.

"I know a man who is at his breaking point. It's my

specialty. How many men do I need to send to that building?"

Shit. I lost count. "At least ten, if not a dozen."

Alfonzo paled. "You killed all of them?"

"Yeah. You're welcome. You are officially the only Conti left standing in the city... Except me."

His jaw worked. "She got a call from her sister. Something about checking on a house."

Allie's house, I knew where it was. "I've got to go."

Edward stepped between me and the door. "You are going nowhere until I know what's going on."

I put it as succinctly as I could. "He's going to run Chicago. I'm going to pick up my girl." Then I had to go to Sardinia and explain how I missed killing Johnny Porciello, but managed to wipe out an entire faction of the Conti's business in under two weeks. That should be fun, not.

Alfonzo smiled as I slipped away.

When I got to Allie's, I spotted the agent's car. That made me extra cautious. I slipped in through the back to avoid the sticky front door. I heard Ellie's voice. I waited to listen to the conversation, and heard enough to bury me. Porciello was here. I had him in my grasp again.

If I could kill him, I wouldn't have to return home in total shame. I'd have accomplished at least one of Don Manca's goals. I might be forgiven for the rest.

But I also heard the agent's voice. Perkins sounded like she had control over the situation. I couldn't let her keep that, because sending Porciello to the cops would cement the downfall of the Left Hand's reputation.

I had to channel the ruthless nature of my biological

father. I cursed my luck. Just when I had a good life in my grasp, it was snatched away. If I killed the agent, there wouldn't be a corner I could hide in. If I didn't, someone would want me dead for leaving loose ends dangling.

Or, if I let her kill him, which she wasn't going to do, I'd be a laughing stock. The guy who was nothing without his handler.

I stepped in and took Bridget's gun.

"Ringo." Ellie breathed.

There was a knife in her leg. "Who did that?"

Forget asking, I knew who it was.

Johnny Porciello was waiting for his chance. He was actively gauging whether he could jump the gauntlet of women tied to the chairs, and beat me to the trigger.

I lifted an eyebrow to let him know he was shit out of luck.

"Ringo? I need to probably go to the hospital?"

Yeah, she did. "How are you still conscious?"

Ellie shrugged. "I guess when it's my own it doesn't matter."

"Like Hell it doesn't." I lined up Johnny in my sights.

"Dude, I don't know who you are but—"

Ellie cut him off. "Shut up Pornstach. Nobody said you could talk."

"Babe…"

"Bridget, are you okay?"

Trust Ellie to worry about someone else rather than herself.

"I'm okay, I'd be better if I could undo this damn knot." She was working furiously on the jumble of electric wires wrapped around her legs. She'd been through a bit. Johnny roughed her up good. The blood on her shirt had dried to a dull reddish brown. Head wounds bled a lot. Luckily, that looked like her only problem, save the chair hobbling her legs.

I couldn't let her get free.

"Ellie, look away." I didn't want this haunting her like Venice did. I wouldn't be there tonight to keep the nightmares at bay.

"Ringo, don't. You don't have to."

Yes, I did. "I'm sorry. Look away."

"Dude, please? Don't pull that tr—"

His words cut short. I sent a second shot through his skull.

Then checked to see if Ellie had listened.

Her eyes were wide. Her face was almost white. "Why?"

I couldn't tell her that.

She collapsed in her chair, dead out.

I turned to the agent.

I should kill her. "Take care of her." Having a federal law enforcement officer handling the questions at the hospital would speed things up.

"But..."

"No buts. If you don't get her to a hospital in the next twenty minutes, I will hunt you down. And you know I can do it. Good luck, Agent Perkins."

I slipped out, wiping and dropping the gun in a muddy puddle just outside the back door. If the agent searched my exit, she'd see it. I got in my car and didn't look back.

The airport was a half hour away. I dialed Edward. "I

need your plane. It will be in Sardinia. Make the arrangements and bill the Left Hand."

"Did you get your girl?"

I debated how to answer that. "She's safe. That's what matters. If you want our continued service, make sure she stays that way. There's a federal agent with her."

Edward made a strangled noise. "Godspeed my friend."

I'd need it.

As the sky turned black over the Atlantic, I stared at my reflection in the window. "I had it all."

Was it Loppa or was it Don Manca who told me that eventually I'd have regrets? I didn't believe them. A month ago, I thought I would when I accepted the bounty for Mario's head.

Maybe that was a premonition?

But it hadn't worked like I thought it would. Instead of burying my best friend, I'd lost something more precious.

I winced as the breadth of my purgatory unfolded. I'd lost Ellie. She'd tell her sister, who would ban Mario from ever talking to me. And even if he did talk to me, that would put a wedge between him and his new wife. And I couldn't do that to him.

By the time I landed, I knew what I needed to do. I approached the citadel where Don Manca reigned. He was up early, feeding chickens.

His guards took my weapons. I wouldn't need them back. My fate was sealed. "Don Manca." I knelt in the muddy grass.

He tossed a couple of handfuls of grain toward the flock, scattering it as they fought each other for the kernels. "I hear the pig boy with the ugly mustache is dead."

"Sì."

He shook the bucket and dug out a few more handfuls. "And I hear that there is one beaten Conti struggling for scraps."

Did he mean me or Alfonzo? I kept my head down just in case he meant me.

A moment later his gnarled fingers dug into my hair. "You failed, yet succeeded." He shook my head.

"Sì."

He sighed and let me go. "Get up."

I brushed my knees off and walked beside him. He handed me a rake as we reached the sheep pen. I got to work, mucking out the night's excrement and laying down clean bedding. He worked beside me, putting fresh grass and water in their feeder.

A spicy ram got a little too close with an attitude ready to pick a fight. I caught it by the horns and tugged it away from Don Manca.

He noted my protection and spoke. "An agent from the FBI took Ellie to the hospital."

The question on my lips took a moment to form. "Is she okay?"

He sent me a glare from the corner of his eye. "No thanks to you."

I hung my head in shame. "I figure your son needs a shepherd for a few years." His oldest son eschewed modern life and the family trade, making a simple life high in the mountains. He made cheese. The goats ran wild, or near wild on the rocky slopes all summer long. Living rough in the hills would be better than getting cast out. But it was as close as I cared to be to being removed from the family. I hoped Don Manca thought me useful enough for the job. Otherwise, I'd be alone.

He nodded absently. "The newest generation is too young or still preparing to be born, and the current generation is itching to leave the nest. Firenze will take your place."

He deserved his chance. "Mario's going to keep working on his knife skills, I hope?"

Don Manca laughed humorlessly. "You care?"

It wasn't my place. I remained silent.

"Goats? That's your choice?"

"When I first came here, I thought they were punishment."

He smiled. "They were. You and my grandson were wild boys. I needed something to tame you."

"It didn't work."

He slapped at the dirt on his pants. His chuckle died. "No. It took women to do that."

My heart ached.

"Truth," I said.

I felt his eyes on me. "I never thought I'd see this day."

"I'm sorry, Don Manca."

He nodded once to accept the apology. The skin around his eyes wrinkled as he tried to look through me. "You were the best of us. There won't be another like you for at least a generation, maybe more. I want you to know that you were *never* the bastard son of Gesualdo Conti. You were *always* one of ours. The gods willed it so. Never forget that."

My heart was too wounded to sing, but his words helped. "Anything you need. Anywhere you need it, I'll be there. I am not retiring."

He smiled. "I know."

Thank goodness. I don't know what I'd do without a purpose. Even if it was the worst possible one in the world, I needed death. I needed this family, the work, the blood…the finality. Otherwise, I'd go insane.

"Go. Hide. I know where to find you."

I bowed my head and wished him well. "Happy hunting, grandfather."

He touched my sleeve. "Keeps the wolves at bay, my son."

The tears in my eyes were shoved deep. I'd have plenty of time to cry once I reached the summer peaks where the goats grazed freely.

25

ELLIE

A limping bartender, a retired cop, and a disgraced federal agent sat together in a bar. But it wasn't a joke. Collectively, we made one hell of a somber trio. Jameson was the poison of choice. Silence was our confession. I poured three glasses and raised a glass toward the bar.

"For each petal on the shamrock this brings a wish your way. Good health, good luck, and happiness for today and every day."

The words were automatic. The sentiment was no longer a balm.

It hurt too much to feel joy.

We drank.

Bridget set her glass down and confessed, "They offered me my job back."

I barely paid attention.

Casey, however was. "You turned them down, right?"

"I can't do it. I can't anymore." She slammed the remnants of her drink.

"Is bartending difficult?" she asked.

"Horribly difficult," Casey replied.

"Why do you do it then?"

Casey thought about her question. "Because I'm not made to kill people. I can't hold a grudge long enough."

I could. I sipped on that thought as they chatted.

Bridget needed this. Commiseration with a fellow cop who'd lost his way and his purpose. She was struggling to find her path.

Lying did that to a good person.

"Did you know I only discharged my service weapon once?" Casey was trying to be helpful, but he didn't know the truth. If he did, he might have said something else. Or maybe not been as sympathetic.

Bridget took the blame for killing Johnny.

Her confession was scrutinized for two weeks as I recovered. We'd gotten the story straight before we even left the house. It was her decision. Not mine.

He'd left me.

I wasn't worthy of love.

The knife Johnny buried in my thigh missed most of the vital parts of my leg. But the damage to the muscle took a while to heal. I'd only been mobile without aid for two days. Bridget had a severe concussion. She spent three nights under observation.

The prosecutor reviewed Bridget's case and examined the findings on our injuries. They deemed the shooting self-defense.

My lawyer had her free within 48 hours. The mob lawyer.

And yes, I paid for her defense. It was the least I could do since she almost died because of me. We made a pact to never again mention Johnny Porciello. Ever.

She didn't want her job back.

Which was why she was considering bartending. "We need the help." St. Patrick's Day had been a madhouse with Kat and I missing Saturday night. She showed up at the hospital for me. Edward in tow.

He didn't have a plane, so he couldn't leave.

Which hurt, too. Ringo flew almost halfway around the world to dump me.

I talked Kat into taking the Sunday parade shift. It didn't take much. Casey had gone above and beyond managing the Saturday puke fest. He hid in the downstairs bar while Kat tossed folks to the curb when they got too drunk. We had our best revenue day, ever. And I wasn't there. It made me realize the bar didn't need me, it was me who needed it.

It felt like a shoe that had been outgrown.

Familiar bagpipes filled the air.

Some regular customers stood as the mournful song played over the noise coming from the TVs. Tall Bob removed his hat.

"You put this on, didn't you?" I accused Casey.

"I figured it fit your mood." He licked his lips.

A cheer went up as the song ended and the normal volume of the bar returned.

"Don't be that way." I slammed the contents of my glass and grimaced.

"I should say the same to you. Drinking won't get him out of your head."

I met his eyes. "It will if I drink enough."

He shook his head. "Nope. It won't. I learned that's true because leaving the force felt like losing a limb. And it broke my heart. Don't think love's any different."

Bridget lifted her glass and muttered, "Amen."

He pointed at her. "She knows. You feel lost. No job, no reason. It sucks. And your heart? That's the worst part. It wants hope. And there ain't none."

"That's supposed to cheer me up?"

"You're still alive. Some folks ain't as lucky." He glanced at Bridget with a funny look on his face. Like he had a secret, and she should somehow know it. Yet both her and I knew he didn't know the full story.

He cleared his throat. "Things are awful quiet now that there's only one boss in town."

How in the hell? I glared at him.

He tipped his head and pretended innocence.

Bridget smiled. It was her first in a long time. "You think he's hiring?"

"You don't want that job." Casey scanned the bar. All was normal. "You want to escort Ellie on her next trip. Make sure your passport is good."

"What in the hell are you blathering about, old man?" I asked.

"You. You're going to go to Italy or wherever your sister

is and stop moping around here. I never figured you as someone who gives up. I thought you were a fighter."

I digested that advice. "I didn't give up."

"Bullshit." He pointed at the bar sign. "I'll call you on that if you try to argue with me."

I was drunk enough already. "What if he doesn't want me?"

"You won't know until you go."

That's what scared me. I'd much rather remain in this limbic state of denial than find out the truth.

"Maybe he thinks you don't want him."

Bridget wasn't helping.

She ignored my glare. "He did ask me to make sure you got to the hospital. He cares. I know he does."

They needed a reality check, fast. "Both of you need to stop comparing notes. It's not healthy."

"I figure if he wanted me dead, I'd be dead. Same with Casey." She shot a thumb at him.

"Hey now, I cultivate a good cover story, don't go dragging me into your demise."

Bridget studied the table. "What's Sardinia like?"

I resented both of them. I resented Kat, who was currently in Macau or somewhere obscenely exotic and rubbing elbows with the most subtly notorious circles of power. I resented my sister who had just celebrated her second month of pregnancy drama and issue-free.

And, I missed her terribly.

I turned to Bridget. "Do you have a bathing suit? The water is crystal clear. You can see a hundred feet down."

"Really?"

Don Manca was going to kill me. I couldn't bring a former federal agent to his doorstep, could I?

I wasn't a quitter. I wasn't a fighter, either. I was a complication. It was time I acted like one. I filled Bridget's glass, then mine. "Two days or as soon as I can book the flights. We're going in."

"Hear, hear! Let's storm the castle." She clinked glasses with Casey.

What a funny way to put it.

Loppa met us at the airport. I couldn't exactly keep the trip a secret. Firenze shadowed us from the bar that night. At least he knew how to keep a professional distance.

"Signora Perkins, Ellie. I hope your trip was smooth?"

I glared at Firenze behind us, then addressed Loppa. "Don't tell me that I really needed a bodyguard. Because I'll kick your shin if you do."

He smiled. "It's good to have you home."

"I'm not home."

He sent me a little shake of the head as if correcting me. Then addressed Bridget. "And you, Miss Perkins, where do you call home?"

She glanced around. "I don't know. What's the hunting like around here?"

His grin widened. "I'm certain we can find entertainment for you. This way."

That went better than expected. Although, I doubted Bridget would leave the island for a long time, if ever. I'd made the introduction. It was up to her to figure things out.

Allie was well. Not showing, but glowing. Even Firenze could tell us apart at this point. Me being the morose twin, and Allie being the happy one. I hugged her for a long time. Mario must have cleared his throat at least three times.

He could wait for his. I was mad at him.

I left Perkins behind with the crew to climb a long-ass mountain trail. Firenze followed at a distance, only catching up and pointing to the right path when I got lost. It was lonely up here. The goats danced from rock to rock making it appear effortless. The bells around their necks clanged under the relentless sun.

I caught sight of a man in a ball cap sitting next to a circular hut. Stones piled on top of each other made up the bottom half of the cuile and the conical roof was shaped by rough boards bound together by brush and plants.

It was a far cry from a lakefront penthouse. Or that beautiful villa in Italy. The whole thing would fit in the atrium with that naked statue.

I tromped up to announce myself.

"What are you doing here?" Ringo stopped whittling a pointed stick and flicked his knife shut.

"I'm exploring a new career in goat shit testing."

He glanced down at my shoes.

I knew my toes felt too warm. I scraped the tip of my boot in the dust to get the worst of it off. Then I straightened my back.

"Looks like you stepped in enough."

"I also climbed a fucking mountain." I swung my arm at the vista. There was nothing but trees, rocks, and steep slopes under the fluffy white clouds in a too-blue sky.

He glanced at my leg. "You're limping."

"Duh." I was stabbed in the leg a month ago.

He frowned. "You shouldn't have come."

"Why?" I spread my feet apart, bracing for the worst.

"I'm not good enough for you."

"Bullshit. Try a different story."

He took a breath and stared at the slopes. "How'd you find me?"

Firenze scuffed a toe against a rock, giving away his position.

"Traitor." Ringo threw down the stick he was destroying.

"Don't bitch at him. Don Manca made him follow me."

At the mention of Mario's grandfather, Ringo winced. "I can't be the man you need."

"Don't I get a say in it?"

He shook his head.

"So, that's it. You're just going to give up on me. On us?"

He stared at me with haunted eyes. "I killed someone in front of you." He laughed once. "He was your fiancé for crying out loud."

"Ex."

Ringo squinted.

"Ex-fiancé," I clarified. "And I'm glad you did. In fact, I can pay you a half a million for it." I glanced around. "Lord knows you could use some money to renovate the hovel."

He shook his head despite laughing. "There's a reason I'm here. You realize that, right?"

I stared at him. He needed a good reality check. "Are you on the lamb?" It was hard to keep a straight face at my pun. Yet I managed. Barely.

One of the little bastards bleated, which made me lose my shit. But the tears were also too close, so I sobered. "Bridget lied her ass off to keep your name out of that mess with Pornstach."

For the first time since I walked up, he looked me in the eye. "She shouldn't have. What did that cost her?"

"A calling. Life on the light side of the force, that sort of thing. But I think she's happier now. Not many people can suffer a stick up their ass for an entire lifetime."

He smiled. "Speaking of…" His voice trailed off, letting me pick up his unspoken question.

"It's-a-me-Mario is his usual surly self. My sister is happy, though."

Ringo dipped his head to hide his expression, and yet I caught his smile. "Does he still frown when you call him that?"

"Every damn time."

Firenze snorted, reminding us both we had an audience. When we turned to glare at him, he composed himself. With his finger pointed toward the the ridge, he said, "I'll be over there. Scream if you need me."

Ringo waited until he was out of earshot. "Seriously, Ellie. You wasted a trip."

"I stepped in goat shit. More than once. Isn't that worth more than what you're giving me?"

"I can't give you a life."

I sat on a rock, checking the surface first. I also checked the crevices and overhang for snakes. Finding none, I crossed my legs and studied him.

He'd grown a full beard. "Are you going to keep growing that scruff and become a hermit?"

"You know what I do." He tossed a rock he'd picked out of the dirt.

"You're the best hitman I know."

His eyes shot to me. "That's the point, Ellie. I kill people. I can't marry you." He didn't pause long enough for me to disagree with him. He stood up and gestured at the horizon. "Where are we going to live? You can't stay at the bar with your friends because I can't live in Chicago. You're not going to want to live here because it's too… rustic for you."

"I'm marrying you."

He frowned and lifted his cap to scratch at his hair. That had grown longer, too. "You're not listening."

"I stepped in goat shit for you. GOAT SHIT!" My voice echoed against the hills.

"There's goat shit on my shoes, Ringo."

"That's the point. Eventually with me, you'll step in shit. Those nightmares you have? Try multiplying them by a thousand if someone wants me gone. You'll be in danger. You'll be watched just like you were when you were a kid."

"Why are you telling me what I want and don't want? And fuck you if you're not going back to Chicago, you have a family to run. Don-fucking-Conti-Messina was in *my* bar trying to find you. You're lucky I'm a damn good liar and told him Don Manca had a job for you because he was ready to do something and I don't fucking know what."

Firenze stepped into the clearing, "Everything okay? I heard yelling."

"Goat shit."

Ringo ignored my outburst. "She's just working stuff out. It's cool."

Firenze turned but Ringo stopped him.

"Hey, you were supposed to let me know if there were people coming after me. Ellie says they aren't."

"You said, warn you if they come after. Not tell you you're a free man. Be clear."

Ringo held up a finger. "Listen, just because you got promoted doesn't mean you get to be a smart-ass to me. I can still slice you up faster than Loppa and his favorite Zimino."

"What's Zimino?" I asked.

"Intestines. You cut it with a scissors." Firenze's comment made me gag.

"Great. Bad enough you eat that awful cheese, now I have *that* image in my head." My stomach didn't want to settle.

"Go away," Ringo grumbled.

"Me or her?" Firenze asked.

Ringo stood up. "Are you sure you brought the right one up here?"

Now he was just being mean.

"Of course I am. Allie walks around the goat shit."

"I hate you." I didn't say it with malice, but Firenze chose the wrong time to mess with me.

"You'll love me eventually," Firenze shot back.

"Over my dead body," Ringo warned.

"That can be arranged." Firenze's voice was colder than I'd ever heard.

"Not likely!" Ringo's raised voice spooked the nearest

clump of goats. They scampered up the slope and stared down on us from the rocks.

"Boys, stop." I stood up and pointed at Ringo. "You, come with me." I took a step and the distinct squelch of poop rapidly expanding under my toes made me cringe. "SHIT! Fucking goats!"

Both men laughed.

"Where are we going, Ellie?" Ringo asked.

"Home. That's where. I'm not going inside whatever that is." I pointed at the shack.

"It's cozy in there. I remember this time when Maria—"

"Shut up, Firenze." Ringo picked me up.

"What are you doing?" I grabbed his shoulders so I wouldn't slip out of his arms and land on my ass.

"Making sure you don't step in shit."

"Put me down," I begged.

"No."

"You can't carry me all the way down the mountain."

Ringo stopped walking. "The hell I can't."

I pointed out the obvious. "It's steep. You're going to hurt yourself."

He set me down and caressed my scarred thigh. "Better me than you."

My chin quivered. "You mean that?"

"Always." His cheeks stood out in sharp hollows as he gritted his teeth.

I touched them, enjoying the rough hair along his jaw. "Johnny couldn't grow a beard."

His eyebrow shot up.

"I'm not comparing you. You're far superior."

But I was worried. He'd lost weight, but honed his muscle since we'd been apart. He was more feral and less happy. I could see it in his eyes. There was sorrow there that hadn't fled despite the soft touches we simply couldn't stop.

His fingers touched my lips. "I've thought about you every day."

I nodded. I had, too. "I'll make you a deal. Help me but don't carry me."

"I want to carry you."

That was an opening I had to exploit. "You can carry me over the threshold on our wedding day."

He sucked in a breath and held it. Softly he said, "When will that be?"

"How does Christmas in Ireland sound?"

His jaw flexed, and I caught the hint of a smile. "Honeymoon?"

I weighed the logistics. "Chicago?"

He made a face. "It'll be cold."

"Then we'll flip them. I want the gang there. No streaming this time. But we have to figure out coverage for New Year's. That's the bar's busiest night."

He chewed on his lower lip. "Conti was looking for me?"

I nodded.

"Does Don Manca know that?"

"What? Do I have to report everything to him?" I was being sarcastic, but apparently neither man understood me well enough yet to tell. They both answered, "yes" in unison.

Ringo asked another question, "I thought St. Patrick's Day was your busiest night?"

"Oh sweetie, you've not seen anything like New Year's in Chi-town. We're going to set up a blues band in the basement."

His eyes bored into mine. "You walked all the way up a mountain, for me?"

"And stepped in goat shit."

"And you're okay with me being a hitman?"

"Absolutely. I don't faint at the sight of blood anymore."

He studied me. "Not at all?"

I shook my head. "Not at all." I lied.

He smiled, the light finally returning to his eyes. "I love you."

Good. Because my leg hurt like a mother.

26

RINGO

The luckiest man in the world was in second place as my bride walked down the aisle. She had shamrocks woven into her hair. The gown she wore was lace, almost completely lace. The gaps between the flowers and vines woven into it were such a fine mesh her skin peeked through. She must be wearing something underneath that matched because despite my best attempts, I couldn't see what I wanted under there.

She climbed the three steps to the altar platform and I snapped my eyes back to her face. Her eyebrow was quirked with knowledge that she'd caught me staring.

For a laugh, I leaned a little to stare at her backside which faced the cathedral. Sure enough, that lace appeared see-through, as well.

Beside her, Allie shook her head. Her dress had the same lace, but only on the sleeves. Both bridesmaids wore soft silk gowns. Floor-length and fully covering them from neck to toe, only allowing the hands to peek free. Kat winked at me. Her escort, Loppa, grinned like a proud papa. Then sobered, mouthing "pay attention" as the priest began mass.

Ninety minutes and a lot of sweat later, I was a married man. Our flight to Ireland left in three hours. While we waited, Ellie held her nephew.

Mario's boy looked like him. All serious scowls and dark eyebrows. Ellie admired his tiny fingers as she bounced him on her lap. "Isn't he the cutest?"

No. Ours would be the cutest.

"What?" she asked because of my silence.

I spoke what was on my mind.

That was met with jeers from my side of the family.

"He or she better not have that Conti nose," Ellie muttered.

The chatter stopped. "That nose has been there since Pope Leo the tenth." In addition to being a pain in my ass and my newest competition, Firenze was also a history buff. If it was Italian history, that is.

"I didn't inherit it." Luckily. But it made me pause. I glanced at Don Manca who was silently watching his family from the corner. I brushed my nose once, asking a question of him. He'd taken the package I'd given him, deep-sixed the photo inside the yellow folder, and never spoken of it since.

His grin lifted. He sent me a knowing wink.

Shit. He'd likely been waiting for this moment since I dumped it on his kitchen table in March. "It's obvious the luck of the Irish is on us. Our little Devlin, whenever they show up, is going to be as pretty as my wife, or as handsome as I am."

I grinned at Ellie.

She ate my bullshit up and spat it back out tenfold. "He'll have ladies lined up for miles as soon as he turns eighteen."

"She'll need seventeen bodyguards."

"Twenty, at least."

Mario butted in. "My son will be the best shot of them all."

He was quickly booed down.

"How can he be the best shot when that is me?" Firenze chimed in.

I stood up to set him straight. Ellie frantically tugged me down. "Let him hang himself," she whispered.

Soon the bragging reached competition level.

Firenze lined up against Molly, who'd taken Kat and Ellie's mantle as the mistress of the Blarney Zone. With her strawberry blonde hair and those freckles, she was a hit. And when her shots were lined up, Firenze eyed her with appreciation.

I leaned over to ask my wife. "Do those still taste like lemon vodka?"

"Molly prefers light rum with her tea."

A second later the tumbler hit the wood, and Molly flourished each pour of that evil concoction with a boast. The sign behind her flashed as the countdown began. The patrons pounded on the bar.

Fool he was, Firenze drank the first glass down, not realizing the danger he was in.

Molly swept down the line, pausing at the fifth, then filling his glass again. She offered, much like Kat had, but Firenze didn't take the bait. Instead, he took a ride he wasn't going to enjoy. I laughed as Molly drank down the final shot and threw her hands into the air to celebrate.

Firenze looked a little green.

I tipped my head at Mario, daring him to drink one.

He stared at the bar for a moment before walking up to collect his son. He leaned in and asked, "The glasses the woman drank, they didn't have alcohol, did they?"

"Oh, they had alcohol. Just not a lot."

Firenze stumbled from the bar.

Mario frowned. "He's going to embarrass us."

"Better get someone to show him where the alley is," I suggested.

Mario handed his son to me and took off to find a willing sacrifice. I stared at the kid in my hands for a minute. "Hey."

His little cross-eyed stare tried to focus on me. It was cute. "I want one."

"Give it about nine or ten months." Ellie sipped on her drink.

Something in her tone made me study her. "You went to the doctor last week, didn't you?"

She nodded.

Where was the nearest coat closet? "You know we can't have sex on the plane. Edward frowns on that shit."

"And the limo to the airport is going to be… cramped." Ellie's eyes darted toward the stairs to the downstairs.

"Do you still have your key?" I asked and indicated the door to the basement.

She nodded, slipping off her stool and around the corner to deftly unlock the door. I waited until a roar of laughter rose from the back of the bar before handing off the baby and joining her on the stairs. I pulled the door shut behind me. I quickly flipped the deadbolt locked. "That won't stop Loppa. He's an expert lock picker, but—"

"Shut up and follow me before they miss us." Ellie dragged me down the stairs by the tie.

She kicked off her shoes and flopped onto the largest sofa.

I slid my hand under the yards of lace. Finally, I found the top of her stockings. She wore a garter belt at the top. With a little flick, I snapped the band against her skin. Then I forgot about teasing her and lifted the mass of delicate lace and the flesh toned skirting high enough to duck under.

My wife wasn't wearing underwear.

And she tasted good.

"You're not getting me pregnant doing that." Her fingers tightened in my hair, telling me she wasn't as unaffected as she tried to sound.

Yet, if she could talk, I wasn't doing this right either. I spread her legs wider and flicked my tongue against her clit while fighting the fabric that threatened to smother me. I freed a hand to push up her skirts, and she took the opportunity to wrap her legs around my head.

I was trapped and loving every minute of it. It was a pleasure to trace through the intricacies of my wife's pussy with my tongue.

My wife's... wow. It was finally real.

That would take some getting used to. Me, the consummate bachelor, the guy tasked with getting in and out without entanglements or complications, had hung up his spurs, settled into a quieter life of business and neighbors, and I embraced the ever-expanding circle of friends my wife attracted like a magpie. She was my North Star, my joy, and an unexpected gift.

Her gasps grew louder and the fluttering of her pleasure was sweet to taste. I drew my tongue across her clit once more to test her patience.

"Stop."

"Stop?" Her skin was flushed and the meticulous wedding updo was falling apart.

"I mean... not stop. But not that? Please." The quickness of her breath interfered with her ability to speak full sentences.

She was so beautiful. I set my hands on my belt and relayed a question to her with a lifted eyebrow.

"Yes. Now."

Since she demanded, who was I to deny her? I unbuckled and slipped my pants down. Then dragged my boxers to join them.

She fussed with the dress, getting it out of the way and welcoming me between her thighs. I slipped inside, holding on to the rush of sensations as I stilled.

"Ringo?"

"A minute, baby." Patience wasn't her strongest asset. While I had enough patience to make me a good hunter, that flew out the window when I was bespelled by the sensation of being inside her. I adjusted as I began my slow glide out, then in, over and over. All the while, I watched the subtle shifts of her expression. I studied her, the things that caused her eyelids to flutter closed, or the sharp thrusts that made her gasp.

Mine. Now and forever. An emotion I thought I'd lost a long time ago overwhelmed me.

I belonged. Not just to a family, but to someone I'd give my life for. Someone I could create a life with, not death. It was incredible and frightening.

Some might call love a weakness, yet I felt stronger than I ever had before. My mind and heart were aligned and tuned to a greater purpose. I was a husband. Someday, maybe even a father.

My skin prickled with awareness that this day pushed me into a deeper connection with life. No longer was I just an instrument of death, of finality, and solutions, but now I was part of creation.

The majesty of it made my breath catch and my knees weak.

This woman took me there. She initiated me into a rare gift.

With her cries of passion and the sharpness of her fingernails digging into my skin, I was reborn. And with the last thrust and the pulsing of my orgasm, I answered her call, falling or rising, I couldn't tell which. But it changed me.

In the peace after, I caressed her skin. As my hand slid away, I lifted it to look at my palm. It was my left hand. The same hand Don Manca taught me how to memorize the history of assassins dating back to their service in Egypt and possibly before civilization kept records. With their left hands, they toppled empires, created dynasties, and most importantly, remembered that life and death are bound. Like the thumb and the pinky. But in between there is honor, duty, love…

I touched my ring, the first I'd ever worn. It would be the last I'd ever wear, God-willing. It sat between home and innocence as symbol of an oath.

"You like it?" Ellie asked about my ring.

"Love it." Just like I loved her.

The noise from above got louder. Quickly I scrambled off Ellie and pulled up my pants. Meanwhile, she fussed to get her dress straightened out.

By the time Loppa tromped to the last step, she stood beside me, trying in vain to fix her hair. It only made the waterfall of her temporary curls fall apart faster.

"Forgive the interruption, the guests are asking for you two."

"You're lucky I didn't shoot you," I growled.

"If you'd been upstairs not—"

I slipped my knife from its holster and brandished it to silence him. "You were saying?"

"Nothing."

"That's right. Nothing."

I turned to Ellie and plucked a bobby pin dangling from one of her curls. "Here. Go find your sister or Kat so they can help you fix your hair. I have to kill this guy."

Loppa made a noise that sounded suspiciously like suppressed laughter.

"What? We're married. Don't tell me you've never snuck off with your wife."

He turned a shade of red I'd not seen on him before.

Well, I'll be damned. "You have?"

"That's enough out of you. You can't wait for the honeymoon?"

"No. Duh." Ellie flounced past him, carrying her shoes. She turned with a mischievous smile aimed at me. "Ringo?"

"Sweetheart?"

"Don't kill him today. I don't want to make Molly mop up blood."

"I'll think about it."

"Think harder. Okay?"

Loppa grinned. As soon as she reached the top of the stairs he said, "I like her best."

I slapped the back of his head. "Mine. And I'm going to tell Mario you said that."

"Please don't. I value my life."

"Yet you picked the damn lock."

He shrugged. "Don Manca asked me to. But I'll have you know, I did it very slowly."

"Why didn't he make Mario do it?"

Loppa chuckled. "We drew lots. I lost. I was unlucky."

"You're still alive. I'd say you're lucky enough."

"Like you could kill me."

I stuck my fist against his back right where the blade would do the worst damage. It was a damn good thing I'd dropped it into my other hand before I did it.

But Loppa jerked away, hands up and wary. He stared at

the knife I could have killed him with. "Firenze needs to learn that trick."

"I'll teach him. Have him ready in three weeks."

"Are you going to have any energy left in three weeks?"

He was yanking my chain. "Marriage didn't slow you down."

"That it didn't." He studied me for a silent moment. "You've always been welcome as one of our own. But now, I believe you know why we fight so hard to stay alive and protect each other, no?"

I nodded.

"It is not blood this family fights for. It is love."

With that, he left me alone to ponder his words.

Love.

Family.

I was lucky to have it. Even if it came with its share of cutthroats and criminals, I wouldn't trade it for anything.

To quote from one of my favorite movies,

The end is only the beginning...

If you're like me, you want more...
[Looks around, puts a finger on her lips...]
Tell you what, go to this super-secret web page to read a bonus scene. You may be asked to sign up for a newsletter there. If you do subscribe, you will get two emails a month with what's coming next, freebie links, and other great content, but you can unsubscribe at ANY time.
shh...
caliawilde.com/lucky/
The password is: Ringo

To find more Wilde stories, visit:
https://caliawilde.com

Thank you for reading!

— *ANNOUNCEMENT* —

If your tour of this fictional world was less than a 5-star experience, please don't tell my villains. They get sentimental and silly when not taken seriously. And if you don't care what they think, please go online and review honestly. I love 5-star reviews, but I love YOU more!

Did you leave a review? Tell Calia about it here:
   theauthor@caliawilde.com

ABOUT THE AUTHOR

Calia Wilde believes the hero isn't always the good guy. She believes some heroes and heroines cannot play by the rules to get their happily ever after.

She is a writer of misfits, anti-heroes, villains, underdogs, fringe elements, and other tropes that will likely get her barred from polite society.

As a feral Gen-Xer, she spent numerous hours roaming the woods in search of elves, fairies, dragons, or anything that would take her away from the dreaded curse of doing dishes. She once fell off a wardrobe, but instead of landing in Narnia, a very emphatic order of *"Don't tell Mom,"* was decreed. In case you are wondering, yes, she did land on her head.

Rainy days and dark nights landed the author in other worlds between written pages or immersing in her favorite space and time travel TV shows. Whether it was exploring the final frontier or simply disappearing down rabbit holes with shapeshifting aliens, the escape was the same, only the moonscape differed.

One time in Sturgis, she was offered twenty bucks to climb a ladder. She declined as there was some fine print regarding the quest that went beyond conquering a fear of heights and some activities which were definitely illegal for someone her age. But it was there... in that magical realm of bikers, booze, and foul language, that she came into the possession of her very first item of armor... aka, black clothing. The forbidden was in her grasp and became an life-long obsession to avoid anything pastel.

As she searched for a career that would indulge this penchant for wearing black, she stumbled upon the world of special effects and excitedly pursued the art of sleeping in strange hotels, working ungodly hours, and handling anything that could, and would, burn, blind, explode, freeze, or otherwise entertain wildlings like herself.

Her current fictional worlds are forged in a hippie world where music and nature peacefully co-exist away from modern conveniences, like bathtubs. Okay, there's a shower, but she has to share it with spiders. Yuck. Which is why she looks forward to going on the road once more where the hotel may have a real tub. Or a hot tub... maybe a heated pool... please?

So, she **BEGS** you to leave a review and do a good deed by encouraging others to read her books. With enough fans scattered across the globe, she'll have to travel, right? Then she'll have an excuse to leave the farm.

**Want a FREE BOOK? Sign up for her newsletter.
CaliaWilde.com/newsletter-sign-up/**

or

Become an ARC reader and get all the books FIRST.
CaliaWilde.com/become-an-arc-reader/

Walk on the Wilde side here:
CaliaWilde.com

ALSO BY CALIA WILDE

Destroyers Series

Motorcycle Club Romance, Contemporary Action/Adventure Romance Novels and Short Stories

Devils Handmaidens Motorcycle Club

Motorcycle Club Romance, Contemporary Action/Adventure Romance Novels — A shared MC universe with other MC authors

DeSantos Trilogy

Contemporary Romance/Romantic Suspense

Bones Series

Paranormal and Fantasy Romantic Short Stories, Mythology-inspired Romantic Tales

TKI Logistics

Contemporary Romance, Military Romance Short Stories

The Sinister Legacy Duet

Contemporary Mafia Romance Novels

Visit CaliaWilde.com/book-backlist for a full list of current publications.

www.ingramcontent.com/pod-product-compliance
Lightning Source LLC
LaVergne TN
LVHW040042080526
838202LV00045B/3443